EMMANUEL

The Boy Whose Name Meant 'God Is With Us'

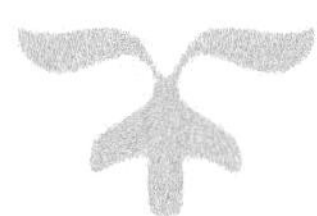

Melissa Crickard

ISBN: 978-1-951482-06-0

1

Later, they called him Dolly.

But this morning, he still went by Emmanuel Ayala, or just Manny, the kid from one of those small ranches northwest of Juarez who started every day at four a.m. on the farm, or at the *Mercado del Mundo* where his brother sold fish, loads of *pescados y mariscos,* like the big sign read, painted and chipped, above Juan's storefront. Fish and shellfish, nothing more—*dorado* and *cabrilla* caught from the Baja peninsula, and *carpa* and *jaiba.* The blue crab was his favorite, but he rarely ate anything from the market. He awakened hungry on that morning, like so many others. He chewed at a piece of jerky as he hung the longhorn skull that had fallen twice from the teal wall of the shopfront. When the daylight came, he'd wander to the stand where Alena's *abuela* made *ceviche, vieiras,* and *calamar* chopped with tiny flecks of red pepper and crushed *cilantro*, embalmed *con limon*. Maybe Alena would be there. Maybe she'd see him and smile and look away and look back at him again.

But at this early hour, even before the sun cracked its tangerine lens—before the blackness began to lift from the night, piling layers of blue on the eastern horizon—he sat on a wooden crate beneath Vega and Orion and he brushed the dust from his *charro* boots. He chewed the jerky and spat it out and then threw it into the trash, and he sighed as he waited for

1

the delivery. Juan was expecting a promising load of corpulent salmon and swordfish.

The seafood trucks arrived in Ciudad Juarez to stock the marketplace. The Juarez market was one of the largest in Mexico, third in size only to *La Nueva Viga* in Mexico City and the *Mercado del Mar* in Jalisco.

The demand for wholesale seafood now outstripped the traditional markets' ability to supply it. The market had grown so vast that it spanned the perimeter of a street block, crossing it on its northern border and projecting two more city blocks. Its inner workings took place in the core of the rectangular block, with the big sales and the orders of crates iced and packed with shrimp and soft-shell crab, lobsters, manta rays. The sellers external in the shopfronts radiated peripherally like a corona of spokes, these satellite markets revolving from their universe central and entire that now, due to the sheer size of the enterprise, seemed to stretch ever-distant. The spokes now reached vast latitudes that capitalized on the demand for product coveted by owners of restaurants, tourists, diverse entrepreneurs.

Warehousers, whetting their knives, signaled the dawn as they prepared thousands of tons of black sea bass, large-scaled and smooth-gilled, the soft ray portions of their dorsal fins continuous and foundering inward as their innards lay gutted at the feet of the fish mongers. Eyes glassy.

Bodies dead, lifeless.

Juan seemed to enjoy the task of filleting the biggest ones and always said that having the sharpest tools and the gumption to slice the unfortunate and lifeless creatures—rather than pushing at their flaccid bodies—was the key to the chore. Juan also told him that pushing with a dull knife, not fully committed to slicing the flesh—when and where it needed to be—might lead to mistakes that could get him into trouble.

"*Permanacer fiel la tarea,*" Juan had told him. Stay faithful to the task.

Juan honed the knife now a few times over his stone and then over the steel sharpener at acute angles and then wiped the stone with a cloth and blew away the steel dust. Juan examined the knife before hacking the flesh of another mackerel from the tail end through the breast. Then Juan picked up a yellowfin tuna and looked at its clouded eyes and its body that had all but lost its turgor, lay in Juan's hands like a squishy spineless mess, and Juan ran his rough palm over its scales and chucked it into a blue tub of plastic filled with ice and water.

"What's wrong with that one?"

"No good."

"Why no good?"

Juan said that he had enough sense to know which fish were no good and that those spoilt and rotten might sour the entire catch. Bad fish had to be removed from the shipment, at the risk of losing all the others. And Juan said that the biggest customers could sniff out the bad fish from a mile away, and if they found too many, the word would spread. It would mean the end of his whole store.

Manny nodded. "*Si.*"

Juan again took the curved blade and its tip pointed at the gills of a tuna enormous and fresh and then cut it back along the meat of the fish toward the tail. After carving out the meat, Juan felt along the bones of the tuna, with his blade and his fingertips, and sliced around them on both sides, angular and precise. Juan neatly lifted the bones, antediluvian, primitive like the remnants of Neanderthal tools. Juan peeled them from the dead animal, let the delicate relics fall to the floor. Sometimes, Juan chucked them into the pail, sepulcher of aquatic martyrs, or smelled the meat before cutting it into beautiful fillets for sale. Manny began to sweep the floor now as his brother removed the white vinyl apron covered in fish innards, the Mexican *futbol* cap, the black rubber gloves that covered the arms past the elbows.

"Get those off the truck," Juan told him. "Luis will be here soon."

Manny hoisted another load of fish slurried in ice-filled plastic crates from the next truck and he stacked the fish on the wooden ledges, one green crate on top of another. The inventory today was good. The restaurant owners would be pleased. They were always the first customers of the morning.

Juan smiled when he saw Luis on his scooter turning from the *Defensa Popular* onto the *15 de Septiembre*. Luis owned the largest seafood restaurant in Juarez, the *Casa de los Peces*. After dark, the restaurant hosted live entertainment, flamenco dancers adorned in the *traje de Gitana*, red and black ruffles billowing from waist to ankle, cascades of dark curls down their backs, and navels tinkling with tiny cymbals and bells. *Casa de los Peces* was home to the best margarita in the city. Manny had been there a few times, including once when he was barely able to see over the counter at the bar. Maybe today he'd ask Luis if he could work there as a bus boy. He could mop the floors, wipe the bar, clear dishes for the servers and the bartender— anything to be in that restaurant. It had such an energy about it. He grabbed the broom again now and swept the front. Then he set the broom down and wiped his hands on his apron.

Luis came speeding into the center of town, past the carts where men sold knives, and he approached the *escaparate,* the showcase, got off the scooter and examined the piles of snapper and swordfish and mahi, their eyes staring—clouded and glassed as marbles, cold and dead—back at the owner.

Luis looked Juan over and rubbed the stubble on his chin. Then he turned to stare across the street, as if watching the cart where the tamales and fish tacos were already cooking. The woman standing there turned in a quick, uncomfortable hurry.

At the bank directly across from the fish market, the white stucco on the buildings was torn in patches and the Spanish tile broken from the rooftops. Posters taped to the telephone poles offered rewards for missing women. An old woman in a dress blue and wrinkled with gray hair pulled into a bun sat, barefoot, selling culinary supplies from a second cart. Her copper pots clanged with the breeze, dusty and humid, that blew in through the center of town every so often, carrying the smell of the fresh fish everywhere with it. The side of the old woman's wooden cart had been vandalized with yellow spray paint. Every so often, as a potential customer would walk by, she would stand and pretend to polish her pots, and when they passed, she would return to her seat and just rock, her arms crossed, staring back across the street at the men.

Manny looked away.

To Juan, Luis said, *"Tu has hablado del menu del restaurante."* You've been talking about the restaurant menu.

Juan shook his head. *"No."*

"Tu has hablado del menu del restaurante,.." Luis said again, tilted his head back and looked Juan over. Manny saw Juan sweat from his forehead, pausing. Then Luis laughed, and Juan sighed, and Luis shook Juan's hand firmly and Juan wiped his palms on his apron and Luis said that it was okay. They talked about his order for the day and Juan told Manny to gather the order. Luis tipped his chin up and to Juan, said, *"Quieres ir a comer conmigo?"*

Juan acted as if he had not heard Luis correctly. Luis repeated himself, as he often did, and Juan said that he would be honored to eat with him. Luis said that he admired the way that Juan ran his business, and that it was the most efficiently run shopfront at the fish market, said that he was thankful that Juan was such a good supplier, and that he would not buy from anyone else in the marketplace. Then Luis shook Juan's hand and he slapped his back and he said that they would share a meal later that week. Juan said he was looking forward to it, gave Luis crates of lobsters and giant crabs and much more fish than he had purchased that day.

When Luis turned to leave, he put on his sunglasses and swung his leg over his scooter. Then he paused, climbed back off the scooter, tucked in his white T-shirt. Luis took off his sunglasses, said to Juan, "*Vamos a hablar ahora*." Let's talk now.

Manny swallowed.

Juan looked around, said, "*Si*," motioned for Luis to join him in the back of the storeroom.

Then Juan called to him to watch the *escaparate* before he walked down the wet floor of the back hallway to the back room, closed the curtain.

Manny listened at the door, perched, avian and precise. His neck rotated, hawk-like, and he shifted his eyes between the front of the shop, where he was attentive for thieves or customers, and the door, behind which his brother talked business.

Luis asked Juan about the buckets of brown shrimp, coiled ellipsoid like fiddleheads, and about the largest giant grouper Juan had ever received as product, and what the markup was, and what it had finally sold for. Juan told Luis about the largest wholesale orders taken and where he shipped them. Juan said the largest orders that came in regularly were for more than 40,000 pesos. Luis questioned Juan about *salmon salar,* salted salmon, and about capelin and white barracuda and giant squid and scallop. Luis purchased additional tuna loins and silver pompano and pangasius steaks, and there didn't seem to be a question about the product that Juan couldn't answer.

Luis seemed pleased, and Manny was proud of his brother. He thought that if their father was alive, he would be proud of him, too.

Juan and Luis talked for some time while Manny stood, listening. His heart was beating very fast and sweat had formed in cold pools on his palms that he wiped on his jeans. Soon, the men were laughing, and from the door he heard glasses clinking, and he figured Juan had poured Luis some tequila. Juan toasted to business. Then without warning Luis' voice changed, and Luis said that he did not want to talk about fish anymore.

Manny pressed his ear to the door.

The voices grew hushed. He could hear very little. Then the bell in the front of the store rang, calling him to help the customers. It was busy that day in the center of town, with Volkswagens and scooters filling the street. Customers lined up now, tattooed men in leather vests, and *abuelitas* who could not see well that he had to read the prices to, and children with pesos in the pockets of their ripped clothing, who had just enough money to buy one or two smelt to feed them for the day. When he had served them all, he went back to the door in the core of the shops where his brother was still talking with Luis. He tried to listen again, but he now could not hear what was being said over the bustle of the busy marketplace. The horns of punch bugs and the voices of the shopfront owners calling out to the trucks up and down the *Avenue* made it impossible to hear.

He cracked the door so he could see. It creaked. Juan immediately set down the glass rimmed blue half-filled with tequila. Luis rose from the table, reached around his back.

Manny opened the door, stepped inside.

"Manny," said Juan. "The storefront."

On the table, he saw the bag. Clear plastic stuffed full of white powder. It could have been flour or sugar or powdered sugar, but it was none of these.

"Manny."

"Manny?" asked Luis. "*Es ese su nombre?*" Is that your name?

Luis walked toward the door. He put his arm around Manny's shoulder and led him out of the back room, down the hallway to the front of the store.

"Yes sir," he said.

"Look at that doll face. No scars, no missing teeth. Not even a pock mark." Luis tilted Manny's chin up and examined him, smiled. "No ink, either. You look more like a Dolly."

Manny remained quiet, swallowed.

"He's my brother," said Juan. He had followed them down the hallway.

"Your brother?"

"My brother. He's fast. Like a jaguar. A hard worker. Smart, too." Juan looked at Manny and scratched his head and looked back at Luis.

"Manny, you see we have a lot to talk about. Not only about fish."

"*Si,*" he said. "*Mi gustari ser apodado jaguar.*" I would like to be called jaguar.

"*Muy bien, Dolly.*"

Then Luis said that he did look smart, and that he looked like the kind of kid who kept his eyes and ears open and that he reminded him of a falcon. Luis asked if he knew what kind of bird a falcon was, and he wanted to say that of course he knew what a falcon was, but he just swallowed and nodded, didn't take his eyes off Luis, and he said, "*Si.*"

Luis asked him if he could keep his eyes and ears open, and he said that he could. Then Luis smiled and handed him one hundred pesos and shook his hand and told Juan that they would speak later. Luis shoved the bag in his jacket and climbed back on his bike. Then he disappeared down the *Avenue de Septiembre.*

~ ~ ~

Later, Manny walked past barrios and rows of homes vandalized with paint, their foundations crumbled away and vulnerable, through the city, to his bus stop. He took the bus that ran down Federal Highway 2 along the *Rio Grande.* After some time, he got off the bus and walked home along the red clay of the stream, with the sun at his back. He found the road by the old farmhouse and he started up it. The sunlight was fading when he came to the ranch where he lived, painted brick red and rimmed with windows painted white, rounded at the top and squared at the bottom. He walked along for some distance and then he crossed over another stream. Today it was dry in the spot where he crossed. He hopped over the unstained agricultural fence and the stone border surrounding it. Every day he did this. He made his way up the graded lawn and the steep driveway where he was higher in elevation and could see out clearly over the land. He looked out at the lights of Juarez, now illuminating the dark, as if he were a foreign being watching

Earth from the moon. Then he looked at the driveway where Juan's truck, cherry red and dented on its rear end, was parked on the gravel. But Juan was not home.

He hung his cap and he sat down at the table of wood stained turquoise and tiled on its surface. His mother gave him frijoles and a tamale, and he asked her if he might have a beer, and she hit the back of his head and put some more beans on his plate. She came to the sink and she washed her hands and she dried them. Then she sat down across from him just watching him, eating, and she shooed the flies from the food. He looked up, asked where Juan was, though he already knew, and she said that he had gone to see about a job.

"A job."

Her eyes squinted into suspicious slits then. He should not have tested her.

He turned his head down and he shoveled rice into his mouth, and he drank some water and he ate more rice. She stared at him from across the table and when he looked up, she asked what was wrong.

"Nothing is wrong, Ma," he said.

"Nothing?"

"Nothing."

"Juan works hard so you can keep going to school." She said Juan was going to get another job at night and she said that she was proud of Juan for his work at the fish market, but that she did not want him quitting school like Juan had. "Did you go to the school on Friday?"

He said that he had.

"We go to the church tomorrow," she added, as if that was an option. She couldn't force Juan to go anymore, mostly because Juan was too big for her to beat with her slipper in the morning to get him out of bed. Sometimes, though, Juan went on his own.

Manny had grown taller than his mother, Enriqua, but not by much. She was heavier now than she used to be, and her dresses burst at the seams, and her chin was full and doubled in profile, and she still had a way of towering over him and insisting that it was her home, even though *padre* had been dead only a year now. She had a way of defining the once-profitable dairy ranch by everything that it wasn't. It wasn't a hotel, she reminded him. It wasn't a restaurant. It sure wasn't a club.

Elvie came running up to him now, pulling at his leg. The girl was two, with dark eyes and hair like his. She was beautiful and always made him smile—his reason for going to church, his reason of praying to Mary, the reason he felt at home with them every time he looked up from the table at the rectangular picture of *El Ultima Cena*. He scratched her head and she smiled, and he picked her up and set her on his lap.

"Something's wrong, Manny," his mother said.

"Nothing's wrong, Ma."

"Yes. Something's wrong."

"Nothing's the matter. You got more beans?"

"No, you tell me what's wrong."

"I told you, it's nothing."

"You're sick. It's something. Have some more frijoles and rice."

"I'm not sick. Everything's fine. You gotta relax. You don't want Elvie to end up crazy like this, Ma."

"Crazy?" She got up from the table. "Is that what you think?"

"I just think you worry too much."

She took out two long glasses and a bottle of mescal and she poured some for both and she set it on the table.

"This will make you feel better."

"I'm not sick, Ma. You don't want me drinking beer but you're pouring me a glass of liquor."

"It's not a glass. It's just a taste. It'll settle your stomach."

"Ma, it's a glass."

"Emanuel, don't you lie to me."

"I'm not lying, Ma." He sipped the liquor. It burned and he set down the glass and then he shook his head and he picked it up again and he downed the shots. Then he set down the baby, stood up from the table. "I gotta go."

"Where do you think you're going? It's dark. Eat some more beans."

He took another scoop, put a large forkful in his mouth.

"Some friends from school are going to play paint ball in the city center."

"You just got home." She picked up Elvie, who started to cry. He put on his jean jacket and kissed her, headed for the door.

"I know. I gotta go. I'll see you later, Ma."

"You kiss your baby sister."

Elvie held up a plastic toy and shook it coarsely at her wrist and he smiled and picked her up and he smoothed her hair.

"A pony, huh?" He took the toy animal. "I tell you what, little lady. When I grow up and become a famous soccer player, I'm gonna buy you a pony. Maybe two."

His mother laughed, "How you going to do that?"

"She should have a pony. A Shetland. Maybe a pinto with some beautiful brown and white patches or an Appaloosa with spots. Would you like a spotted pony, *princesa*?" He smoothed her hair, looked into her eyes. She had stopped crying. "Would you promise to take care of it?"

"It's a unicorn," said Elvie.

"A unicorn, huh?" He took the animal and he examined it and he frowned. "It is a unicorn. Everybody wants to find a unicorn. I'd like to find one."

His mother snatched up the child then, said he shouldn't put such ideas in her head.

"I love you, little lady," he said. He set down the unicorn and he ran out the door and ran beyond the fence where the smell of the animals and the grass wrinkled his nose. The sky was clear, cloudless. Then he hopped the fence and started running, away from the *granja* where sheep wandered far from the house, under the moon and the great hunter which was nearly sideways on the horizon. He stopped for a moment and shuffled his feet in the dirt. Then he ran back into the house, and he grabbed Juan's keys from the hook on the wall next to his mother, who was washing the dishes. Elvie stood on a chair beside her, clapping her hands between clouds of bubbles. Before his mother could stop him, he left the kitchen, and on the driveway, he started the truck, began to back away.

She came running from the house screaming and swearing to Mary, calling, "Manny!" He couldn't hear everything she said, but he was sure she was cursing him for being fourteen and not old enough to drive yet. He kept going and he drove off, heading back into Juarez.

2

Manny drove south on Highway 45 until he came to Boulevard Zaragoza, headed for the paintball center. The Terminator was already there—one hundred-ten kilos of useless adrenaline, pug-round face, gold cross hung around his neck over his black T-shirt. The Terminator was good for running around the field like *un pollo con su cabeza cortada*, a headless chicken, or for firing off shots aimless and inaccurate every time he heard a sound, popping up from cover and running clear across the middle of the field with his *vientre* sloshing side to side.

The Terminator was useless to his team because he always got eliminated in the first two minutes of the game, but they'd been friends longer than Manny could remember. It was hard enough to hit targets with the liquid projectiles made uneven by dents and seams, streaming out of the straight barrels, without him shooting at anything and everything in his path. The Terminator was always early, gun hopper loaded, double trigger Trilogy Sport paintball gun slung across his body, obstructive breathing moving it ever-so-slightly up and down on his *vientre* with each breath, where he sat on the wooden bench, arms crossed, legs spread apart.

"Manny," he said, rising to shake his hand.

"Ramiro, check this out." He fought back a smirk, crooked and gap toothed, as he nodded toward the gravel lot.

"Put on your helmet, man. It's almost go time." The Terminator donned his body armor, looking the part of a 'roided-up Mexican armadillo.

"But you gotta see this. Check out my ride."

"You took your brother's truck again. Jesus, he's going to beat the shit out of you Manny." The Terminator broke into laughter.

"Shut up. After the game, we're gonna take a ride."

"You're gonna get arrested, dude. The *Federales* are going to have their guns up in your face like this," Ramiro said, put the butt of the gun to his shoulder and placed his third finger on a trigger, pulled the safety and yanked off the safety case on the end of the barrel, and pushed it into Manny's temple.

"Get the hell out of here, you fat fuck." He swatted the barrel away and slapped The Terminator on the back.

"It is a very nice truck, Manny." The Terminator ran his hand down the hood.

"I told you it is. We're going to take a ride. I got some money."

"You got some money.

"Yeah, I got some."

"Where did you get money?"

"Never mind. I got enough pesos to have some fun."

"Then why don't you buy yourself a paint ball gun instead of borrowing Piranha's?"

"Why don't you just stay down under cover instead of running like a pregnant Rottweiler on a land mine?"

"That was harsh, Manny."

He pointed at him. "We're going out later."

The Terminator sighed and he checked his hopper as he put on his polycarbonate mask, shined luminous and fastened, and tied a bandana around the top. Then The Terminator turned his gun sideways and aimed it at the group of *muchachos* hopping off the back of the black truck that had pulled up beside Juan's truck.

"The ammo doesn't come out when you turn it sideways, dumb ass." He slapped The Terminator on the back.

"I know that," Ramiro breathed, raspy and muffled, through the mask. "I was just playing Matrix with you, Manny."

"Well cut it out. Everybody's here."

"Okay, Manny."

"Okay."

The center was dark now, with no lights in the open, four-acre field that was crisscrossed with obstacles of corrugated pipe tubing, wooden planks, and forts built at ground level. Some forts were vertical in Mesquite trees, adding another dimension to the game. Once, The Terminator had fallen out of one of the tree forts and Manny had had to drag him back to the center and call the *ambulancia* and haul him onto the back of the truck because they'd sent two women who couldn't lift his immobilizer-boarded fat ass up from the ground.

So Ramiro was no longer allowed in the trees.

Mostly, though, the field was sparsely forested without a lot of coverage except during rainy season, when the Palo Verde got some leaves and the elephant trees looked like scrub brush. The Ponderosa Pines weren't much help, especially for Ramiro, because their coniferous leaves were nettles that grew from long, thin trunks far above the ground. The field made for a game that was played mostly on the ground, often in a commando crawl across the desert dirt, snaking forward slowly until a target was localized at fifty to one hundred yards or so.

His air system was set up now, gun loaded. When the game started, he reminded The Terminator to try to win by not losing the game for them, and Ramiro told him to fuck off, and he nodded to Piranha and Justin and they spread out over their side of the field. He knelt behind a barrack of rotted wood, sighting down the barrel. Everything about his upper body was steady, almost too stiff, as he took aim. He kept both eyes open, weighing the distance to his targets, and he took a few shots to gauge where his balls were landing. Then he shot some more in succession.

The four guys on the other team were league champions who took things seriously. He got the impression they'd shot more than paintballs. It wasn't easy to shoot even the best of those guns with precision, but the one they called Ricky had The Terminator out before he could materialize from behind the pipe tubing, which lay oblong through the field in pits of thick mud. Ramiro took a slow walk off the field, shaking his head as if it was a surprise.

Losing was always a surprise to him.

Piranha crept forward between the inflatable targets, stood and positioned his fingers on the trigger and aimed down the barrel and shot Ricky out with a clear hit to the right shoulder as Ricky peered over a wooden hut. Piranha's birth name was Josef Calderon. Some people thought his nickname was Piranha because of the paintball gun he used, a Piranha, but that wasn't the case. Piranha had once bitten a chunk out of a kid's leg so large that it required hospitalization, *antibiotic,* and stitches. He couldn't say for sure, but he thought it was during the time that Piranha had been experimenting with methamphetamines with another kid, Piranha's best friend at the time, a violent and feral boy who didn't even notice that he'd been bitten until three hours after the notorious bite. The kid's leg was swollen and bloodied and by then, infected-looking with pus and fluid weeping yellow like viscous gelatin.

Nothing screamed amphetamines like being bitten bloody in the leg and not taking notice of it until three hours later. And when the kid did come out from the effects of the drugs, that was pretty much the end of his friendship with Josef.

Piranha was so skinny that any medication or drug affected him twice as much as any kid with a normal amount of meat on his bones. This made it easy for him to hide behind the scrawny trees on the playing field and snake between the barracks. Piranha could even fit inside the pipe tubing, crawling through it to reappear at the other end. The Terminator had tried that once, but he'd gotten stuck and instead called out "Jam!" as if his gun was jammed so no one could shoot him, and he'd laid there screaming for help until they stopped the game to pull him out of the tubing by the legs. Piranha's parents were always on drugs themselves, and they never fed the kid a thing. Everything Piranha ate he pretty much stole, and when he did eat, he seemed to burn through his meal with the metabolism of a desert shrew.

Manny glanced at Piranha and Piranha glanced back, nodded. Manny advanced forward where none of the other players were visible. Only the moonlight and the lights jaundiced and dingy from the building lit the field. A wolf howled. Where he crouched motionless for a while, a shadow moved sinuous across the field. He hoisted himself up into a tree fort and lay there on his abdomen, his breathing shallow, his middle finger poised on the trigger, the gun held strong. He moved it at his shoulders, keeping his sight between the two eyes on the shadow.

Piranha shot a few balls, gauging his distance to their target, but they fell short.

They were about the same distance from the player. Manny arced his gun up and he kept the player in his sight, and he squatted in a troll-like stance and he held his gun where the trigger was stiff and just about to click. His gun averaged fifteen to twenty balls per minute. He shot a hail of balls, keeping his finger on the spot where he could reload quickly.

The player fired back, his ammo landing beneath Manny. He was visible now in the fort. He tried to fire again as his target crept in closer, behind twenty yards of pipe tubing, laying there in the mud. As he popped up, Manny fired again, but his gun stuck. He shook it and he hopped down from the tree fort.

He knew the kids on the other team from school, but he could no longer remember their names, no longer see their faces clearly. Their features began to blur, and their forms moved, continuous and marked, faceless, inhuman targets.

From where he crouched now, the adrenaline, testosterone, raw anger, was working its way through his blood.

He fired more shots to test his range and his target swore, covered in yellow paint.

His target swore again, and the lights flashed, and the target moved off the field, out of the game.

"Nice," Justin called.

He and Piranha took fire from the right, the left. A hail of paintballs came at them. At once, he pulled back behind a wall of logs. Then he advanced on either side of two stacks of monster truck tires that offered some protection.

Piranha laughed, "You're a great shot, Manny. A great shot."

"What's so funny?" He shook his head. "We're taking fire on all sides here. Reinforce Justin."

Ahead of them, Justin raised his gun in the air and yelled, hit at close range in the right thigh.

"Bastards. That wasn't no hundred yards, Manny," said Piranha. "It's you and me."

"You and me," he said.

"Okay. Go."

"Anybody over there?"

"Nothing."

"I'll stay back and reinforce you," he said.

Piranha crouched down and moved forward into a dusty depression, a small arroyo where Manny could see him from behind the thickly treaded tires that concealed his gun, his narrow shoulders.

He fired off a few balls that landed just ahead of Piranha. Piranha was taking fire from both sides again.

Manny pressed the butt of the gun into his chest and he held it steady and he kept his finger stiff on the trigger where it was ready to fire, and he fired on the target on the left. He could see the target moving closer to Piranha. He nailed him and he shot him out. Then he fired at once to the right.

"Piranha, get out of there," he shouted.

Piranha ran out of the arroyo and crouched and ran toward a wall of logs, two meters long and ten high, and he dove behind it.

Manny's gun stuck. He shook it and followed his sight to the target, to where Piranha was still taking fire. One more to go.

His mask was fogging up. He lifted it and wiped it off. He pulled it back down over his face.

The field was quiet.

In the distance, the wolf was howling again.

He breathed heavy on his mask. It was the closest he'd come to war. In that second, he might have been at war, and it was thrilling, and he could feel his heart pounding faster than his breathing could keep pace with, and in that same quick moment his eyes swept the field, and he remembered that his life did not depend on the win.

His breathing settled. His mask cleared then.

He could see the mask of his target again.

He could imagine the face beneath it.

He looked toward Piranha, nodded.

Piranha moved forward again and crouched beside a metal grating, vertical and cuprous with greened residue tainting its surfaces, a dented hull with sheared edges projecting like the teeth of a monstrous beast. The other team took fire.

Piranha shot out a hail of balls, aiming beyond the arroyo and then pulling up his gun and shooting forty or fifty more. More balls grazed the metal grating. As Piranha stood and aimed to shoot, the balls burst and covered his shoulder. He was out.

"Up to you, man." Piranha shook his head as he walked off the field. "Finish him off."

"Uno a uno."

Wisps of clouds like clumps of pulled sheep wool covered the moon now. It grew pitch dark. The wind picked up, blowing the smell of savage sweat, a primal scent of body odor regressive to centuries of communal tribes who existed only to hunt and procreate, to times of long-haired men who squatted around a fire with sticks sharpened to a point, eating game killed fresh and marbled with fat and gristled white. It was a pungent odor. His own sweat beaded hot inside the helmet and ran down the back of his neck. And the sound of his breathing against the polycarbonate shield made his sweat drip faster, hotter.

The paint balls came from behind a stack of tires. He could see the final opponent between the treads, which curved like shark teeth arced from the black rubber. He took off, closer to the target, moving up his right side of the field.

Fire came at him, at closer range now.

He lost sight of the target.

Yellow paint splattered against the rusted metal where he stood, his gun clutched against the hollowed pit of his shoulder, the paint balls rattling as they settled in the hopper. He ran and dove and rolled on the ground and he sprang up again and repositioned the butt of the gun. He held it steady and he looked right, left. He fired off ten or twenty balls, gauging their distance in the vertical and horizontal planes.

Too far.

He brought the barrel down.

The scrub brush rustled. He located his target behind it. He shot off more rounds as he moved. He could see the shadow, sinew drawn out slender and oblique in the moonlight, and he stayed with it and he fired.

The target could see him, too.

It ran from behind the scrub brush and fired at him.

The shots went over him. He moved closer.

He saw its mask, felt his breathing.

As the target lowered the gun, Manny had already fired and covered its left shoulder in yellow.

From the observation deck behind the field, he heard The Terminator and Justin cheering. He slammed his mask cover up on his head, panting, sweat dripping salty down his forehead into his mouth.

He caught his breath.

Piranha was already on the field, slapping him on the back, and the smell of body odor like the musk of animals had dissipated, and now the heavy scent of Piranha's aftershave and the faint wheeze of crack off Piranha's breath was in his face, and Piranha was hollering something in his ear, jumping on his back, pounding his ribs. There wasn't anything his eyes could focus on beyond a tunnel of vision, until the face of his target cleared. Slowly, the target's features reemerged where it stood down the center of the field. The boy was the youngest on the opposing team. His name was Javier and they had played together as children.

— ⋅ —

3

Manny drove down *Avenida Juarez.* He turned onto *Paseo Trunfio de Republica*, behind the wheel of Juan's 1954 vintage red Chevy pickup truck with its bulbous fenders, chrome shining the reflected lights of Juarez. He referred to it as The Apple, which Juan hated. Piranha was riding shotgun. The Terminator was in the truck bed of the five-window vehicle.

The Terminator rapped on the glass of the truck, his mouth moving in dramatic gestures.

"I can't hear him. What the hell is he saying?" Manny asked, glancing in the rearview.

"Slow down, I think," said Piranha.

"Slow down, Manny," shouted Ramiro.

"I don't know what he wants, man. We're fine. There's nobody around for miles." Piranha smiled, stuck up his middle finger. Ramiro turned around, shaking his head as they bounced over potholes.

"He's fine."

"Yeah. I don't know what he wants."

"Probably ice cream. He always wants ice cream after paintball, and potholes make him think of Rocky Road."

Manny looked back. Ramiro's hair was blowing up into the wind, whipping at his face. In the distance, the faint blur of a motorcycle appeared, a phantom speck of dust. In the rearview mirror, it grew larger, louder, as it approached the truck, tailing them.

Piranha turned on the music. Club vibes, heavy beats. "We gotta check out this DJ, Manny. He's playing at Lotus."

"You're crazy. They'll never let us in there. I'm thinking if we go downtown to Kentucky Bar and maybe walk over to where Juan's working, Luis will give us some drinks."

"Luis."

"Yeah, Luis."

"I'm crazy? You stole your brother's truck and you want to go drive by him and say hello to an underboss." Piranha pulled his hair back into a ponytail and he ran his hand down it and he took out his cigarettes and he took out his lighter.

"What the hell are you doing?" He slapped the lighter out of Piranha's hand. "You can't smoke in here!"

Piranha laughed. "You worried about me smoking in Juan's truck. Christ. It already smells like an ashtray in here. You really are crazy, Manny. You better get this truck home before Juan gets there. That's what you'd better do."

"I know what time Juan gets home. He doesn't have to know a thing."

"You don't think your mama's going to tell him?"

"Nah. She doesn't want him upset. My little sister will be sleeping. By morning, she'll forget about it."

"She's gonna tell him."

"I know she won't. Shut up. Maybe we should go back."

"And who's gonna take me home? You aren't driving into my neighborhood with this truck. At least if we go downtown, you can give me some pesos to catch a bus back home."

"You got your own pesos."

"I don't have any pesos."

"Jesus, Piranha. Let's just go out."

"Ramiro has some money."

"Yeah, he does." Manny checked the rearview. "Let's just go out."

"Downtown."

"Yeah. Downtown."

"With this truck."

"Yeah."

"There's a reason Juan doesn't drive The Apple downtown."

"I know. It'll be fine."

"Because you say it will."

"Yeah."

"There's a girl." Piranha took a drag and ashed out the window, exhaled. "A girl."

"Put that out, I said."

"Marisa."

"Not Marisa. Put that out."

"Who?"

"Alena Maldonado."

"She's beautiful."

"I know. I have to see her."

"What makes you think she'll be out? A nice girl like that."

He glanced in the rearview. The motorcycle was now visible, approaching on the driver's side of the truck. Carbon-tempered Ducati Diavel with forged wheels and coated exhaust pipes with conical ends. Driver straddled over the seat wearing a black jacket and black leather pants. No one else on the road. The driver pulled what looked like a Colt 1911 pistol, covered in a grip adorned with a skeleton's upper body, the skeleton's rachitic ribs peeking out between the driver's fingers.

"Holy shit, Piranha."

Piranha ignored him, ashed out the window again. "She won't be there. You're dreaming."

He looked at Piranha and back at Ramiro, who was lying in the truck bed, sweating, rubbing the St. Christopher medal that hung from the gold chain around his neck. The motorcycle driver, who had both hands back on the billet aluminum handle grips, still held the machined black and anodized pistol in his right hand as he drove alongside The Apple.

The driver's head was covered in a black, full-face helmet, black-tinted visor. He motioned for him to pull over.

"What the fuck does this guy want?"

"Holy shit, Manny. Pull over."

"No way. He's got a pistol."

"If you don't pull over, he's gonna shoot you with it."

"He's might shoot me with it if I do." He gassed The Apple, but the Ducati kept pace.

"Put the window up!"

"What the hell does he want?"

"Run him off the road."

"I can't do that. I'll kill him. I'll go to prison and I'll be violated by inked-up, hundred-fifty kilo men nicknamed *Bambino* and, and *Mariposa*."

Ahead of them a police car blocked the road. Two officers, one with an MP5 submachine gun across his chest, the other with an AR and a square-brimmed cap covering his eyes. Crumples of camouflage uniforms, faces covered with black cloth revealing only eyes came into focus as The Apple slowed.

"Holy shit. That's what he wants. He wants me to try to run him off the road."

"He wants you to stop."

The Terminator popped up his head from the back of the truck bed and opened the back window, "You can bet that's not light bore ammo in there, Manny. Manny, I bet that's 158 grain in .357 Magnum, full metal jacket. He's gonna empty that chamber into our heads, Manny. Right through the glass. He's gonna kill us!"

"Shut up! Stay down," said Piranha. "This has to be a mistake. They're *Policia Municipal*."

"I don't think those are *Policia*, Manny," Ramiro said.

"I gotta pull over. There's too many of them around us."

Piranha laughed. "Definitely not Municipal Police. Not with those magazines."

"He's gonna kill us!" shouted The Terminator.

"You got a gun?" asked Piranha.

"No! I don't have a gun. Where would I get a gun?"

"I don't know. I got one."

"Where?"

"At home."

"Manny, pull over," shouted The Terminator.

"Ramiro, shut up," he shouted.

The Apple slowed to a stop. Plumes of opaque dust kicked up from its tires as it pulled over to the shoulder. "You got a gun at home. A lot of good that does me."

"What about Juan?"

"That's right. Piranha, you're a genius. Open the glove box."

Piranha opened the glove box. Colt 1911 .45 ACP. Gold-plated handle.

"Give me the gun," Manny said. The windows in the car fogged.

"I don't need it anyway."

"Oh yeah?"

"I've got a Piranha." Piranha picked up his paintball gun and rattled the balls, flashing a wry half smile.

"Put that shit down. You'll get us killed."

The men in police uniforms approached The Apple. The Ducati driver pulled off in front of them. As the Ducati driver started to move the bike again, his foot slipped on gravel and he nearly dumped the bike. Piranha laughed.

"Shut up," said Manny.

"Get out of the car." Automatic muzzle up against the glass. "You, too, fat boy."

Ramiro got off the back of the truck bed. They stood up against the side of The Apple.

"There must be some mistake," he said.

"No mistake, *amigo*. We've been looking for you, your truck." said the shorter police officer. He had squinty eyes like burnt almonds. He pulled the bandana down from his face revealing two silver top front teeth, and an unshaven face. The police uniform was bursting at the seams where it buttoned over his abdomen. Sleeves too short. Definitely not *policia*.

"This truck? This is my brother's truck." He shifted his feet nervously in the dust, wanting to bury himself in the cuprous dust that covered his shoes. A coyote howled. The moon disappeared behind wisps of cirrus.

The shorter officer looked him over. "Your brother's."

"Yeah."

Suddenly, the shorter officer dropped his grip on the AR that was slung over his chest, picked him up by his shirt and held him up against the door of The Apple. "You're full of shit. We followed you and your brother from California last week to keep an eye on the shipment you promised to move. Your brother dumped his piece of shit car there and bought this truck in Nogales. And your fish market is not in Mexico City, *compadre*."

Manny looked sideways at Piranha. Juan had been gone four days last week. He'd watched the shop and handled every shipment that came in. When Juan showed up with The Apple and refused to drive it downtown, he hadn't asked why.

"My brother was here all week, wasn't he, Piranha?"

"That's right. He bought this truck at the dealer—what was his name? At *Automotriz Juarez*."

"Now I know you're full of shit, because I talked to the dealer who sold this truck. And you know what I did after we talked?"

He swallowed.

The Terminator was hyperventilating, sweat glistening in the moonlight like dew drops. The hair on his chin bristled like the Opuntia cacti. His eyes widened. "Manny, just give him the keys, and—"

"Save your breath for your sleep, you snoring son of a bitch." The taller officer shot Ramiro in the foot.

Ramiro dropped to the ground, screaming, holding his foot. A curlicue-tailed lizard raced away from the back wheel of The Apple.

"Why'd you have to do that?" Piranha screamed, got in the shooter's face.

The other man put the butt of his gun against Piranha's temple. Ramiro was still panting, screaming. Calmly, the man said, "You're bold, aren't you?"

"You looked better with the bandana over that grill." Piranha had taken something, alright, to be talking like that. Meth, maybe, or a line of coke. Manny forced an elbow into Piranha's ribs, his rachitic chest, washboard and skeletal, and knocked him sideways into The Terminator's lax pillow of flesh.

The other said, calmly, "After we talked to the dealer that sold this truck, I gutted his bladder with a fishing knife, and I sat him down at a table and I put a lobster bib around his neck, and I fed his bladder to him in small little pieces. Then I slit his wrists and I left him where he would bleed a slow and remembered death."

Manny's heart pounded in his chest. He shook his head. "There must be a mistake. I don't know what you want from me—or my brother."

"Your brother was carrying over one hundred thousand dollars' worth of totoaba bladders."

Juan had never mentioned anything about fishing totoabas, an endangered Asian delicacy.

"My client, Mr. Yokushimu, got calf livers, not the product he paid for, and you got a full payment from whoever you sold them to. I haven't met the lucky bastard yet, but I can tell you what I'm going to do to him when I do. I'm going to secure his arms behind his back. Usually, I would duct tape his mouth, but I'm going to leave it open, and let Hugo pull his hair back, hard."

Hugo, the shorter man with the silver teeth, nodded, gave a smirk.

"Then, carefully, I'm going to put on gloves—the ones you wear up to your elbows to slice the fish. I'm going to make an incision—much like a surgeon would—right down the middle of his abdomen, until I find his bladder. I used to want to be a surgeon. Have you ever wanted to be a surgeon, little boys?"

"No." Manny made a hard swallow, as if his larynx was pointing sharp against the inside of his throat, trying to escape.

"Totoaba?" said Piranha.

The officer made a squeezing motion with his fist. "When I have his bladder, I'm going to rip it out of his belly and squeeze the piss out of it, into his mouth."

"Totoaba are like aquatic cocaine," Manny said to Piranha. To the officer, he said, "Juan doesn't sell those. They're illegal."

"Juan is his name, Jose," Silver Teeth said, nodding.

"Juan. *Si*, Hugo."

"Where do we find Juan?" Jose tipped up the brim of his cap and stared him down.

From the ground, Ramiro sat, rocking back and forth, holding his foot around the upper of his leather boot, where the bullet had blown a hole in it. "Go to hell."

The man called Hugo with the MP5 pulled the charging handle and engaged the bolt and put the butt of the rifle against his chest and looked down as he fired two rounds into Ramiro's chest. Ramiro fell back against the car before he could speak.

Manny's ears rang so he could no longer hear the man shouting at them just then, and his vision tunneled like it had in the game he'd just won, only an hour ago. Only this was real.

This was war.

He panted, staring at Ramiro, his best friend. Ramiro's blood was spattered all over The Apple. His body was growing lifeless. His face was blank, hungered for air. He reached for his chest, eyes half sighted like his future was dimming into memories on exponential decline and flashing before him subliminally toward their end from some fantastic hand cranked black and white projector.

Manny's teeth clenched hard. His eyes bored into the killer, as if he could tunnel through him face first, as the Pacific cold-water hagfish does, a horrid creature with tentacles capable of burrowing into solid flesh. He would've enjoyed that.

His skin clamped down, moist with sweat. Piranha was reaching over the side of the door, inside the truck. As the man, Hugo, with the MP5, turned to train the gun on them, Piranha grabbed his paintball gun and fired it at Jose's face, then at Hugo's eyes. The rounds rattled in the hopper, came out quickly enough to blind both the men for a moment with yellow paint while Manny reached behind his back for Juan's Colt. He aimed it and fired it at the man beside the Ducati, who was now running toward them. He hit the left side of the man's lower abdomen with a wild shot.

Then Piranha hit Hugo with the butt of the paintball gun and tore at the MP5 strap and the gun fell from the man's hands and hung around his body, but Piranha could not tear it from him before Jose hit him with a pistol, his eyes still smeared yellow and blurred. Piranha ran around to the truck's passenger side and climbed in, screaming, "Get in!"

Manny jumped in and shot the tire on the police car, shot Hugo at close range, grazing his shoulder enough to knock the MP5 from his hands. The weapon hung across Hugo's chest as the man held his wound. He tried to lift the MP5 again, but his shoulder was limp.

Now Manny started The Apple and he gassed the pedal and the tires squealed and they peeled away as a cloud of dust covered Ramiro's body. It fell toward the ground where it had been leaning, breathless, pulseless, on the back tire. He prayed for his friend and he crossed himself and he swore, and he looked back once and then he drove on fast toward Juarez.

He was not thinking about his friend's death in those immediate moments to follow, not about the loss, but he thought about missing the shot. He had meant to send a bullet through Hugo's chest, and he still wanted to kill him. He thought about how he'd failed, failed Ramiro, failed Juan. He thought of the pistol of the man on the bike, its handle adorned black with the skeleton, and he looked at his brother's pistol, gold-plated, and he clutched it now and it shook in his hand.

He turned it sideways and rubbed off the man's smudged blood from the handle. Piranha sat silent. His own breath heaved heavy now as he drove, and the techno music rattled the dashboard, the militant beat of electronic machinist chords behind a whimsical female chorus singing vocals, pulsing through the radio as it had been playing before he'd stopped the car.

He went straight to the club.

There seemed to be no other option. He only hoped he'd get to Juan before the men did. He hid The Apple behind the building, parking it in a series of maneuvers so awkward that had even the drunks—whose pores seeped of tequila and who could not walk straight on the cobblestones—looked at him as though something terrible was wrong.

If only they knew how terrible.

He took the Colt and he put it down his back and he put on Juan's jacket, a calfskin brown leather worn soft and thin, and he walked down the alley with Piranha. His face was tense where the boyish smile of the paintball game had been wiped from it, forever maybe, and his eyes were heavy upon the ground, and his brows knitted together where his head ached most. His mind wandered somewhere else entirely, confabulating in conscious dreams how this was going to be alright, somehow. Somehow, he would not paint his own canvas with the past and the sorrows of this majestic country. He would not.

4

Ramiro was gone.

Ramiro, who had gotten beaten by his dad for him the day they'd stolen snuff from *Senor* Pablo Jose Dominguez Cervantes store, which had a wooden Indian out front. They were only eight when he'd paced the aisles of that store slowly, passing over gum and candies and wooden crates of cactus paddles and prickly pears and specialty fruits, when he'd waited until the grocer was on the phone before he slipped the Skoal into his pocket. The old man had looked suspiciously in his direction, but he was tied up on the phone and still nodding, saying "*Si, Si*," over the line, when Manny left the store with the chewing tobacco. Ramiro had nothing to do with it until they got it home and Manny pulled it out of his jacket and opened it up in plain sight and chewed it and spit it into Ramiro's mother's ceramic vase with the potted lilies. His fat mother had screamed bloody murder when she discovered the clumps of viscous black tar, congealed and still moist from their mouths, and she'd grabbed Ramiro by the back of the neck and hit and kicked him down the hallway of sienna tile all the way over to his fat father, who woke up and took off his belt and went at Ramiro.

Ramiro never once blamed him. He'd taken the blame for the whole thing.

Now he was gone.

One unconscionable act and that was it. And Manny had called him fat and told him to shut up. If he'd known he was never going to speak to him again, he would've listened better to what he was saying, heard every note of his raspy and hungry and wonderful voice. He would've had something better to say, because he couldn't pick out a friend like Ramiro, not like he could pick out the limes or pears or a can of Skoal at the grocer's that day. Friendship wasn't something he shopped for. They'd somehow found each other.

He looked back at the mountains, streaked caramel across their dry peaks, the lights of Juarez blurring out the stars. Somewhere off in the distance, he saw his life as it was, predetermined, unmoving. He breathed heavy and he walked into Luis' establishment. Tonight, it was sexy and dark and awful. Heads turned and stared as he and Piranha walked past white linen-covered tables of guests. The white glass bar glowed blue beneath it and the lobster tank bubbled with red and blue lobsters armored in chitin useless against the instruments of their fate, the hot boiling water and stainless cracking claws. Piranha's white T-shirt and cargo pants were covered in yellow paint. Manny's clothes were sloppy, wrinkled, too. In the back of the store, he walked through the swinging doors, through the kitchen, to the back room, where he knew he'd find his brother.

Luis was standing by the line, inspecting every dish that went out. He was dressed in black pants and a black shirt and a thin belt and his hair was slick and his face was clean-shaven. Manny ignored the stares from the cooks on the line, ignored the smells of lemon butter and fish and grilled steak. He stopped where Luis stood.

"Dolly," Luis said, smiled when he saw him, put his hand on his shoulder.

Manny smiled reflexively, pulled away. Swallowed. The words balled like the pit of an avocado was stuck in his throat that with a ball valve effect, choked him as he breathed, sucking back the words and his air into his windpipe along with any sound he tried to materialize.

Luis squeezed his shoulder, laughed. "What's wrong, Dolly?"

"I need to speak to my brother, please. This is my friend, Josef."

"Josef." Luis examined Piranha and shook Piranha's hand, and said, "Luis," and Luis whistled and ordered the line manager to watch the line.

Manny was trembling then, sounding quite the opposite of the way he did with the adrenaline racing through his blood when he'd faced the men on the road, and entirely removed from his triumphant rush to fight on the paintball field. In the restaurant, a strong flight response operated in him, a fear that the men hadn't harmed him, but that Juan might.

He wanted badly to leave, but he did not, could not.

Luis ushered him to a small room in the back of the restaurant. He opened the door and there was Juan, counting a suitcase full of money. Juan closed the lid and stood up and said, "Manny."

"Juan, I'm in trouble."

"You're in trouble."

He nodded.

"I told you not to come here. How did you get here?"

"I'm sorry, Juan. I'm so sorry."

"What did you do? Who's with Mama and the baby?"

"I need your help. Your truck. There were these guys. These cops."

"They were fake cops," said Piranha.

"Fake cops," Luis said.

Juan stood.

"What's wrong with my truck?"

"Nothing. It's fine. I took it. I took your truck and—"

"You can't even drive. You probably gave Ma a heart attack."

"Listen, Juan. Please, listen. I never meant for any of this to happen."

Juan patted him down and searched his jacket and pulled the keys to The Apple. Juan felt the Colt in his back. He grabbed it and he said, "My gun? You took my gun? Manny, what are you doing with this? You didn't—you didn't shoot someone—"

"No," he said. "No."

Juan's exhaled, shoulders falling.

Luis put his arm around Manny and told him to settle down and he told Juan that he had something very important to say and that they would listen. Then Luis poured some mescal into tall glasses rimmed blue, floated a lime wedge in each.

Manny told the story of what happened, and he told him about how Ramiro was shot and how the men were looking for Juan, and he told them that he'd shot them but not killed them and he told them what they said they did to the car salesman in Nacogdoches. He said the men wanted their payout for the totoaba bladders. He sighed, expelling all the troubles of his world in one breath, and he took another breath that filled his lungs with Piranha's secondhand smoke, and he looked at Juan and said that he was scared.

Luis held his chin and looked at him and Luis' pupils poured suspicion upon his face that flickered prisms of light as the pull-string lightbulb on the ceiling flickered, as though he spun faster around the sun just then, until before him he could only see the centripetal blur, a solitary line of whirling light blended congruent, this revolution aging the innocence of his complexion, adding years that were not to be recaptured in dreams nor hopes nor prayers. Now he started to understand why Luis didn't talk about his business, why its machinations were an unspoken mystery, advertised nowhere but known everywhere. And he understood why Juan wanted to shield him from it.

This complex machine Luis operated—the cogs and pistons and cranks and gears interdependent, the tiniest parts indispensable to the whole of his masterpiece, each piece, however small, with its own price—seemed now to be swallowing him, slowly, engulfing him. And yet he was drawn to it, washed in with the mass of the ocean tides, as if at once he were inside the palate of a terrible beast that watched, licking its lips as it chewed, dissolving him in delicate pieces within taste buds flat and massive—a monstrous fish, perhaps the giant squid of the ocean spoken of in a hush but remaining forever unwitnessed, or a behemoth whale with all of the analogues of the anatomy of man, but without the reserve of man, if man had any reserve.

"*Eres capaz conducir*," said Luis.

"No, he *can't* drive. He's only fourteen," said Juan.

"Dolly, do you know when I learned to drive?

He shook his head.

Luis said he'd learned to drive when he was nine and Luis said that he would like it very much if he would help him with his deliveries and that they were very important deliveries. And he said that he and Juan had some important business to take care of that night and he thanked him for keeping calm and reporting everything that had happened just as it had happened. Luis said he was terribly sorry for the loss of his friend Ramiro and that he would see to it that Ramiro's family was taken care of and that the boy would have a proper funeral.

By that time, Piranha had chain-smoked the rest of his pack and finished the glass of mescal and his hands were jittering and he was pacing the room.

But nothing more was said in the back of that room.

That might have been the beginning.

The first thing Juan did when they left Luis' restaurant was nothing. There was no yelling, no fist fighting. Not even a word the whole way home in The Apple, whose breaks were screaming, "Say something already. Anything. *Hablame.*" Metal on metal, hissing out chards of composite, cast iron splaying at every rolling stop.

It was terrible.

The next morning wasn't much better.

Manny sat at the table with his head against the wall and he picked his eggs and he kept looking at Juan, but every time Juan looked up at him with icy globes, he looked away, ashamed.

"You're not eating," said his mother. She placed two tortillas on his plate. She took a sip of guava juice. Then she set down the glass and she swallowed, and she looked at him and then she looked at Juan. Her hair had once fallen in black whorls that bounced proudly about her shoulders. Today, the strands coiled tight from humidity into frazzled clumps that stuck out in stubborn nonconformity. Her cotton dress lay starched but wrinkled in stiff polygonal shapes, hanging asymmetrically on her frame.

Juan pushed his chair back, scraping it against the wooden floor. He stood.

"Where are you going?"

"I gotta work."

"You gotta take me to the church."

"Manny can take you. He can drive."

"You know, then."

"Yeah, I know, Ma." Juan kissed her on the cheek. "He can drive my truck."

"He's not gonna drive. He's fourteen, and I should've told you. You're gonna take me, and Emmanuel, too. And Elvie." Her eyes narrowed as she looked across the table and she called to the bedroom, "Elvie!"

Elvie appeared in the kitchen doorway, her pink cotton dress scalloped at the hem, with white shoes that looked leather but were vinyl, buckled across her feet, hair pulled into ponytails that whipped laterally each time she turned. Her long eyelashes weren't only adorable, they were a prescription for getting out of mischief when batted against her puppy dog eyes.

There was a song on the radio, *Noche de Ronda*. Elvie didn't know all the words, but she sang a few of them and she spun around, hair twirling as she asked for something to drink. His mother loved old Latin love songs—the cornier the better, especially if they were coming from a popcorn Victrola or a vinyl album full of white noise and static and clicks.

Monday morning, with all the bookish structure and regulations at *Preparatoria 64*, always came too soon. His weekends, especially when he followed Juan, were novel and limitless and sometimes dangerous. *Secondaria* was rigid, and all roads from it seemed to lead to an existence that would propel him off that revolving cycle, flinging him in some alternate direction to chase a truth or a fortune or an understanding of the world that would never be realized in the mundane. This morning was apoplectic with uncertainty, because Juan hadn't spoken to him since Friday night. Normally, he went to school for four hours. Then he worked at the seafood market in the afternoon.

Maybe the excitement of seeing the teenage girls with their knees showing just below the hem of their uniforms, and the testosterone of fist fighting in the courtyard over them, or fighting for no good reason at all, or the lure of doing what he wasn't supposed to do—stealing a cigarette from Ms. Munoz's purse or skipping a class—might be enough.

Just maybe.

This Monday was different, though. Ramiro wasn't there. He should've been there. Ramiro should've stopped at his home before school to drink his mother's coffee burnt and black, and Ramiro should've been there when they said the Pledge of Allegiance to Mexico as they did every Monday morning. Ramiro should've been there as he walked through the metal detector and opened his bag for the safe-bag check at the entrance to the school. All they ever found in Ramiro's bag were potato chips and mangos and whoopee pies. Ramiro taught kids how to swim at the community center, even though all he really did was float, and he was going to go to the *tecnica* to learn to fix cars if he could fit under them. But today, Ramiro wasn't there, and he wouldn't be there tomorrow, either.

Yesterday, Father Guillermo DeNardin had swung his golden thurible, metal censer jeweled and suspended from chains and smoking with incense of patchouli and cedar and myrrh, over Ramiro's casket. Sister Mary Magdalena Montenesco had prayed over the casket, and Ramiro's mother had sworn at Luis in church and thrown at him a lighted votive from the gilded stand of beeswax candles when Luis brought his offering forward to her. The glass with the light of the world smashed against the rose marble of the cathedral floor and shattered and took down a silk-screened drape of the Virgin and child as she sank to the floor crying. But then soon after, she rose to accept Luis' offering, which more than covered the costs of the service.

It was a terrible day.

Mayo was warm and the mountains of El Paso to the north appeared prouder today. North Franklin peak looked down upon her sister, South Franklin, whose own shadow descended into the valley between them, and both appeared to be frowning upon Juarez sadly. Beneath their points, the Mesilla Valley was sunless. His eyes followed the ridgelines of the volcanic triangles and the steep pitch down the west side of North Franklin as he walked along the sidewalk to school. North Franklin's Precambrian summit peaked in a scalene, spear-like, with tilted sediments of iron-rich rock dating back before Mexico shed her blood upon it, skimming red dirt along its side. Green vegetation spurned the beginnings of trails along the horizon. These seemed, from Juarez, impossible passages, climbing among the twisted subterranean pockets and tunnels of rock, and recesses concealing army munitions and skeletons and the histories of the dead. All paths branched toward the peak of the mountain, Indian's Peak, alternating rocky and smooth, between intersections and switchbacks, and descending again.

Maybe he would go to *technica* or *baclaretto.*

Maybe he'd continue to take on Juan's business at the market—if Juan ever spoke to him again. He'd take the route he always took to the market later, and maybe Juan would tell him to leave, but maybe he wouldn't. Maybe it would be the same, like nothing had changed, even though everything was different.

Ramiro didn't attend the same classes that he did, but Piranha did, and since Friday night, Piranha's face looked even more skeletal, reminiscent of the dolls of the carnival of *Dias de Los Muertos*, only sacrilegious, an unholy, hollowed-out vessel among ripened beings: White shirt and black pants of his uniform stained in patches that told the story of everything he'd eaten in the last week. Ponytail slick and tight. Rachitic chest lost beneath wrinkles of cotton and beltless pants. He could tell Piranha hadn't showered all weekend, because he could still smell the incense from the church on his hair, and there were streaks of yellow paint on the back of his neck. He sat a minute with Piranha and there didn't seem to be much to say, and then he got up and walked back to the cafeteria, and Piranha looked back at him from across the courtyard and tipped his chin and kept walking, out of the school.

After classes that morning, he didn't go right to the fish market.

The café was full that afternoon and he went there looking for Alena. The afternoon was gorgeous, the restaurant was gorgeous. Copper ceiling and shining copper coffee bar, espresso machine gleaming silver just inside. Doors rolled up into the ceiling and leading out to open-air tables covered with prismatic tiles, plates of strawberry mango salsa and *biscochitos* cookies and café Americano. And sitting there waiting for him at the table by the Boulevard Zaragoosa, Alena Maldonado was gorgeous.

A white cotton *huipil* rested on her shoulders and a tangerine sash encircled her waist over her black cotton skirt, bunching softly in wide ribbons, with embroidery down its left side in pink and red and yellow and turquoise, twisting in geometric strands. Her *rebozo* shawl was folded into a square on the table. She twirled the delicate golden chain doubled around her neck, elongated in miniature rings and hanging to her navel.

He sat with her and he kissed her cheek and after some time, the waitress brought their coffees and some apple wedges sprinkled with cinnamon. Alena pushed them before him, and he bit one and she drank some coffee and she looked down and then looked back up at him.

"What will you do after all of this?" She was staring off at the mountains.

"After what?"

"*Secondaria*."

"I don't know," he said. "*Tecnica*, maybe."

"To do what?"

"Fix cars."

"I think you are better than that."

"You do?"

"I do," she said. "Grandmother says I should marry. She is old. She worries about me."

"Do you want to?"

"Do you? I mean, not with me, but—"

He smiled, because he couldn't have imagined marrying anyone else, but it seemed impossible that she would have thought of this possibility with him, even in the distant future. It seemed he could've been soaring over this moment, detached from his life like a falcon, eyeing it from North Franklin. "It would be nice. Someday, I mean."

"Your brother, Juan. He makes a good living."

With her words, his stomach knotted, descending, bottomless in disappointing free fall. "You like Juan?"

She shook her head no and regarded him with romantic eyes that spoke their own language, with their corners angled at gentle diagonals, and her velvety eyelashes closing over them in flirtatious draws. "Manny, I like you. Juan makes a good living. You could do what he does."

"Alena, you don't know what—"

"I know there are some things I don't need to know. Your friend, Luis—"

"He's not my friend, Alena."

"What is he?"

"What is he," he said. "How did you know I know Luis?"

She stirred sugar into her coffee. "People talk."

"What are they talking about?"

"Do you believe in God?"

"Yeah."

"Are you sure?"

"Yeah, I'm sure. I don't know if he believes in any of us, no matter how much I'm in his ear."

She said that while men did many bad things, the only thing that mattered was whether they doubted Him and if they possessed humble thoughts when they laid down their heads at night, and she said that that was something between a man and God and for no one else to say. She said that often, people who appeared outwardly holy could be filled with doubt and not truly believe at all. And she said that a murderer who repents and does not doubt God but believes in Him unconditionally might be saved by Him, and that it was impossible to know which one of us that might be by looking at a man or a woman from the outside.

"Have you ever killed anyone?" he asked, laughing.

"No," she said. She said that men were not the only ones who took the lives of others, though, and that women who enjoyed lives that appeared free from violence and sin were sometimes also guilty of the same evils.

He should've been getting home.

He should've been feeding the cow cereals and grass and silage, feeding the pigs turnips and swedes and mangolds. Chasing the mice whose hearts fluttered as fast as his did then just sitting there with her, chasing them from the barn, and sweeping the barn—and of course, repairing what was broken with Juan. He could hear his mother's voice yelling, smell her cooking beans that would be on the stove when he got home. She'd scream and tell him that if he left the animals out at night and did not lock them up before nightfall that the *chupacabras* would come and slaughter them. *Chupacabras*, mythical devil dogs. He fought a smirk, but the conviction with which his mother believed this could not be argued, could not be reasoned.

He should've been halfway there by now.

Instead, he took Alena's hand.

He was aware that his gap-toothed smile was plainly visible, but she was smiling back at him and for a moment there was no concern about the future and her smile healed everything inside him, even the pain of Ramiro's death.

She said that the worst thing any man could do was to think that he knew better than God.

He said he thought there was something worse.

"Oh?"

"To proclaim that to others," he said.

"*Si,*" she said. She squeezed his hand.

"I'm not trying to tell God what to do." A white cat had butted its head up against his leg beneath the table. He scooped it up and scratched its head. The fur on its neck bristled and it licked him with the dry prickles of its tongue. "I'd like to know what the hell He expects me to do with the hand He dealt me sometimes."

There was a silence between them. Then she asked him, "Why are you laughing?"

"You remind me of my Ma."

She made a strange face, scrunching and wrinkling her nose like a jack rabbit. She probably wore red panties every day in some bizarre ritual to extort what she wanted from God Himself. Probably had an altar full of candles and a tiny statue of Saint Anthony of Padua turned upside down or hung from a noose of kitchen string, blackmailing the canonized mortal in a strange and tortuous tradition, holding him hostage until he helped her find true love. Probably realized no conundrum of lining up false gods to rationalize her every whim. Women sure got some crazy ideas, yet he kept returning to the thought of her in red panties. He sighed, and he drank some of his coffee, and he ate another apple slice, but he inhaled the cinnamon dusted across it and he coughed, and he sneezed and they both laughed so loud that others in the café turned to stare.

5

It was almost three days before Juan spoke to him.

It was two days after the service at the *catedral* for Ramiro, where he'd laid down The Terminator's paintball mask outside the closed casket. It was a day after he'd washed and waxed The Apple until he could see his distorted reflection in it, that kid looking back at him that he barely recognized in the red paint. After an entire afternoon of working at the fish market stocking tuna and hauling crates of ice, removing the scales and tiny bones from the flaky fish and scrubbing the innards from the floor and washing out the plastic barrels, without a word.

And then, at the end of the third day, when the other shop owners were packing up, pulling down the wooden doors over their shopfronts, Juan spoke as if nothing had ever happened.

"I need to take care of something," Juan said.

"Okay."

"I'll be gone a few days."

"I'll come with you."

"No." Juan turned and padlocked the door and he checked it and he put the keys in his pocket. Then he turned back to him. "Manny, I need you to be in charge for a few days. Here."

The cords in his neck tensed and his jaw settled. He swallowed, nodded. "You're going to take care of those guys."

"No," he said. "Luis is going to take care of those guys. I'm going to take care of my customers."

"Your customers."

The women across from the *mercado* on the *Avenue 16 Septiembre* selling *guayaba* popsicles and serapes and leather boots with spurs and sombreros were beginning to pack up their carts. The women waddled about, sweeping street dust, with *rebozos* wrapped tightly and ruddy faces and hair pins holding back wires of black and gray, flat sandaled feet spread apart the width of their doughy shoulders.

"I'll be back in three days. Take Ma to church, the market, wherever she wants to go." Juan pulled his keys out. "I'm going to get The Apple. You're going to drive us home."

"But—"

"But what? You wanted to drive my truck, right?"

"Yeah, but I thought you were—"

"What you had with Ramiro can never be made right. And that probably wasn't the first time you took the truck and went out with him, was it?"

A wry crescent formed at the side of his lips, but he held it back, stopped it from merging into a full grin.

"You probably had some good times in it with Ramiro, Piranha, and who's that other kid you go out with?"

He nodded. His jaw tightened, clenching his teeth into a taut vice of disbelief. "Justin."

"Hang onto those memories, Manny. Never let them fade. When they start to go away, peel that truck out in a cloud of dust and tear up a stretch of desert where the sun is setting like a blood orange and you remember every one of those times you had. Don't you let anybody steal that pain from you. It's yours. It's your pain, it's your life."

"You remember Dad that way. I was too young, mostly."

Juan turned. "Hang on to those memories, Manny."

He nodded, wrapped some tilapia and shrimp in white paper and he taped it closed and he tucked it under his arm, and he waited for Juan to pull up the truck, and he drove the truck back to the farm. Nothing else was said on the drive home, except that Juan said that he did not want The Apple to smell of smoke ever again.

He learned from those days—from what was said and what was not said—that there was not a man in Juarez who did not trust Juan, and not one who trusted Luis. When he spoke of Juan and he introduced himself as Juan's brother, warm smiles passed the faces of customers, both the young women with plump cheeks and the ones who were aged, etched by time. On the first morning he watched the market, a young mother with soulful eyes, barely twenty, lingered at the shopfront. He thought she might be a gypsy or a thief, and he kept close watch on her hands and her child's hands where she loitered. The woman strolled with the barefoot child, whose face was smeared with cocoa dust. The feverish-looking boy yanked at her skirt, and she ignored him. She batted her coal-rimmed eyes, and she tossed her misshapen curls, and she asked where she might find some cilantro and red pepper and lemon. She chatted a while and looked to the street and back at him, looking as if she were waiting for him to say something that he could not discern. There was a silence and she smiled, and she seemed not to care about anything as she examined the racks of the day's catch.

Suddenly, though, the moment changed. In the woman he saw the way fear could be omnipresent of nowhere and then hawk-like, ubiquitous. There was a sharp whistle from a rooftop where a boy sat on the parapet across the *Avenue*, and this fear materialized.

Luis' motorcycle was peeling down the *Avenue.*

Luis parked in front of the shopfront. The woman turned to the street and though her flirtatious face was young, it withered years in a moment, a glance. She pulled her child close and tightened her *rebozo* over her breast, and her fingers trembled, and she turned from the carts of mackerel and deveined shrimp. Her dust-covered huaraches disappeared into the crowd and she said nothing and everything with a hesitant smile, a timid, elderly wave. She yanked the rosy-cheeked boy along as he looked back at Manny.

He wanted to ask someone. Luis, maybe. No, not Luis. He could ask the ones who spoke in whispers, perhaps, the ones leaning on streetlights, smoking quietly and scratching grayed mustaches and tipping their sombreros in a respectful gesture and shuffling their cowboy boots. No, not those either. He wanted to ask those men who did not speak in words at all and said everything in their reticence: What did Luis *do?* How many people did Luis employ? How did they come to work for Luis? How did Luis' life come to be a far-reaching empire in which Luis asked things of people in the form of questions that were not actually questions but orders, without room for the elevation of an eyebrow?

The sun rose and it set on Ciudad each day, and yet there seemed to be a separate world, removed, revolving around another set of men, and these men were not ones he knew, but Luis knew them well.

He did not ask, but the answer began to unfurl in those days when Juan traveled.

Luis climbed off the bike now and stood the bike and smiled wide and fluid and shook his hand and patted him on the back hard. Manny took off the yellow apron and underneath, his white shirt was covered in sweat. He wiped his brow and he asked Luis what he could get him, told him he had *Almeja chiluda* clams and *casrilla* and Pacific tuna, things Juan had told him to say, and he showed Luis the crates of whole fish and filets he had cut that morning before the sun rose, and he showed him the jumbo lobster tails.

"Juan is gone for a few days," Luis said.

Manny looked down at the scallops and considered their size and he felt a similar size knot rising and falling in his neck, balling up tighter. "*Si.*"

Luis lit a cigarette and he leaned on the iced carts of swordfish and he smoked. He looked at the shopfront beside Juan's, wood painted teal blue and chipped, with yellow and orange and white pictures of fish, their pointed teeth carnal and their backs scaled and finned, names painted beneath them, many misspelled. The owner, Aristeo Ortega, was hosing the floor, shaking his head.

"You like to watch fights, Manny?"

"What kind of fights?" His feet shuffled beneath him. Juan was probably helping pull a huge catch off a fishing boat now, a giant swordfish reeling in the net, hauled in still flailing in wild, parabolic arcs, flopping futilely—outmuscled, perhaps, but not outwitted in its capture.

"I have a special pass," Luis said. "To the bullfight. The fights have returned to Juarez, and you can watch it with me in a special place, Manny. We can go into the *callejon.*"

He wiped his hands in the stiff folds of the apron and he felt his face grow ruddy and his expression tried to hide his inexperience. Luis lifted his chin and it felt like a gesture vaguely paternal, but it was not.

"The *callejon* is the hallway connecting the bull ring and the stands, the screaming fans, the spot where the matador and his team of *cuadrillas* wait."

Manny smiled, swallowed.

"Would you like to go with me to see the fight, Manny? I planned to go with Juan, but he will not return tonight. There may not be another fight for some time."

"Where is my brother?"

"Your brother is fine, not to worry."

He said that he would like to go, and Luis smiled and nudged him with his elbow, and Luis said that they would have a great time and that he would pick him up directly from the shop at sunset. Luis took a large order of lobster tails and tuna and swordfish for delivery to the restaurant and Luis said that the fight would be spectacular, that he would remember it forever.

Manny asked if the bullfighter was good and Luis winked and he promised him that the matador would not be gored, said that it was guaranteed.

"How?" he asked.

"Shhh," Luis said. "Now, Manny. You're a young man. Probably, you'll be the youngest man with such credentials to stand near the fighters. It is a big favor to Juan, for you, I mean."

"Thank you, Luis."

"*Si.*"

"Thank you."

"Can I ask you a favor as well, if I need one?" Luis patted his back hard again, squeezed one of the lemons from the iced scallop display in the wooden crate and bit it raw and ate another.

"Yes, sir."

"I'll see you later." Luis threw his leg over his motorcycle and started it and crushed his cigarette. Then Luis sped off down the *Avenue.*

There was a lizard racing about Manny's feet where he stood and a man with a tattoo on the back of his neck talking on a cell phone beside the street and a Jewish man walking quickly by as he looked around him where the street was now shadowed. Bare-shouldered *senoritas* stood sipping hard lemonade at the cantina next to the bank. They looked like it was not their first time in the cantina, like permanent fixtures. It was already time to reel down the aluminum door and close the iron padlock on the store for the evening.

The day at the *Mercado del Mundo* had been lucrative. Juan would be proud. He would have felt independent and destined and liberated that day—except that now he felt pulled toward a certain confinement, an employment, to a cause that was less unknown to him the closer he came to it. He wondered if it was inevitable, and if he possessed only the illusion of autonomy.

His mother would've loved the *Espana Cani*, the simultaneous fanfare of *Gypsy Spain* and the gore of the fight and the anticipation insatiate of the spectators and their impossibly loud shouts of *"Ole!,"* and even those of the Americans who had wandered from El Paso to witness the bullfight. She did not possess an ounce of sympathy for the magnificent animal, nor for the PETA protestors crowding the entrance to the Globe-like, Shakespearean arena with its plebes packed together. Enriqua, in her best *puebla* dress, would've sat with him to try to recapture twenty revolutions around that brilliant sun that illuminated their *sol* section, where she would've sat fanning herself and looking across toward the entitled guests, where Manny and Luis now sat comfortably in the shadows, the *sombra*, cool and protected. She embraced every delicious barbarism of the *corrida de torros* tradition.

But he did not tell her that he was attending it, because he was attending it with Luis.

In that space of the hour before the fight, with the guitars and castanets of the *mariachi* music playing and the entrance of the *picadors* on white horses cloaked in purple by men in sombreros of black velvet and sequined gold, followed by flamenco dancers—during that time when he stood quietly next to Luis in the *callejon,* sipping *anejo* aged tequila, waiting for the matador to come out, young and narrow and light-footed from Malaga, Spain, he tried to find a solution for his loneliness, the exactness of this irony of being surrounded by nineteen thousand five hundred fans and still knowing he could've fallen away unnoticed and dissolved into the earthen ground of the ring, morphing into the dust from which he came. He tried to find a cure for the emptiness, but he could not.

And so, he followed Luis, stood by his side. And when the flags of Mexico waved proudly, he stood and he sang and he felt the veins rush in his temple when the parade of the *toreros* and *bandellieros* passed them, massive and unyielding. Then it was time to sit in Luis' box beside the judge, and as they went up into their seats, Manny's heart beat fast and terrified when he saw her. She was waiting in white cotton, her hair pinned with a gardenia, wearing an unbelievable smile, warm and white, with the same destructive power of the bull itself. He looked, perplexed, at Luis, and Luis slapped him on the back and told him that he knew Manny fancied Alena and that he had arranged for her to be there, too, and that he would be very pleased at the outcome.

"How did you get here?" he whispered to her, but the fight was starting, and in all the noise and pageantry, that detail was soon forgotten.

Alena clapped at the first spear plunged into the rump of the bull, shiny and slick and vulnerable. She squealed in childlike analogues with the beast, wincing and cheering with a disregard for the creature that sent a coldness through his skin, which came and passed as his own elation disappeared into hers, her breathing, her excitement, her hair that bounced out in rolling curls from a high ponytail atop her head.

Before the bull was impaled, she stopped and looked at him, perplexed, watching her. She furrowed her nose and she told him that the fight was not a cruel affair. She said that the way in which the *matador* covered the bull's face with his cape, in a serene and gentle pass, was quite religious, and that it was done in the same way that Veronica wiped the face of Jesus Christ before his death on the cross. She said that the bull shared the same passion.

He reminded her that the bull was not the savior of man, and she told him to hush, and she leaned forward on the rail of the box and looked on and he looked at her and finally, he smiled.

"She is yours," Luis said, in a whisper. "*De nada.*"

Manny looked at him strangely, with envy and confusion and innocence, and they were interrupted by the hawker who brought a special plate of paella and tamales and another who brought glasses of sangria and apologized to Luis for the humble nature of the gifts. Manny sipped his drink and a laugh escaped him as the smell of the grilled food filled him with a comfort remembered. The Terminator would've ordered seconds and eaten Manny's meal first, and then his own two portions, afterwards.

Luis made a toast. Then he introduced Manny to another man who had entered the box.

Gusto was a heavy man with a young and bored wife. He had glassy eyes, grey like dolphins, that stared off, raking the crowd in horizontal and continuous, distinct passes. He looked as though any smile would betray his own conscience. His wife, Anna, was loud. All her teeth showed when she smiled. She kissed Luis on the cheek when he entered the box. Gusto had a Colt that was not meant to be concealed and he was missing his pointer finger on his left hand. Although Gusto said very little that evening, Luis told Manny not to be fooled, said that he was called Gusto because he was long-winded and told stories with life and vigor. Upon hearing this, a smirk escaped Gusto's face, though his eyes did not cease scanning the crowd.

It seemed a long time to watch the bull trounce about, imbedded with spears jeweled and golden, wielded by the *picadors*, preparing it for the savage and gallant and final death with the impaling sword of the *torero*, but Luis kept his glass of sangria full and Alena's face was mysterious and lovely and awestruck, and he could not say that he did not want to be there. The bull was a feisty animal, resisting the lure to its kill, tossing its horns proudly and brushing through the cape, and attempting to knock the picadors dressed in ranchero costumes down from their horses.

The *torrero*, Javier Diaz Reyes, was a true showman who bowed and knelt before the judges at each pass of the bull as it galloped reverently. Diaz Reyes plucked up one of the carnations thrown at his feet and placed the stem of the flower, with its soft crumples of white petals, between his teeth as he strutted before the flamenco dancers, and the judges, and the children who cheered him on, dressed in cowboy hats and *charro* boots.

After several charges by the bull and the elaboration, the bull was weakened in its rump by the picadors' spears, and the kill was imminent. Just below the *barrera*, Manny watched Diaz Reyes take the *muleta* and the sword and enter it into the animal, which contorted and thrashed about before it went down.

It wasn't, however, a long and labored kill.

Diaz Reyes seemed to enjoy the ritual, even the splashing of the sanguine and garish nightmare upon him. It seemed a bath that the *torero* took great pleasure in, washing him in the bull's blood as he stood before the dying animal and bowed. His suit shimmered the color of quicksilver, embroidered red, speckled red now blood. The gentle curve of Diaz Reyes' shoulders tilted downward at the bull's corpse in its respectful defeat.

When it was done, Diaz Reyes looked to the judge.

Luis whispered in the judge's ear and the judge waved two white handkerchiefs. Both ears of the animal were cut off. Manny could not fathom what came next, what would happen amidst the shouting and the cheers from the *sol* and the *sombra* and high from the mirador cloaked in ivy and bloomed bougainvillea, where a family of fantastic wealth sat with eyes cast down at the dust now coppered with a trail of blood. Flamenco dancers spun in delicate lines around the stadium, dresses floating in soft waves of red and black and gold. It was a magical reality, this momentum of his life, the dreamlike direction it was headed. With Luis at his side, it seemed this course could not be resisted even by his own choosing if he did not wish to follow.

As Diaz Reyes' white-gloved hand placed one of the bull's bloodied ears into Alena's delicate and small hand, she covered her face in glee and looked to him and to Luis, giving thanks eternal and disbelieving. Manny, too, felt this disbelief, and he felt through her happiness the tears of Mexico raining ashes upon the stadium, upon him, titanic drops of the dead.

No sooner had he imagined the night that would follow in the *zocalo* that would be filled with tequila and plates of grilled shrimp and celebration and toasting, when suddenly, Gusto whistled, pulled him by the arm.

Luis drew his pistol, shouted to Anna, Gusto's wife, "Take her." Then he pointed to Alena.

A bang erupted in the crowd, a smoke bomb, a firework of hot chemical soup filling the stands in vicious vapors of sulphur.

Spectators began screaming, rushing the exits, but they were packed in tightly, and the splendor rushed from him. He could not ignore the tension below the surface any longer, because it was no longer below the surface, no longer imagined, nor longer deniable, nor surreal. The edge of an ocean of blood approached him now, another horizon irrefutable where the violence was god and all the saints its slaves. It was what his mother had warned him about and had prayed would not be so. It was what Juan had made a vain and knowingly futile attempt to shield him from, to thwart his entanglement in, like the porpoises sacrificed to the fishing nets thrown out vast and wide, ensnared in with his illegal totoaba catches.

There were children in the venue, placid and red-cheeked, waving little flags of Mexico. The music of Gypsy Spain kept booming through the speakers of the amphitheater from all sides. People hopped over the wooden backs of the seats and scrambled away from the smoke, out of which appeared the men he'd encountered on the highway. Gusto's eyes passed over the men. He pulled a Super Red hawk .44 Magnum pistol from his back and he put it in Manny's hand, and he said, "Here."

6

Manny stood, frozen, gripping the gun, watching as Alena was hustled from the crowd, down the cement hallway and out of the stands, looking back over her shoulder. She had the bull ear wrapped in a *serape* and gripped tightly against her chest. Two men, both armed, walked toward them now, ignoring the commotion. From his right, Gusto held his Colt with his ring finger on the trigger.

"Where's she going?" He started toward the hallway. "Alena," he called.

Luis pulled him back.

"She'll be fine, Manny." Luis' eyes were hostile. "They'll go to celebrate with the matador, and they'll enjoy churros covered in chocolate and giant strawberries and some absinthe. We'll join them shortly. You'll see. You'll enjoy it very much. I need you to help me here now. Can you help me?"

He nodded, as if there were a choice in the matter, as if he had a free will that he could in fact, exercise. He looked at Luis and looked at the men who he realized were meant to see him there, the men who thought he was Juan, and he thought of how they'd shot Ramiro, mercilessly and without remorse. His breathing quickened and he coughed from the smoke of the grilled meat, and the wafting blood of the bull's ear nearby, disappearing with Alena, and right then, this decision to follow Luis became his own.

He held the gun. His heart pumped into tense blood vessels, clamped down and high pressured. He held the gun as if this were paintball, serious, controlled.

Hugo—Silver Teeth, he called him. A vile piece of work if he'd ever seen one, still unshaven, with yellow paint flecked in his dark hair from Piranha's paintball gun, a gauze dressing bulging beneath his orange T-shirt, over the bullet wound. Manny had made that hole in him, had shot him.

"Your sidekick is a bit young."

"Who hollowed out your shoulder?" Luis slid a line of grilled shrimp off a skewer, into his mouth.

Hugo spat. "My client is owed a debt by him. What's his name?"

"Dolly. Dolly is his name." Luis smiled, lips that settled wide upon each other like clamshells. He slid another shrimp skewer, drunk with lime and cilantro, off his teeth, chewed the shrimp.

"What's his real name?"

"Have some shrimp." Luis waved to the waiter.

"I prefer it to veal, and so does my client."

"I don't know what you're talking about."

The waiter, shaking, lowered the cast iron skillet to serve, steaming with grilled peppers and shrimp skewers. Hugo reached beneath the tray, hurled it upwards. Food sailed, the young man faltered, shielded his face from the hot plate. Hugo swore. "Get out of here."

Gusto aimed his pistol. Silver Teeth mirrored his action, his teeth clenched, urgent and tense.

The smoke had cleared, but a sulfurous odor remained. The spectators were still filing out of the stone exit. The bull was being pulled away by a chariot while noisemakers exploded all around.

Gusto was calm, he frowned. "Your client doesn't know who he's threatening. Give him some time to consider. This has been an unfortunate misunderstanding."

"A smoke bomb entrance—a little juvenile, no?" Luis coughed, looked to the stands, where the smoky soup of gray air still dissipated. Judges shuffled their papers together, exited the box.

Hugo aimed his gun, crowns gleaming in a twinkling snarl that narrowed his eyes. A woman screamed. "You asshole, the firework was set off by some kid. We sat up in the *mirador*, watching your friend here, Dolly, looking forward to our meeting. He owes us a considerable sum of money."

"Gentlemen," said Gusto. "There's been a misunderstanding."

Both lowered their weapons. "My associate, Juan, is an exceptional businessman. He supplies wholesale seafood as far as Chicago. His marketplace and connections are vast, and he's known for delivery of nothing short of exceptional product. He would never intentionally deceive your client, Mr. Yokushimu. Your accusation insults me."

"It would be an odd coincidence for hundreds of thousands of dollars' worth of a delicacy like totoaba bladder to disappear, only to be replaced by calves' livers. Is delivery of such a valuable delicacy not insured?"

Gusto laughed, clicked the pistol back. "The only thing to be ensured in this world, *compadre*, is death, and God's love."

"Now, *Espera un minuto*, Gusto." Luis was pacing the penumbra of the stadium wall, its cracked mortar and gray brick shading away the midafternoon sun from the men, obscuring his expression. "*Espera un minuto.*" Wait a minute.

"*Espera un minuto*, he says. Let's hear it." Hugo, with his almond eyes light brown narrowed into slits, stepped back.

"I'm losing my patience," said Jose, disgusted.

Gusto said, "I never had any. Better for you."

"Of course, Juan stands by his business, and Juan and I do business together. I stand by Juan." The waiter, who had left them, returned, offered tall glasses rimmed blue and chattering on the tray. He set them down and filled them with *reposado* tequila, hands still shaking. "We have a matter to settle here."

"You're the matter." Jose reached for his pistol. "We're here to settle it."

"Settle the debt, or we kill you. Unless you want to leave this world, today, that is. It's an obvious choice."

Luis sipped the tequila, set down the glass on the waiter's tray. "*Gracias.*"

Gusto smiled at the men, nearly laughed.

He was silent, and there was nothing comical about that moment, and his life could've ended just as quickly as The Terminator's had, by the hands of those men, but he was thinking of how the steam off the shrimp smelled now and how many of the grilled shrimp Ramiro once ate at the all-you-can-eat buffet on *Paseo de la Victoria.* He was watching the flamenco dancers exit the stadium waving scarves adorned with golden charms and hearing the finale through the speakers at its crescendo, and he wanted to believe that standing beside Luis offered him protection, immunity.

"We both know that Luis' head is worth more than yours, *compadre*, and your family's lives, and your children's, your *abuelita*. Don't we?" said Gusto.

Hugo smiled. *"Mi abuela murio de fiebre tifoidea en un burdel."* My grandmother died of typhoid fever in a brothel.

"I believe that," said Luis, raised his shot glass of *reposado*, lowered his head. "To *Abuelita.*"

Hugo started at him, held back by Jose's ropy arm.

"Gentleman," said Luis. "Juan is working right now to remedy the misunderstanding."

"Misunderstanding."

"Coincidence."

"By coincidence you mean lie. Theft. Dishonor."

He examined Jose's face, deep wrinkles lighter where they creased, browned dark at the surface, sun-aged menacing squint, even in the shade.

Luis licked his wide lips, clamped together those clamshells and spoke as though his voice were a vice, tight and direct. Then, he said, "Juan is fishing. He is to bring back a new, larger, shipment of totoabas. Mr. Yokushimu will have twice the original amount by Friday."

"You want me to depend on you to deliver twice the amount, when you didn't deliver the original shipment."

"That's correct."

Gusto ran his finger along his gun. His hands had wrinkles horizontal and continuous like the segments of brown earthworms, except where he had lost the finger and the scar remained, white and shiny. The men appeared to consider, but Manny was learning that there was a great deal of acting taking place, the expressions of which he studied in meticulous detail. There he learned that Gusto was correct in saying that the repercussions of harming Luis or those who stood with him there were far reaching and had greater consequences than the loss of these men named Jose and Hugo, and the lives of all their families combined. Manny shuddered to think so, and he wondered why Luis wished to guard him, but he did not ask him now or ever.

It was late in the evening when the celebration after the bullfight started to wind down. He should've been getting home, knew his mother would be pacing the wooden floor of the kitchen and scrubbing the same pot with anxiety repeated and unsatisfied, looking out the window, smoking, thinking he was smoking, too, or drinking, or dead.

Tonight, he could've been.

The night had not cooled the air much since the afternoon. At Luis' ranch, he looked over the escarpment and the landscape of flowering saguaro and aloe and agave. A coyote howled between the songs pumping loud from the speakers. From an iced mug that he melted on his sweating forehead, he sipped a *cerveza* with a lime fizzled on top. An old man with a white beard cooked his fish on the outdoor grill. The man just nodded at him and placed a piece of snapper on his plate, seared, steaming. Manny took a bite and he looked out over the rock cliff of Luis' ranch at the lights of Juarez in the distance. The smell of the night balmy, humid, and the grilled snapper, warmed his thoughts. But there was a coldness filling him that he wished to ignore but he could not.

It bristled the hair on his arms, his neck.

The pool was illuminated with LED lights changing teal to red to royal blue, dimming out the stars in a navy sky, vast-reaching and unknowing. Luis drank tequila with women in bikinis and women not in bikinis, all of them laughing too loudly. Gusto came up by his side and squeezed his shoulder and there were shots of mescal passed, and he understood then what Luis meant when he told him that Gusto was long-winded. Gusto shot his mescal and he paused and then he began to talk, talked for a long time. It could've been all night with the way the alcohol blurred Manny's sense of minutes and hours into epochs of times that existed in Gusto's story threads, and periods in and out of his own experience.

Gusto told him about the time when Luis shot the priest, Toribio Cristobal Aristeo de Jesus Martinez, in his church, set fire to the mural of Juan Diego on the Lady's Feast Day, because the priest had refused to baptize Gusto's daughter, the child of a "*Narco.*" An entire congregation gathered amongst wooden benches in white dresses—little *senoritas* with buoyant curls and *chicos* and very old women hunched and skeletal in their waning *Deciembres*—had given witness to the only natural consequence of such humiliation. Six magnificent white columns rimmed with gold and suspending the three structural arches leading to the tabernacle, splashed maroon with blood, the priests body falling sack-like in a thud on the altar.

"He treated me like I'm some trash from the highlands of *Badiraguato*, Dolly. My mother was singing *corridos* at the altar and had to witness that beautiful statue of the Lady of Guadalupe destroyed. Can you believe that?"

He said that he could not.

"My wife, she took it hard." Then Gusto pointed to his wife in the pool. "Isn't she beautiful?"

He nodded, examined Anna's hardened features, but not for too long. Gusto's galvanized expression was watching him.

"Anna cried for days, prayed for the bishop's life, prayed for the baby. She was so upset. She did not leave the house for weeks."

"Upset that the priest was shot. Yes, that is terrible."

"No, *compadre*, for our daughter, our beautiful baby. Can you imagine having to take a baby out of the house, not baptized? Waiting for months to find a priest to baptize her? Imagine what could've happened to my daughter." Gusto made the sign of the cross, swallowed another shot of mescal, rubbed his protuberant abdomen where his banana-print shirt was moist, wrinkled over his gut. He was gazing out over the parapet of the rooftop at Juarez with the clouded eyes of some old and wild dog cloaked with cataract, only he was not old, forty maybe. "My sweet Maria."

Manny feigned a smile, shot his mescal slow and awful that so it burned, so that maybe this would numb his thoughts somewhat. "Do you have a picture?"

"Do I have a picture?" Gusto smiled, pulled out his wallet. "Maria is five now, see. Look at that smile, those doll eyes. They're just like yours." Gusto nudged Manny's cheek playfully. "I would like to have a son like you. Maybe people would think you are my son if we were out walking."

He swallowed. "She's beautiful."

"Dolly," Gusto said, in a hushed tone. "Never keep pictures of your loved ones on your phone, do you hear me?"

"*Si*," he said. "Gusto, I don't have a phone."

"I'll take care of that."

"You want to know why you're here, why Luis is taking care of you, protecting you, doing you favors. A fourteen-year-old boy who, to others, looks like he has nothing to offer. You want to ask me about Luis, what he does, who he is."

He nodded, sipped the tequila. He scratched his face.

"You already know."

"*Es un capo.*"

"No, Dolly. *No es un capo*. The *capo* is imprisoned. I'm sure you've heard. We have a job to do while *el capo* is away, an empire far-reaching that must keep running. The sun does not stop turning, the ocean tides do not cease. *Luis es un lugarteniente.*" A lieutenant.

"But he is important, as you see."

Gusto smiled as he looked around at the old chef and the outdoor grill and the pool, the bar, the women, showing his demineralized teeth rotted black from the smoke of cigarettes and crack, like Piranha's mother's teeth. "You want to know what Juan does, how deeply he is involved. Ah, Dolly, look at me. Look here, at my eyes."

He looked at them, still clouded and soulless. "*Es el un soldado?*" A soldier?

"*No exactamente.*" Gusto began to smoke a cigar. "*Luis es un asociado. Tambien es muy importante. No cometes errores.*" Luis is an associate, also very important. Make no mistake.

Anna had climbed out of the pool then and wrapped her body in a towel so only her bored and aged face and shoulders and calves and feet were revealed where she walked in a sultry gait toward Gusto. The rebellious beats of the techno music pulsed loud through the stereo, discordant, overpowering their conversation.

Manny leaned in closer to hear.

"I can see the eyes of others, compadre. They reveal you. You wonder why I allow her to walk around here, with these women." Gusto tasted his cigar, looked at the pool, his dripping wife approaching. "*Ne le confio en casa. Las mujeres, enganan. Recuerda que. Pero ah, eres joven, no te preoccupes acerca de estos asuntos. Que te diviertas. Tienes diversion?*" Don't trust women, because they cheat. Remember that. But you're young and don't have to worry about these things yet. Have fun. Are you having fun?

He said that he was having fun, it was the truth.

Anna spoke. "*Mi amor, no estoy teniendo diversion.*" My love, I'm not having fun. The bored pout, wrinkling her chin into a hallowed peach pit, swept Anna's face. She looked better wet.

Gusto kissed her and he told her that it was almost time to go. He told Manny that they would speak more, soon, and that he was happy to protect him while Juan was away. Gusto said he knew that he would be happy to repay the favor to him and to Juan. Manny swallowed, looked out at the valley and then back at Gusto. Gusto told him to enjoy his time there with Alena, and Manny remembered that Luis had said that she was his. He was still confused about this, and very unsure how Luis had arranged Alena's presence at the event, but he went now to search for her, searched where his thoughts had never left her.

Inside the modern ranch, Alena sat alone in one of Luis' bedrooms, rooms that resembled those of the hotels where his mother cleaned rooms and had brought him to work with her as a child. The back walls of the ranch overlooked Juarez, and they were made of glass only, and when he looked out over the mountains and the city, he could see lights speckling the landscape as though he was looking into a jar of captured fireflies.

She turned, brushed her hair from her shoulders, her eyes softly falling in a conquered look that was not like that of the Alena he knew from school or the café, the confident girl with theories on saints and love and vampires. One day at school, she'd corrected him with an attitude patronizing and condescending, a swish of her long ponytail that was falling down her back, and she'd said that she in no way believed in vampires, because that was *ridiculo*, but she'd said on the same day that the legend of *El Hombe del Saco* was true and that everyone knew that it was true. Then she retold the entire story of *el Moruno* in detail, the man thought to be dying of tuberculosis who was advised to drink the blood of children and to rub their fat on his belly to cure his disease, and she told him of how the man once kidnapped a boy in a black sackcloth to slit the boy's underarm so that he could drink the boy's blood, and how *el Moruno* still roams the streets in search of children who misbehave.

"You know what?" he had said, walking to class with her that day, her books held close to her chest, him walking a step behind. She had only smiled. "I'm going to tell that one to my little sister one day."

"You would not dare." She poked his chest.

"I would, just to mess with her, at bedtime."

"Elvie is so sweet, so innocent. You would not."

"I would. She's got to stay tough, or she'll fall for anything." He laughed, kept following her to class. "It's a cruel world, Alena."

If only he'd known how cruel.

Now her eyes looked up to him as he sat beside her on the edge of the bed, clutching the bull's slain ear to her chest, still wrapped.

"That was some fight, huh?" He was conscious of the alcohol on his breath, the gap in his teeth, the smell of his sweat on his skin, the perfume behind her ears, of being that close to her.

"Manny, what would our parents say, my grandmother?"

"I thought you liked all of this. You said it was a better life. You said Luis was—"

"I know. I didn't know. I still don't know." She kissed his cheek. "Look at me here. I haven't even had my *quinceanera* yet."

"It's next week."

"I know."

"I don't work for Luis. He's protecting me, somehow, from something, for now."

"Protecting you."

"Juan is in trouble. I should know more of the details behind it. Believe me, I'm not hiding anything from you."

"I know you are not."

Outside the moon was high, bright. He thought about how Elvie had run up to him yesterday, wearing her jammies, before he'd left for the market, and told him that the moon was missing a piece. She'd pointed to the gibbous satellite and insisted that someone had bitten a chunk out of it, stolen it, the nerve. He'd said it was Juan who'd stolen it, and that Juan was keeping it in his heart for her until he returned, and he told her to take another piece of that waning rock and keep it in her heart and that when Juan returned, they would both put their pieces back. He worried about his sister, worried about Alena, his mother.

He sat closer to Alena now, nudged her shoulder. He was trying to gain the nerve to say something to her, compliment her, maybe, when she leaned in close and kissed him, hard, on the lips, for a long time. She did not resist him as he pressed closer as he'd have guessed that she would have, and too soon his belt buckle clinked and loosened and his jeans fell as did her cotton dress, and their rogue garments lay on the floor. Then he advanced, awkward and humble, moving about her soft flesh, and yet she was gracious and supplicant in this microcosm so removed from the one made by the God that she worshipped unconditionally.

That evening in Luis' bedroom, he left his childhood a few steps farther behind, somewhere in the desert over the escarpment of mountains, beneath the tragic and champagne landscape of Mexico, buried in honeyed dust and aureate cacti and skeletons from the wars of rebellion in Chihuahua, fought by generals and armies of Mexico's people and the Spanish and the French, who spread smallpox and typhoid, who traversed her by railcars and horses, during a time equally savage and lawless. Across the ambergris backdrop, beyond North Franklin, so close to El Paso, and the United States.

7

When he awakened on Monday, The Apple was gone from the driveway of the ranch and his mother was singing to *La Llorona*, a ballad of life angst, but absent was her own angst interjected into its melody, and her voice had sweetness in its pitch. The kitchen was filled with the aromas of fried plantains and cinnamon and warm milk and other scents that he did not smell from his nose, but rather his heart. The rosemary plant in the window had been refreshed from the rains the previous evening, too. She cut a stem off the aloe plant in the terra cotta pot and she applied the salve on the small laceration on his forehead. He had fallen, drunk after Luis' party. She probably knew this, but she did not screech at him, she only muttered under her breath, and he knew from this and from the way that her eyebrows had loosened apart from one another, and the way that her shoulders had relaxed, that Juan had returned.

That morning, Piranha picked him up for school in a Dodge Charger. Manny wanted to ask where he'd gotten it, but he already knew, so he did not ask. Piranha smelled of woodsy cologne and soldered metal and cigarette smoke and had on the shirt of his blue work uniform from the garage in the city where he did brake jobs and oil changes for the owner. Manny told Piranha about the bullfight and he told him about the men, Hugo and Jose, returning, and Piranha said that if Luis was protecting him, the men would not go any further, and he said that it seemed like a misunderstanding, as Manny had said. Manny said that he was not convinced, but that the evening had passed without violence, and then he told Piranha about Alena, and instantly he wished that he had not.

Piranha's body was slick. He moved vulpine through crowds, poised to steal everyone's wallet and left shoe, if he wanted to—but as far as he knew, everything Piranha had learned about sex had been from the Internet, and once, from a night in a back room of the strip club, *Cebras Brillante*. At first, they'd put forth Ramiro as a pubescent experiment, his cheeks scarlet from embarrassment and his body erecting a specimen of betrayal, of vain attempt to remain composed. But then Piranha, too, had fallen for the girls' impious laughter, fabricated praises, the false adornments on the young ladies' bodies, and he'd hung his wallet out along the flaxen strings of golden cotton connecting their breasts and thighs and buttocks.

Now Piranha wanted to know the details of his experience with Alena, and he was conscious of his feelings for her. It made him quiet.

They got to talking and they did not go to school but rather back to Piranha's house in the most dangerous neighborhood in Juarez Valley, where a soldier just off Highway 2 waved a red flag to stop them but soon saw them as they were, two kids. Piranha swore and gave the soldier all the pesos he had in his pocket and the soldier looked away and then he let them through.

They played video games, *Grand Theft Auto* and *Call of Duty* and *Manhunt.* It would've been the kind of Monday morning that otherwise made him forget that he was alive, forget the habit of breathing in and out and the habit of walking and the habit of everything around him that could've been encoded in ones and zeros and could've been a game-user illusion, with no sense of apprehension over the armed soldiers in the town of El Porvenir in Juarez Valley in broad daylight, their faces masked and the serial numbers of their artillery trucks covered so as not to be identified. He'd lost all sense of alarm over the broken windows in the laundry and the bakery and the gas stations they passed, the torched concrete block homes on either side of Piranha's street, foundations alluvial and crumbling, the neighborhood looking like an ephemera abandoned by macabre Cimmerians, leaving behind only revenants and auguries.

It was the kind of morning that usually made him forget that he was alive, except he could not forget the bullfight and the party and, of course, he could not forget Alena. She'd made him conscious of his own pulse, and of every blemish and the twist of every muscle of the face looking back at him in the mirror. The feeling was lovely and terrible, and it wound his stomach like a clenched fist.

He sat on Piranha's couch and he sipped some orange juice and he ate some bacon and he laughed at the way Piranha played *Black Ops.* Piranha asked him why he was laughing, and he said that it was the way that Piranha kept running and gunning, because it reminded him of the way The Terminator used to play paintball, except that not only was Ramiro a spastic mess, but Ramiro had never been able to utilize cover because he covered the field instead of it covering him.

Piranha wasn't laughing, seemed to have forgotten about Ramiro, his leonine eyes suggesting that he already knew more about Manny's weekend than what he had told.

"This isn't *Donkey Kong*, Manny. Why do you keep jumping?" Piranha hit the remote against the wooden coffee table, and he asked him if he was trying to make him the last man alive in *Search and Destroy* mode.

"You have the Millimeter Scanner attachment, Josef. It's your chance to protect the bombsite."

"You got the PDW-57. So what?"

He switched weapons and stared down the optics of his player's gun, the weapon aimed between stone barracks down a narrow alley, a burning car inferno on the left of the screen, a fresh, bloodied corpse on the right, electrical lines fallen and strung across the street. Oddly, the fifty-three-inch television screen didn't look that much different than Piranha's neighborhood.

Across the street outside, in a periwinkle home with its front burned out, the neighbors were packing to leave town permanently. A king size mattress was doubled in the back of a Ford truck bed, and there was a small refrigerator and clothing piled on top of it, and there was a table-sized popcorn machine packed into the back. A girl in pink pajamas, Elvie's age, was running and jumping about the truck, watching as her mother loaded their belongings. She was eating a long churro stick and she had chocolate and probably cinnamon on her face. He squinted, peering through the curtains.

"Pay attention, man. You gotta hug the walls more, check the corners, Manny. Quit jumping up and down."

"Fuck."

He put down the remote. Piranha's mother, Esperanza, had come into the room. She drew back a flimsy curtain and peered out suspicious and quickly through the metal bars of the front window where alyssum and honeysuckle grew around the crumbling foundation. Her black hair was frizzed up where she'd slept on it and she wore a threadbare nightshirt and bare feet. Creases from the pillow pleated the skin of her face. Her hands shook where she sat with her arms on her knees. Together, Piranha and his mother maybe weighed one hundred kilos.

"Ya no vas a la escuela?" You no longer go to school?

"No hoy pero manana." Not today, but tomorrow.

"I hope so."

"There is no hope. I will go, Mama."

Piranha's mother shrugged and she stared at the game for a while and after some time, she lit a crack pipe tubular and glass with brown burned marks at one end. She smoked, and she sat, counting a stack of bills on the table. On the screen, Manny was shooting outside of a gas station, hiding behind a wall of sandbags, and the gas station was on fire. He had a mini Uzi and Piranha had a sniper rifle. He shot down three of the enemy, hybrids of men and machine, legs formed of gunmetal appliances, hemi-faces soldered into iron veneers. Their kill ratio was the highest he'd seen them play in a while, and he reveled in their score as the last kill played over in slow motion, the target decapitated, its head whipping back slowly and a jet of blood streaming, splattering around. And then the round was over, and he asked Piranha if he wanted to play against him.

Piranha said that he did not, but that he would if he had to.

Piranha's mother was getting agitated, pacing the room now, glancing out of the windows again. A roach crawled across the boot on his foot. The smell of smoked crack cocaine wheezed heavily off her breath then, where she sat back down on the sofa. She bounced her heel repeatedly, finally flipped off the PlayStation. She exhaled another labored breath that whistled heavily off her chest, and she looked to the barred window and she asked Piranha if he was going to go and get rid of the purloined Charger before someone came to get rid of them first.

"Si, Mama," said Piranha.

Later that afternoon at the market, Manny was laying out *marlin ahumado* and *atun ahumado,* smoked fish, on stainless steel bins set on stacks of green crates. The market was very busy that day, with delivery trucks stopped everywhere and horns honking, carriers on bikes with double baskets behind them bringing purchased loads from the stores and bike taxis with drivers sweating like long-coat Chihuahuas in heat. Mostly, they carried obese Americans from El Paso. Kids his own age stood perched on the street corners.

Luis sped down the *Avenue* then and he stopped in front of the shopfront. He got off his bike and he nodded to Manny but did not say hello, walked past him to the back room, where Juan was taking orders on the phone, making notes at the wooden desk.

Manny followed.

There was a storm in Luis' eyes, those lips clamped tightly today like bad clams that did not open when cooked, soured of lemon and the salt of sea water. Luis was not smiling, and Juan was not smiling, and Manny had noticed that the side of The Apple was dented. The chrome fender was bent downward and pulled away from the frame on the driver's side.

Manny cracked the door to the back room.

At first, the conversation was hushed. Luis stared at Juan, eyes boring, said, "What is there to think about?" and then Manny had to strain hard to hear, but things escalated, became the kind of conversation he could hear through the pit of his stomach. Luis' voice was toxic, working its way through the closed door to his bones, putting fear into him as he knocked on the door.

Why had he knocked on that door?

"Emmanuel," said Luis. He rose from the chair where he sat leaning forward with his elbows pinned on the table like an animal poised to attack. His tone changed. "I was just telling Juan how we had a great time this weekend—*la fiesta.*"

Juan looked at Manny and then he looked at Luis. "Manny's just a kid."

"Juan, I'm almost fifteen."

"Emmanuel, please. The shopfront."

He turned to leave, to go back up front, and he should've left, should've kept going, but something pulled him back, not physically, but there was some unfortunate attraction to Luis, to his partly unknowable dealings. It drew him, and over his shoulder Luis was smiling wide and perfect and Juan glowered. Now Manny stopped and he turned, and he walked deeper into the back room until he could no longer see the front of the store.

"There were children there younger than Dolly. Two and three-year-old children with their parents, who kept them safe. They were eating churros and drinking lemonade and enjoying the fight, and they were safe. And I kept Dolly safe while you fished, didn't I, Dolly?"

He'd rather have swallowed *una pastilla, medicina,* just then, *sin agua*—a whole pill, without water—and let it stick, wretched and fixed, in his neck. The lump in his throat felt wooden, unpalatable. Finally, he swallowed, gave a weak nod, certain he had betrayed Juan.

Luis' eyes remained satisfied only for a moment, and in that space of victory, Luis smirked, and then he turned, slammed his fist on the wooden table.

"Dolly could've been dragged dead by the bull with a noose around his neck by a Jap's hitman, or hung from the flagpole, his pretty head of pomaded hair swaying with the flag of Mexico, her national anthem victorious in the background, stanza after stanza alluding to military triumphs of the homeland, while Dolly's defeated life hung severed on her flag, for everyone to see on Sunday morning, as they walked to the *catedral*." Luis' voice was unforgiving, and Luis said that those would not be the worst ways that such a fine young man as he could lose his life, said, "Or worse, he could've been shot, and forgotten by all, *un expendable*."

"*Luis, han protegido a mi hermano. Mis gracias son indescriptibles*." Juan's voice was terrific and humble, and Manny had not seen his eyes speak with such sincerity before. Juan gave Luis thanks for protecting his brother. But then Juan shook his head. "*No tengo la cantidad de dinero que está pidiendo*." I do not have the amount of money you are asking.

Luis smiled wide and his eyes cooled quickly like igneous stones, blackened onyx, but his demeanor was false. A resentment brewed in Manny that rivaled Luis' routine demonstration of power, only his anger was unbridled and raw and it came from a place inside him that he did not understand.

Luis began to whistle, seemed to take great pleasure in the Mexican national anthem, and sang, "*Mexicanos, al grito de guerra el acero aprestad y el bridón*." The war cry of the steel and bridle...

"Take what I have from my humble business, Luis, but I do not have the 200 hundred thousand pesos you ask. I bought The Apple with the totoaba catch."

Luis continued to sing the anthem, and then he laughed, stopping. He stepped close to Manny and he held a cigarette to his lips as one would hold a joint, and he smoked it slowly, and he pinched Juan's cheek. "Do you really think I'd hang Dolly out like that? Ah, no. I will take what you have left of the money from the totoabas today. Juan, I'm a generous man. You'll see. I'll leave you enough to have it fixed, and I offer my sincerest apologies for damaging it. I should not have damaged something so valuable to you without negotiating first. Your business and my business are not so different. You move a lot of product. I do the same. The trucks that leave here, they travel far, to supply a demand. And you know your product, your market, like no one else can understand it. You're not so easily replaceable. My product, too, supplies a large demand."

"I helped you move your product, Luis."

"You will continue to."

Manny felt the militancy in Luis' voice, saw the fear in Juan's eyes.

"Okay."

"I have a job for Dolly, too. Protection is not free."

"Those bounty hunters were Columbians," said Juan. "Not even Mexicans. Their passports are fake. Their speech is fake. Whatever business they are here on is not only Mr. Yokushimu's business. They have business of their own, and it's no business that I've authorized."

"Ah, then when the *policia* stop them, they will sing the Mexican anthem, and if they don't know it—if they don't know every verse of that beautiful song that plays loud at children's schools and football games and the *corridos de torros*—then shame on them."

"I have the shipment I promised them," Juan said.

"No. I considered giving them what they paid for, and then some. I'm a man of my word. I always keep my word. People say *Narcos* have no honor. That's a lie. My honor means everything, does it not? But no, two men so foolish and dishonest would only take an unfair cut of my territory, dishonor my reputable name with their own deceit. We'll give them another delivery of calf liver, not to make them look foolish, as they are, but to ensure that we meet them again."

"Wouldn't it be better for them to just go away?" Manny asked, and then immediately he wished that he had not said it.

Luis laughed, looked around the room as if he'd been asking someone else, and Luis pressed his wide lips to the cigarette. *"Dolly, Dolly. Eres un buen conductor, mantenido a la manzana corriendo mientras Juan pescado. Tengo una entrega para completar mañana con un camión un poco más grande.* You're a good driver, you kept The Apple running while Juan fished. I have a delivery for you to complete tomorrow with a slightly bigger truck. *"¿Se puede conducir un carro más grande?"* Can you drive a bigger truck?

He nodded, swallowed against that hard lump again, the cords in his throat contracted by adrenaline.

"He's still in school," said Juan. "My mother will shit gold."

"Gold has a value, Juan, as we all do. School will be there on Wednesday, and so will your mother, I hope. God bless her. I was thinking, her land is in a strategic location. She must have a hard time caring for the farm by herself with her boys busy and your father gone."

"No, she doesn't."

"Bien entonces."

"Alright."

"Dolly, come with me."

Beyond the curtain, shadows moved about the shopfront, feminine contours inspecting the selection of shrimp and lobster tails, and from out there, voices muffled and unsatisfied, escalated in volume. The smell of the sea off the fish and the lemon surrounded them, and a stray dog began barking, vicious and lonely. He drew the curtain, headed to the front of the store. Luis grabbed his arm as he would grab something he owned.

"*Adelante, Manny*," Juan said. "*Ayudar a Luis. Aydare a los clientes.*" Go ahead, help Luis. Help the clients.

He hesitated.

He picked up the largest sponge, maize-yellow and soft on his calloused palms, and he crunched the labyrinths of tunnels and holes in it, into a ball in his hand, and he wrung out the water into the sink. Then he wiped the back table where Juan filleted the biggest catches, and he remembered his father at dinnertime when he and Juan were very young, telling Juan all about Gulf fish and marine life. The size of Juan's eyes had grown, listening. His father had told Juan about the largest natural sponge he'd seen, the *Monoraphus* sponge, that was over ten feet wide but still just as porous, with adjoining channels to sustain the organism's growth and survival. The sponge let massive amounts of smaller organisms and water flow freely through it while releasing its waste and unwelcome foreign bodies. He wiped the table now, avoiding Luis' cold stare where he stood, waiting. Finally, though, he finished his task, and he threw the porous sea sponge into the stainless-steel washtub near the guts of fish on the tile. Then he looked up, and he nodded.

8

The first trip Manny made over the United States border was in 2012, through a lawless and violent corridor not far from Piranha's neighborhood in Juarez Valley, an area all but abandoned, where the eighteen-foot steel barricading fence that began in El Paso, between the United States and Mexico, trailed off into the desert, near the Guadalupe municipality. The *Rio Grande* was shallow there and he could drive the Ford truck right across.

Luis had assured him that he would not be seen, that there would be distractions—other kids, younger kids, *los expendables*, who were meant to be seen, to draw police attention so that he could get his very important job done safely. He was not expendable, Luis had told him.

"No, not him, not Dolly," Luis had said.

He knew all about the blue crab and bonefish product that he carried for Juan, for Luis, could answer questions about it if he was stopped, and his appearance, clean-cut and unmarred, was too innocent to doubt. Soon, he'd be driving right over the Zaragoza Bridge, looking the border agents straight in the eye without hesitation, handing over documentation. Luis would get him documentation. Luis said that the worst of the destruction in the burned-out towns was over, told him that it was a completely safe area for him, and that in fact, when he was Manny's age, he would walk across to the United States on foot in the same area.

Luis said, "I've done this many times. When I was young, I would kiss my mama and she would not even ask, and I would go across to the United States, and I would return by sunset. It's your turn. Everyone starts somewhere."

It sounded like a vague promise of a better life.

Luis' did not mention that his trips had been before the cartel wars. Before the Juarez Cartel and the Sinaloas and every other rival gang had intensified their fight for control over operating through Juarez, for control of every bridge and tunnel and dust road route that their product could be moved through. This product was methamphetamine and it was cocaine and it was marijuana, and this product was human lives, moved by coyotes, expendable escorts, transporting migrants. It moved in stealth, coordinated advances, across the *Rio Grande,* and through the night desert among the *ghostflower* and the *skeleton milkweed* and the *Devil's lettuce* plants, cold beneath *Libra*, holding the scales of justice in her hand, balanced, and *Virgo*, weakly bright.

It was hard to pinpoint when *Valle de Juarez*, once a middle-class neighborhood, had slipped into the homicidal spiral Piranha described often, with heads unrecognizable and bloodied and rolled out into the streets on some mornings, with charred storefronts, and the flash of fear in the darting eyes of women. Perhaps it was soon after the steel fence was erected that kept much of the drug violence on the Mexican side of the border, or perhaps when the number of border agents was doubled. When Piranha's family moved there to help on a small cotton farm, he could still see ambition, he could still see families, and their dreams, and he could still see God. Now he looked around him where there was tumbleweed and desert only and he saw the optical bending of light that looked like water but was not water. He did not see any future here, or any reason to believe in the ambition or in families or in dreams.

There was an illusion of the law that was no more real than the mirage of light in heat that twisted into a liquid blur, and when he looked at Piranha on some days, he wanted to believe that his life could be put on a path straight and narrow, and that it would be real. But Piranha's family was slipping away, and he could better explain *Valle de Juarez* in terms of what was not there than what was present. He did not see order, nor justice, and if those things were there then they had nothing to do with right and wrong, nor any written law, nor any law enforcer. If the law was there, it was written in some other language, a language that he was learning because it was being spoken all around him, as a child learns vocalizations and phonemes and nonverbal cues, but it was a language that he could not yet hear nor speak nor write in any code.

He had just begun to gun the truck across the river, feeling the passage of the *Rio Grande* beneath the 19.5 inch ribbed highway tires on the wheels of the F450, not made for slick and grainy driving, when he saw the *Policia Federales*, about a mile back, the U.S. Border guards, and the five children, climbing the linked fence at the crossing point, using the horizontal supports and the shoulders of the heaviest child to hoist the smallest child up, farther ahead. Behind him, in low mountains where he could not see, was a lookout. Beside him, a phone, recently wiped of calls and history and contacts. Everything about the *Federales* looked black. Their helmets, black. Uniforms, black. And their weapons, alloys of black metal, HK21A1s.

He'd left the town near Guadalupe that looked demilitarized, drove out where it trailed off barren, and he'd wondered if he were somehow able to drown out the city sounds of Juarez, farther west, if he'd hear a lonelier popping of rifle fire, bodies landing with a thud on the desert ground, and *policia* sirens and *ambulancia* sirens like he heard in the video games that he and Piranha played.

One morning in 2010, shortly after the fence near Piranha's home was completed, they'd found a T-shirt cannon stuffed with bags of marijuana near the steel fence. They'd shared the weed, smoked it, and dumped the cannon, and he'd wondered now if at night, he would be able to hear that, too, the sounds of those cannons launching bags over the border.

He heard the rocks thrumming beneath the vehicle now, some weathered and round, others shale flat and sheared off their ledges. The tiniest pebbles settled in cisterns between them, with the hierarchy of sediment nestled among larger stones, the smallest packed and detained tightly within the confines of the largest rocks.

There were no municipal police. The municipal police didn't come there, Piranha had told him. He was headed for Tornillo, on the other side, the U.S. side. That first run went remarkably well. Luis had been right. The kids climbing the fence provided a distraction and cleared the way for him and the five kilos of cocaine he had hidden with the iced fish shipment. Looking back on that day, he realized that that was a lot of product to place in his hands his first time running it, covered in the back of a truck bed in coolers of fish and concealed only by a vinyl tarp.

And that's how it all started for him.

If there was a day he could've gone back to, a day he could've turned around and run so fast and far away from that he ran out of it completely, that would've been the day, but he did not. He kept on.

One of the shipments did not go as well. That shipment, simple by design, unraveled toxic and threatened all faith he knew. Miles of fence unwound a lawless desert wound. That long border scar.

Manny was driving a manual transmission, diesel fueled, white, refrigerated box truck that day, when the *Federales* stopped it, blockaded Highway 2, further into the valley near *El Porvenir. Porvenir* lay brutalized, like Guadalupe. The middle-class families that farmed alfalfa and cotton, or ones that had moved out from Juarez, were largely chased out of *El Porvenir* by rival cartels, the Juarez cartel, Luis' affiliate, and the Sinaloa, or they had succumbed to drugs themselves, remaining where the Devil needed no introduction because his work was everywhere. These families awakened to rifle fire, automatic fire, homes ablaze, with stars alighted and fallen on a macabre horizon godless and brought forward by the bestial and violent who self-indulged heartily on their own malevolence. The only men he knew now.

He pulled the truck off the road beside a yellow home, its windows barred with rusted metal. The old truck smelled of burning oil, and the fish had been out of the water a few days, smelled too, blue corvinas and salmon and tuna, stuffed between bags of cocaine filling metal cans, blue and welded shut and buried in the interior of the vehicle. His brakes squealed, but they did not drown out the sound of the blood pulsing through his temporal artery. He reached below the seat, tried to appear calm, though he was not. He did as Luis had instructed.

The envelope. He extended his arm far down beneath the seat for the envelope.

The officer approached the truck.

Miguel Cervantes Gutierrez, Corporal of the *Division Antidrogas* of the *Policia Federales*—the Anti-Drug Division of the Federal Police–was a curiously tall man, whose sweat beaded everywhere on his round face. His words poured icy and aggressive, and he had a crisp walk, seemed to turn with sudden surprise each time he changed direction. Gutierrez had small hands. A narrow waist. His uniform was adorned with the seven-pointed star and one chevron. On his collar was pinned a little gold fish, not a Jesus fish like Alena wore sometimes, but an impossibly gaudy little trinket that looked like it was made by hand, like it had an elaborate, almost magical, history behind it.

"*A donde vas*?" Gutierrez eyes narrowed.

"I carry a small shipment of corvinas and salmon to a fish market in Tornillo, sir, to a friend of my brother. He's a fish seller."

"Your brother."

"*Si, hermano*." It was sounding like the night Ramiro left him, and guilt pressed heavily on him now. "And his friend."

"What kind of fish-seller is your brother?"

"My brother sells all kinds of fish. People come from all over to buy it. He ships it everywhere. He buys many lobsters and shrimp. I work in his shop."

"Get out," Gutierrez ordered.

"Please, Corporal." Manny stepped down from the truck, stood at the side of the road. He could not reach the envelope faster than the weapon was against his chest, its barrel ferric and matte. "I come in peace—"

"Open the truck."

When he opened the back of the truck, crystals of misted frost melting into a single gust billowed toward him, but the air from the refrigerated truck did not cool the sweat which poured now from his skin, nervous from his pores, and it did not dry the beady oil on the corporal's forehead. Beside him paced a roadrunner and another whistling bird. Three pink crosses, one draped with a white plastic rosary, rose crooked from the desert with their paint chipped, where they were placed beside the highway.

Gutierrez's partner, Cordoba, was much larger in the arms and chest, though shorter, and just as dark-skinned. Cordoba told Manny to get down on his stomach on the ground with the scorpions. He lifted the huge drums, moving them aside one by one.

There were no scorpions, but he lay beside the molt of a snake's skin and small pebbles and cracked clay dusted dry and beige at his feet. The fish was smelling spoilt. Th men sniffed it and their faces soured and Gutierrez told Cordoba to open the cans.

"I'm not impressed with this shipment."

"It is all I have," he said, with Gutierrez's combat boot pressed across his back where his kidneys lay. "*Señor, por favor*. The fish will not last in this heat. I must carry on or the shipment will be ruined."

"Shut up," said Cordoba, with his weapon trained on him.

"Your fish smells like bullshit. Your story stinks of it, too, little boy, though you are cute." Cordoba rubbed a black-toed combat boot into the crease between his legs where he lay prone on the ground.

There were two more of them, uniformed in black, armed. Together, their voices made a baritone and premonitory hum that he heard behind him, suspended above him. One of the other men had a bandana over his mouth and it was tied up around his ears and the other had a scarf over his head that covered his entire face save for his eyes.

It probably did not take as long as it seemed for them to shear the metal bins open and find the clear plastic, double-wrapped and packed taut with cocaine, but lying on the parched earth, it seemed an eternity and a poisonous moment for him where his life, with certainty, would end.

"What is the value of this cocaine?"

"I don't know."

"Get up."

"I do not know, sir. I'm only a mule, a—"

"Whose cocaine is this?"

Manny was silent. "Sir, an envelope, for you. In the vehicle."

"Whose cocaine is this?" Gutierrez turned, reached around the front seat where the white envelope lay.

"He's not talking," said Cordoba, nodded. "Well-trained."

"Put your hands behind your head."

"Senor Gutierrez, there must be five kilos in here. It's a huge load."

"It is." Gutierrez smirked, made another sudden turn, away from him, toward the back of the truck, his finger running across the top of the cylindrical receptacle. "And how much is in the little envelope here? It is not bulging, not stuffed very fat, ah?"

"Detain him," Cordoba ordered.

The men followed his command.

With his eyes closed, the ripping envelope sounded of greed, of impatience, and he knew, before he opened his eyes, the look that would befall Gutierrez's face. A deeper fear rose, his heart rate rose, too. It beat in him some desperation that could not escape.

"Pathetic." Gutierrez licked the greasy beads from his top lip.

"Secure him," Cordoba ordered. "There is a pistol in his back. Take it."

With his eyes open now, the other two *Federales* came at him, wrestled him without resistance. Another swift turn by the corporal, and more of Gutierrez's militant tone followed.

"Let him go." Gutierrez spun on his heel, the black boot laced tight, spine tight, turned toward the men and waved them off. "There is nothing to see here. He can go, but the fish is bad. He will not deliver such shit product to a customer. Leave the quarter which is good. The rest goes to the Rio Grande."

"Sir—"

"You heard me." Those coarse metal weapons held by Gutierrez rose to aim and relaxed as quickly, as Manny reassured them with his hands up that he would not fight. Cordoba and the other men grabbed him, pushed him toward their truck with the butt of their guns.

"Yes, sir." The man with the bandana around his face secured Manny's wrists.

When he was restrained, the one with the mask kicked him hard in the chest.

"I said get the cylinders off the truck. All but one. There is nothing in them but fish, spoilt fish, rotten and no good."

"But—"

"Nothing. There is nothing in them."

Cordoba said, "Corporal Gutierrez, there is over five kilos of cocaine here."

"There is nothing, do you hear me?" Gutierrez spun away, arborous, as though rooted in the ground with conviction that could not be untethered, but he did not move from where he stood. "Are you seeing things? Perhaps there are unicorns and electric salamanders in this boy's truck as well. They dance and sing, and they are as jovial as he looks, with his smooth skin that he does not even have to shave, horned horses as whimsical and white as his unstained teeth."

Cordoba and the other two men advanced. Gutierrez turned again, holding the envelope high and forward. He removed the money and counted it and he split it in half. From the first half, he gave Cordoba the largest lot of bills, and to the other two, he gave several bills each.

Cordoba asked, "Are you mad?"

"There is nothing in the shipment but rotted dead fish. This fish is not suitable for consumption. It must be disposed of properly. You saw it yourself." Gutierrez counted more bills from the stack he held. He licked the dry skin of his fingers as he counted every few bills, handed several to Cordoba.

"I did," said Cordoba, but the other men began to protest, and Cordoba and Gutierrez lifted their weapons and the men who had their faces covered elevated their automatics weakly in response.

"There is nothing here that concerns us. Do you understand?" Gutierrez examined the men, whose eyes lowered, turned away from the colonel. Then Gutierrez pointed his gun at the open end of the delivery truck.

Cordoba climbed into the back of the truck, hoisted out one of the metal cylinders, and threw it down upon the ground. He did the same with all but one.

"Senor—"

"Are you Sinaloa or are you Juarez?" Gutierrez abutted his rifle to the wet skin of Manny's temple. The metal was hot, grainy.

"*Por favor*," he said, pleading, sweat pooling along the midline crease of his back muscles in sudden, tumbling drops that fell but did not cool him.

"Sinaloa or Juarez," Gutierrez repeated, his lean frame close, unwavering.

He swallowed, vowed to himself that he would not reveal anything more than what he said, betraying enough by saying only, "Juarez."

Gutierrez lowered the Heckler and Koch and removed his vicious stare, turned on his heel toward the truck. Manny sighed, cleansed his lungs, which were burning from the smell of diesel exhaust and all of Gutierrez's heavy and false magnanimity. Beside him, a road runner observed, chirped a snapping sound like a yipping coyote, and ran off into the desert between a Saguaro cactus and the Palo Verde.

"Leave him one barrel of his disgusting fish. Dump the rest."

"Senor—"

"Dump the rest." To Manny, Gutierrez said, "I don't know exactly what this cocaine is worth, but I know its value means more than this pathetic offering. Ask your lieutenant, 'What do you offer for my salvation? What is my life and my salvation worth to you?' Because this, this amount builds your life into the cost of doing business, and today, I have saved you, given you life."

"*Muchos gracias, senor.*"

"Do you mock me, you little piece of shit?"

"No, sir."

"I could kill you. You have faith in your lieutenant, but your life is worth less than this cocaine."

"I don't know how much the cocaine is worth."

"More than you are worth."

"I don't suppose to be worth much. I'm just a kid."

"Everyone has a value. It is foolish to think otherwise. I have a value and your lieutenant has a value and his capo has a value and, see this? This little piece of donkey shit on the ground here has a value. Ask yourself, what would your lieutenant give up for you? Would he give his brother to save you? No, he would give his brother's life up to this product. He loves his product, his dream. He loves this cocaine. I give you salvation, today. You should love me."

Manny was going to say that Gutierrez could not buy salvation, that salvation had already been bought, but he did not say it then. He did not say it ever.

Gutierrez whistled, revolved around semicircular on his heels to face the men, ordered Cordoba to place the metal cylinders on top of the *Federales* truck. It had gunmetal bars crossed about the truck bed for standing and bull bars across the front and the star painted on the side that said *Policia Federales* in white. They lifted the rusted receptacles. The cans were blue and red and yellow and dented. They rolled heavily onto the back of the pickup truck. The men whose faces were covered secured them with metal straps on their sides and one of the men pushed the butt of his rifle into his back and told him to get onto the truck bed and he did.

"*Por favor*," he said. "Please do not dispose of this fish. I must get this fish to Tornillo."

"I'm not going to dispose of your rotten fish. You will dispose of it yourself."

"Please do not, I beg you."

"I never liked beggars." The rifle rose toward Cordoba's sights.

He swallowed and looked at the cocaine and he lay face down on the hot metal of the truck bed with the rifle at his back. His mouth dried of all its moisture and he breathed heavily. The sun was turning the heat in the air into waves in the distance and the roadrunner called from somewhere out there again.

Then Cordoba got into the driver's seat and the other two men got onto the back of the truck and stood with their rifles across their chests and Gutierrez sat. Cordoba drove them over to the river where it ran fuller and the truck slammed into park and he got out and put the tailgate down and told him to roll the metal drums off the truck and to dispose of them in the Rio Grande.

"Sir, please, do not do this. This is a huge load of fish. If the offering is insufficient, I might consult with my brother to—"

"Your brother has already insulted me."

"But sir, it's a large shipment here that I'm responsible for. Please allow me to talk to him before you—"

"Go ahead. Rid my truck of your soured catch." Gutierrez's rifle rose.

In his mind, he'd already begun to work with street-smart acumen, confabulating how he would explain the loss to Luis, set it right like a painful twist of a broken bone, but he knew he could not, and he shuddered at his betrayal, feeling wicked and disloyal for not lying down and allowing Gutierrez, with his hands on his narrow hips and his expression of alacrity and pleasure, to trample him before he shot him. He closed his eyes and knew that Gutierrez still might, and that brought a brief revolt of obstinacy. He wanted to spit and throw a punch at Miguel Cervantes Gutierrez, that almost half of a man with tiny hands, and he wanted to fight that corporal shit of the *Division Antidrogas* of the *Policia Federales,* not with guns, but with his own rough and large hands, until this feeling passed. Now above him there were black birds of prey circling the sun, and a red-tailed hawk, which slatted the sunlight into columnar rays and made shadows behind the huge saguaro. The birds cawed loud and intermittent for something but he could not say for what.

He rubbed the dust off his hands onto his cargo pants, moving slowly, and pried the hammered-down lids off the drums with a rusted crowbar to reveal the cocaine, pristine and packed. The men set to the bags with their knives gleaming and ripped the product open and began to dump it into the river at a point where is flowed faster, carried away the crystalline powder, this river of drugs streaming a white line until it dissolved into the murky rush and the *Rio Grande* reflecting back in sunlight like a mirror in which he saw himself, defeated.

He picked the bags, seared open, and dumped each of them, with the men prodding him and watching and taunting him. Gutierrez was turned toward the desert, not watching them, but when they were done, Gutierrez spun around, flippant and satisfied. The *Federales* left the receptacles and the lids and the plastic beside the *Rio Grande.* He thought they might drive him back to the truck where the one drum remained undamaged, but they did not. Cordoba drove off and Corporal Gutierrez only looked back at him in disdain.

9

He supposed that Luis would hear when he did not come through with the full shipment, but his cell phone rang, and he knew that Luis already knew. Beside the river, back in the shrub of curly mesquite and honey mesquite and lotebush, he heard a *chachalaca's* raucous call and he heard another call back in chorus, and he looked out onto the floor of the Chihuahuan Desert for the brown birds and he spat and he looked around in the other direction, but he still did not see them. What he saw was a rotted shack, the lookout. Outside, a pair of binoculars eyeing him, and in the far distance, an armed man in fatigues whose face he could not see from where he stood beside the river, alone, beside the mess of plastic and the rusted drums, stranded some distance from his truck.

He answered the phone and the voice on the other end was not Luis. He might have been expecting a savage and angry voice, a hitman, a *sicario*, or another lieutenant whose voice spelled a violent death for him that he had only momentarily been spared by Gutierrez, but the voice was none of these. It was Juan, who said, "I saw the deal go bad. I'll be down to the valley to pick you up."

"Who's at the market?"

"The market's closed."

"Closed."

"Manny, this is not the time."

"You saw the whole thing? Why didn't you do anything?" His breathing deepened and suddenly his sweat was no longer cooling him. The suffocating odor of the fish made him gag, and he coughed on the fine dust of the dumped product around him.

"Stay there a moment. I must make sure things are quiet. I'll come."

"Juan, why didn't you help me?" He choked, coughed.

"Manny, just stay there. No, walk slowly, in the direction of the truck."

He looked around him, up at the hill where Juan stood, the top of The Apple once shiny, now a battered red, was visible from a small arroyo. "Okay."

"I'm coming down."

Enriqua made roasted potatoes with cilantro and garlic and lime that night, and she had made taquitos and set on the table with tortillas and grilled chicken. There was cactus juice with flecks of green in it in a large pitcher waiting when he and Juan came home after the sun had gone down. Elvie was spinning about the table and making her green dress flare out around her knees and twirling her hair around her fingers and twirling the ties of her dress where they made a bow over her shoulder. He could tell that she had not eaten yet because she kept reaching for food on the table and his mother shooed her away twice and told her to wait.

"Where have you been? Elvie's starving."

He looked at Juan sideways and Juan looked at him and then he looked back at his mother, eyes blazing, Narco *corridos* playing on the radio.

Juan kissed her on the cheek, slid into his seat. "Ma, why did you wait for us? You know Manny and I are busy at the market."

"You lie. You were not at the market."

"Ma, we were at the market. I swear. Why are you listening to this stuff?"

The song played on, with chords of guitar and the sounds of the accordion playing the *adorno*, interrupting stanzas of ferocious lyrics romanticizing illegal activities like drug trafficking and drive-by shootings. He sighed.

"Juan, my own son, why do you lie to me? And Manny." She scooped potatoes and placed them on his plate.

Juan was looking down and eating, quiet and shameful. He sipped his cactus juice and Elvie jumped up on his lap, her wrists twisting, flailing, as she reached for a tortilla, shaking water from her sippy cup in all directions as a priest blesses his congregation with the silver aspergil filled with holy water. He wiped his forehead, but he did not make the sign of the cross, though he felt he should.

"Elvie!"

"She's fine, Ma," he said, kissed his sister.

"Emmanuel, tell me the truth."

"There's nothing to tell, Ma. We're fine. It was a busy day."

"It is almost nine o'clock. You were not at the market. And you know what else? You were not at school."

"Ma, I was at school."

"No, no you weren't."

"Juan, please, tell her."

Juan chewed at his chicken and took a sip of cactus juice, and said, "Ma, he was there. Relax."

In Juan's eyes, he saw his own fear of God now, but he was thankful for that instant that her anger was directed at Juan. She got up and took off her slipper and beat Juan repeatedly over the head with it, crying. His chair made an abrupt scrape backward against the tile and he spilled his cactus juice and the glass shattered on the floor and Elvie rushed from his lap to see the broken glass but he held her back. Juan was holding Enriqua, devoted mother who appeared strong but was easily broken into fits of hysterics and tears and fanatical misgivings, holding her at her waist, at her pleading elbows, as she swore and screamed that Juan was supposed to look out for his brother now that Papa was gone and supposed to make sure that he was on the right path and that neither one of them was to leave her like Papa had left her.

Juan just let her run out of steam. He tried to hold Elvie back as he watched them, and when his mother had exhausted her obsessive worry and she had no more blows to give with the pathetic slipper, Juan did something brilliant. Manny thought then of what Alena had said about a man's thoughts and a man's humility being a thing between him and God. He could not be sure if Juan was sincere, but there was a part of him that hoped so, and there was the other part of him that thought he was foolish for even thinking that. Juan hugged his mother's head close and smoothed her hair with his palm and what Juan said was that they should all pray a Novena.

His mother's eyes widened and shined obsidian, as though that blackness in them was pouring anguish from her heart, warming her boys. She looked hopeful, as though she had already made the sacred requests and that they were granted, then and there. Juan said nothing, let his mother hold his cheeks, with the electric fan rattling and Elvie paused in rare silence. Outside, one of the animals groaned and the volume of cicadas in a synchronous hum rose and fell, and a crescent of the moon could be seen through the open window of the kitchen. The smell of the chicken and potatoes was strong and he wanted nothing more than to eat heartily, but he did not move from prayer.

"Yes, yes, my boys are good. I know they're good. Let's pray, pray a Novena." A tear fell from her eye, but she did not let Juan's face go where she cradled it in her hands and her stare held resilient to Juan's eyes and it was impossible to tell if it was a tear of joy or sadness just then.

It could've gone on much longer, could've lasted all night, nine hours or nine days, nine weeks, devoting each day to a different cause. It was Wednesday, and naturally this was a day of devotion to Saint Joseph, he who guarded the infant Savior, patron of those who rejoice and suffer, and he sat, and Juan began their intentions to families for their protection and the protection of all children of Mexico and her people.

The prayers lasted forty-nine minutes, but the suggestion alone by Juan had seemed enough to settle her nerves. Juan poured her some mescal as well and she drank it before they began. Her hair that once fell willowy and smelled of shampoo now sat oily, lumped on her head and bound in a coarse rubber band, but she did not raise her creped eyes from the table where her head was bowed the entire time, and she seemed to ignore the sound of Elvie singing in the next room, and the clattering of the child's toy horses against the tile, until Elvie fell asleep on the braided rug in the bedroom.

It seemed a masterful repose by Juan, who said very little. Sacred hour, years of violent pain healed. That long wishful prayer. Juan's face set in angst, with stoic, hardened eyes, her gaze unwound in grace.

The cocaine that was in that delivery lost through El Porvenir was not insignificant, nor was it forgotten by Luis, and it was not without its price due, although this price would not come in dollars or pesos. No, not with those currencies. And he knew that it would not be the last time he heard about his truancy from his mother. The next morning was Saturday, and he awoke very early with the sun and he fed the animals and led them out of the stable. When the sun rose against his back, he sat on the lawn beside a prickly pear tree with his favorite cow and watched her graze. After a while, he got up and he saddled the Azteca mare and rode her around the perimeter of the ranch near the stone fence and near the brook that trickled, soft and pellucid, over wet stones, and he thought about what he had missed in school, and what he needed to do, and when he was done riding the white horse, he got off and he led her into the wooden fenced corral. She threw her neck back and he rubbed it. Then he came back inside the ranch to eat.

Enriqua said that she wanted to go to church. Juan nodded, said nothing. After she had served Juan some coffee and *biscochitos*, she dressed Elvie and she fastened her hair away from her face with pins, and she put on her rebozo. Soon Juan left to drive her and Elvie to church in The Apple. When Juan returned and pulled back up the gravel road to the ranch, Manny was looking through his assigned school book, *Don Quixote*, and he smiled because he knew Alena loved the story. She read it to him sometimes when they sat at the picnic table outside the cafeteria at school, and she would laugh at the ridiculousness of the stories, but he thought sometimes that she believed them, believed in love that way.

He was laughing to himself now, reading about Don Quixote and the windmills, when he heard a knocking coming from the engine of The Apple that drew him to the window. The smell of burning oil from the truck was strong, and he saw in daylight that the side of The Apple that was dented still had not been fixed, though the fender had been repaired, and he saw that The Apple was missing a hub cap on Juan's side in the rear, and he remembered how, when Juan had bought the truck, it had shined. Juan had waxed it, made Manny take pictures of him in the driver's seat, smiling wide, proud and toothy. Now the vehicle was injured, its engine knocking like some primeval brute, its body needing compassion and the tender repair of a mechanic, which he did not know, but he thought maybe Piranha could help him get the work done where Piranha worked at the garage.

Juan poured himself some coffee and sat and he drank it black and smoked and said that he would try to go to the market again tomorrow and that he would need Manny's help, but that he wanted him to be safe more than anything else.

"I have to go back to school," he said.

Juan nodded, ashed into his empty coffee cup, said that it was probably a good idea. But Juan added that if Luis insisted that he be somewhere or do something, then he should probably do it.

"Luis is my boss now? Is that it? I just do whatever Luis says?"

"I didn't say that, Emmanuel."

"Why did you close the market?" He had never gotten to ask him, didn't understand how Juan had ended up as the lookout in the desert for his last run.

"Templars, I think. They had Templar tattoos."

"In Juarez?"

"I think so. Jesus, Manny, I didn't have time to ask with the gun up against my temple. I didn't have the money they wanted. I wouldn't have that kind of money in a million years."

"They wanted money?"

"A lot of money."

"How much?"

"More than I had. I gave them everything I had. They took everything."

"Everybody wants money."

"Control. They want control."

"Control is money."

"The cartels are chasing everyone out of Juarez. Senor Moncato's shop next to mine—it will never open again, I can assure you. He almost had a heart attack right there yesterday on the *Avenue*. They shot two people in the street. Shot them for no reason. They don't want to see Luis near my shop. They don't want to see anybody they don't control."

"Luis doesn't want to see them, either."

"Everyone wants to be seen."

"Why didn't you shoot them?"

"I didn't have time to defend myself, let alone shoot anyone."

"I don't want to do this anymore, Juan. Not anymore."

"Manny, sometimes we don't choose in life. It chooses for us."

"Those *Federales*. They said my life wasn't worth shit, that Luis knew my life wasn't worth shit and that everyone's life had a value and my life, the value of my life, was zero, and that's why he sent me. They didn't like the amount of money that was in the envelope. It wasn't enough. They were going to shoot me because it wasn't enough. Said I should be thankful for them saving my life because Luis almost got me killed. Juan, I don't want to be around Luis anymore."

"Manny, you can try to stay away from him, sometimes, but look around you. Look at what happens. Do you think I wanted to be involved with *Narcos*? Do you think I put up a little sign at the Mercado that says, 'drug deals made here?' Do I have signs for heroin and OxyContin and cocaine and marijuana? I have signs for salmon and tuna and corvinas and tarpon and scallops and shrimps. I slice open their guts and I get up at six a.m., before the sun, and I smell and cut dead and sometimes rotten fish. I am a fish seller, Manny, a fishmonger."

"Luis is going to get me killed."

"Luis doesn't want you to die."

"He does not care if I die. He's going to kill me himself over the lost shipment. Do you know how much it was worth?"

"Four kilos lost?"

"Four kilos, my *hermano*."

"I do not."

"Over a million dollars?"

"Yes, it would be over a million dollars."

"He is going to kill me himself. I didn't sleep last night. I was shaking like the cocaine was in my own blood, trembling, sweating. I fell of bed and landed on Elvie where she was just lying there on the rug, sleeping, and she started to cry. I picked her up and put her in the bed with me and I just held her until she slept but I could not sleep. I just laid there staring at her, sleeping, thinking what the hell kind of life is this? Where is the God we just spent an hour praying to?"

"Where was mama?"

"Mama drank more mescal after we prayed and then she drank some more until she went and laid on the couch and fell asleep there. I could hear her snoring all night. Elvie could hear her snoring, too, and she wanted to go to her, but I just held her until she stopped crying."

"Mama was drinking?"

"She was drinking."

"She does that sometimes now."

"I haven't seen her do that."

"Why can't we just take care of the ranch? It's enough."

"We have to pay for that, too, Emmanuel. Don't you think I have to pay for that?"

"Pay for what?"

"Pay to stay here. Pay to keep them away from Mama, from the animals, the property. They see every opportunity they can take advantage of."

"But it's ours!"

"Luis is right. You are a Dolly."

"Don't say that, Juan! I don't want to work with Luis anymore. He doesn't care if I die."

"Manny, he doesn't want you to die."

"He sent me with millions of dollars in cocaine. He doesn't care if I die."

"That's why he sent you, not someone else. They would take the product before they took your life. They were right. Destroying the cocaine is worth more than destroying you."

"Luis doesn't care about my life."

"He cares about it more than you think."

"Why? Why does he protect me? Protect you? Why take me to a bullfight and arrange for Alena to be there to impress her, or take me to his fancy ranch with the glass windows and strippers and top-shelf drinks and a pool and an ice sculpture? Why send money to Ramiro's family when he was shot by *Narcos* who are no better than he is? Why fix your car that he damaged himself, kicked it in with his own foot? Luis is crazy. To him, I am shit. I am *los expendables*."

"Look at his eyes, Manny. Look at them and see why he cares, at least more than you say he does."

"His eyes? His eyes are black as old bloodied shit. Black like the devil was in God's ear when he made them, and the same devil poured his evil right through his ears and into his eyes."

"They're *your* eyes, Manny. Luis is your brother."

"My brother." He laughed, got up from the table and stood at the window and stared at the Azteca horse in the corral. Her ears were bristling. "You're my brother."

"Yes."

"Luis is shit. I thought he had some honor. He has none."

"*Narcos* have no honor. There is no code. You know that, Manny. They live and die by a thread of their own lives."

"He's going to kill me. I lost millions."

"He might."

"I thought you said he's my brother."

"I did. And that he doesn't want to see you dead. I didn't say he would never kill you."

"Great. You're serious."

"Yeah, I'm serious."

"What about dad?"

"What about him? He was your dad. Just like Enriqua is our mother. He wasn't perfect."

"I just wanted to make sure he was still my dad, because, you know—"

"Yeah, I know."

"Okay."

"Listen, I have to pick up Mama and Elvie. Go with me to the market and we'll set it up for the week. I'm going to start taking orders again Monday and open on Tuesday. If those Templars set foot in Juarez again, Luis is on our side. There's a lot for you to understand, and you will, someday. You're a great kid, Manny."

"A kid."

"Yeah."

"Jesus, okay."

"Okay."

"I'm going to get a tattoo."

"No, you're not. You're not getting any tattoo."

On Wednesday, Luis sent Gusto to the marketplace. It was after school and he was sweeping the floor and there were very few customers because of the murders on Saturday. Several of the slatted aluminum shop doors were pulled down and locked and had not been opened all day. Even the owners who were there seemed to cower away from the fronts of their own stores, pacing languid and calling only weakly or not approaching the customers at all, as they usually did with vigor and a display of their best fishes. Today, the market smelled of fish that had been out of the sea for some time, and it smelled of cigar smoke and something like abandonment, but there was no odor of grilled fish tacos or Mexican coffee or lemon. Juan was gone for the day to meet with the fishermen and Manny was alone. Gusto was driving a white El Dorado when he pulled up and parked it on the cobblestones.

Gusto seemed to have a different nature entirely from the night they had attended the fight, getting out of his car with a jovial stance and a limp that did not slow his pace. His matte eyes were not scanning, not searching. They still looked empty and clouded, but on his ruddy face, there was a cherubic look. Gusto was wearing jeans and *vaquero* boots and a white shirt and a black leather vest and carried a wooden, Mexican devotion to the Sacred Heart of Jesus, covered on its top with red and gold glass pieces that reflected and shined in every different plane. It was about the size of a salad bowl.

"*Buenos dias.*" Manny stopped sweeping, set down the broom. Techno music was playing on his radio, heavy beats that made the old man in the next shop complain sometimes, but the old man was not there today, and Juan said he probably would not return. He turned down the music.

"*Buenos dias, Dolly.*" Gusto's eyes narrowed.

At once, he thought of the journalists who feared their own jobs, feared reporting the truth that cartels, the murder statistics: more than 2,000 in Ciudad last year. He swallowed hard to push down the balled-up fear that had risen from his stomach, surging beyond his clavicles and into his neck and through his veins. But the fear, the tightness, did not pass.

"Aren't you going to offer me a drink?" Gusto clutched the little heart-shaped box and from it came the vague scents of vinegar and perfumed oils of almond and lavender that seemed soaked into the red wood.

"Of course, of course." Manny tried to think of something intelligent, honest, to say, but he could not. He was sure that Gusto's amaurotic eyes, which no emotion of his could penetrate, would reveal him. Manny stood at the register and poured Gusto some tequila with a coarse tremor in his hands. He thought of what Juan would say, asked Gusto, "How's Anna doing?"

"Good. Good, Dolly. Thank you. My wife is well."

They talked for some time about the bullfight and Gusto said that the matador had been well received and that he would come again soon to fight, and Gusto asked him about Alena, said that he knew at once she was well, because he could read the smile on Manny's face. Gusto finished his tequila, scratched his face with the stumpy and pale remains of the pointer finger lost and healed.

Manny poured another glass and when they had both finished drinking, Gusto asked him how his job was going. He said that the marketplace was not doing well today and Gusto said that he did not mean this job.

From his throat came an explanation that emerged speechless, at first, until his voice broke. His words cracked like stream stones, clinking until his voice thickened over the tequila on his tongue, his teeth, but he said the only thing he knew. He explained the truth.

Gusto shrugged, said that it was a large shipment to lose, but not the largest Luis had ever lost, and Gusto said that it would not be the last, and that Luis was angry at the *Federales*. Then Gusto said that he had an important question he needed to ask him.

"*Que?*"

"Did you tell him how much the cocaine was worth?"

"No. I don't know how much it is worth."

Gusto smiled, and he patted Manny on the back. He squeezed the muscles of Manny's shoulder near his neck, but these muscles did not relax as they would if Alena or Juan or his mother squeezed them. There was no warmth in Gusto's touch. He could not even say that there was loyalty in those hands, but Manny felt his sort of sick camaraderie; he raised his glass against his conscience, and he toasted to Luis.

When he had drunk several ounces of tequila and he'd listened to Gusto's long-winded stories, and his inhibitions were falling away, he could stand it no more. He looked at the item Gusto carried, asked, "What's in the box?"

A pause, a thoughtful smile. "Dolly, I thought you would not ask. It's a gift, for you. A gift."

"From you?"

"From Luis."

"But—"

Again, Gusto slapped his back, and laughed, threw back a large swig of tequila. "Were you afraid, Dolly? No, don't be afraid. I understand that you know now that you and Luis are more than friends. Blood is powerful, blood is binding, forever. Luis is compassionate. Luis understands your suffering. He could not know your father as he wanted to, but he honors you in blood."

"Blood."

"Go ahead, open it. It's from your brother."

"My brother. Juan."

"Luis."

"Luis, my brother." The phrase was uncertain, lacking comfort. It sounded cautious and doubtful, emerging from a place deep his throat. Profane and bloody words.

"Go ahead. Open it."

He opened the box.

"Those bounty hunters, the ones who came for the totoabas. You were right. They were Columbians. They were not Mexicans. They caused you pain, killed your friend. When I found them, I asked them to sing the Mexican National Anthem, honoring our great nation." Gusto shook his head. "They could not sing one note."

Inside the heart-shaped box, honoring the heart of Jesus Christ and His divine love for humanity, His passion, were two meaty lumps the size of human fists. They were fibrous, with whitish, ear-shaped masses at their tops, and branching from them were bone-colored tubular structures, only they were not hard like bone. They were soft, like rolled enchiladas, and another arched out, cyanic blue, over each of the fleshy, maroon lumps, over their tops. He recognized them from science class in *secondaria,* where he'd dissected the hearts of pigs. He recognized the ventricles and the crumpled auricles, which literally meant "little ears," recognized the aortae and the great vessels. Only they were not pig hearts.

They were human.

Each had arteries and pulmonary veins branching from it that had once carried the blood of Hugo, the blood of Jose. Beside the hearts were Hugo's silver teeth, lying mercurial in the hollowed wood carving, and four pearly, fibrous cords, about an inch each. Gusto had ripped out the vocal cords of the men who did not know how to sing the Mexican National Anthem.

He put the lid back on the top, said that he did not know what to say. Really, he did not know what to say.

Gusto smiled, seemed pleased, said, "*De nada,*" and he said that if Hugo and Jose had babies, he would've brought him the hearts of their babies, too.

10

The school year seemed endless. Some days, he was there in class, but many days, he was not. Sometimes he would go to school, but not to class. He would walk with Alena at lunchtime to a nearby café and they would talk, and he would smile and just listen to her talk as long as she kept talking, often about her unfortunate and quixotic brand of Catholicism. Piranha had all but stopped going. He had tried to remain at the same school Manny attended when his family moved out to Juarez Valley, but his parents had lost their jobs, driven out by the violence in the valley, and because they used drugs heavily themselves, they could no longer afford to send Piranha to that school. Piranha was still working at the auto shop, but if he could not drive to school, then he could not go.

Alena never missed school at *Preparatoria 64*, not even when there had been an outbreak of violence near it or a threat called into the office, even if she had to ride her bicycle. One day there was graffiti scrolled across the wall of the art classroom that terrified many of the students who discovered it, but not Alena. The words named the art teacher, Mrs. Hernandez, as a filthy whore for not handing over the money from the book fair fundraiser to teenage extortionists. The three fifteen-year-old girls who first saw the scrawled message ran screaming from the classroom in hysterics and spent the afternoon in the guidance counselor's office, hyperventilating and retelling the story, each time adding another histrionic detail. *No*, this did not affect Alena, who had the composure of a woman twice her age.

He only saw her praying, silently, to herself.

They were not in many classes together, and when they were, his thoughts were never on the class.

One morning, when they were walking on the cobblestone walk in the courtyard, filled with *Ixora* flowers whose petals seemed to flicker as little flames do, licking her shoulders as she passed, passed the orange hibiscus bloomed hot like raging fire—she told him that she wanted to be a journalist or an actress or someone important, and he believed her, believed that she would be, but he was afraid for her. He said that as a journalist, she could be killed by men who killed women just for sport, just because they were women, or she could be shot by drug dealers for telling their story, even if it was accurate and honest and true; and he said that someone could disappear her and he would never again sleep, not knowing what had happened to her. She stopped walking then and her gaze gave pause and she asked him what kind of people would do that to her and he stopped, too, and he thought for a moment, and that was pretty much the end of that conversation.

It was May, a few days from *Cinco de Mayo*, when they were sitting outside of the café where they had talked, really talked, for the first time. The walls were stucco and a goldenrod color with deep red picture frames hung on them, adorned with tiny *Milagros* charms, dangling hands and moons and hearts shaped in silver. They sat at a table eating nachos and *salsa verde* from a *Talavera* plate painted in rings of red and blue and gold and they were drinking guava juice. She asked him how things were going with Luis.

"Okay," he said. "If I could choose not to be around him anymore, I would."

"You can choose."

"He chose for me. Juan says I have to be careful about what I refuse to do for his people."

"Are you feeling bad about the things he does?"

He confessed. "I'm feeling worse that I found out he's related to me."

"Is this true?"

"Yes. He's my brother."

She said that he should go to church. Alena thought that that was the answer for everything. He asked her why she didn't think that this was hypocritical, when it seemed he was on a path to keep doing the same things he was doing day after day, even if he asked forgiveness for them. She said that it was not hypocritical, and that it was the very beauty of the love of the Father and that it was, in fact, not even hypocritical for him to suggest correction to others to change their ways, even though he was not perfect himself. She said that it was not considered judgmental but rather holy to tell others of their wrongs, because it was a Spiritual Work of Mercy required by their beliefs to provide correction of wrongdoing.

"A Spiritual Work of Mercy?"

"Yes," she said, smiled, said it was a divine mandate from Christ himself. "To instruct the ignorant, counsel the doubtful."

He didn't mean to insult her, but he couldn't help the wry smile he felt spreading across his face, and he might have said a lot more, because he heard from deep within him his mother saying all of this, too. Instead, he reached across the table and kissed her soft forehead, said, "I'd like to see how that would go with Luis, with Gusto. I'll just walk into the restaurant and when they give me, not ask me, *give* me, my next assignment, I'll just tell Luis he's got it all wrong."

She said that to offer a hungry man a fish was to provide charity, but to show a hungry man how to fish, or to teach a man who cannot read, who suffers poverty of the soul, was to offer instruction, correction from ignorance. He told her he'd have his head cut off if he said these things and that it would be rolling down *Avenida 16 de Septiembre* with its eyes cold and glassed and as dead as every one of the fishes in the market. She said that he might be a Christian martyr if that happened, like St. Denis and his companions, and she said that St. Denis had been decapitated and that he'd carried his head six miles down *Montmartre* and around Paris, all the while preaching a sermon of repentance. Then she began the hagiology of all the cephalophores, the head-carrying saints, of Christianity that she could list, and he tried to keep listening, but he just looked at her and he smiled; his thoughts drifted.

He said, "I want to go to Paris, to *Montmartre*, with you."

"Are you listening to me?"

He kissed her forehead again. "If there's another way to get out of poverty, I'd like to figure it out."

"You are quite rich."

"My family does okay."

She said that one is only poor if he chooses to be, and she said that they should be going back to class.

The following week, in the north wing of *Preparatoria 64*, Mrs. Abril Torrero stalked the aisles of her classroom, wiping the countertops, the desk, the mini-blinds, with antibacterial wipes. Mrs. Torrero was always ready to pump a clear and bubbly glob of hand sanitizer onto his hands as he walked through the classroom door. Manny, who showered maybe once a week—twice, if he played paintball—was a package of testosterone and growth hormone and pubertal completion at its pinnacle.

He paid little attention. He wiped the sweat from his brow as the fan blades circled the ceiling, propelling the heavy air in thick revolutions that did little to cool the classroom.

He was sitting at his desk in Mrs. Torrero's shiny classroom, thinking of how Alena now had her heart set on journalism after they finished *secondaria*. She had made it her choice for the career fair next week, and he was thinking of how he could get her to change her mind. He crumpled the piece of paper with the note he'd begun writing to her. Then he stood and he aimed the paper wad for a three-pointer, like an American basketball player, an NBA all-star admiring his shot.

The wad felt two feet short of the receptacle.

"You no make the basketball team, Manny." Justin spoke in English, heavily accented, shook his head.

"Justin, be quiet. Emmanuel, take your seat."

"Sorry, Mrs. Torrero," he said.

It was his first time this week in Mrs. Torrero's economics class, and although he was there physically, his thoughts were on Alena and his next job with Luis and the real possibility that Juan might be forced to permanently close his shop at the *Mercado del Mundo*. Monday he'd been at the market. Business was slow; the owners were somber, the customers still guarded, fearful to come out, driven inside by eruptions of vehement rivalry between the Juarez and the Sinaloa and the Templar cartels.

The cartels all wanted control of their product through Juarez, through the Franklin mountains, jagged and fawn-colored, those distant peaks where, on the other side, the Holy Grail called him to some knight-errant journey, past the mountain in Juarez scrolled white with the message: *La Biblia es la Verdad, Leela.* The Bible is the Truth. Read it.

Through the excursions of drug mules and coyotes and warriors, the product moved in this idealized quest, athwart the Rio Grande, to the United States, where its true value was realized.

Tuesday, he'd made a delivery, ten pounds of heroin hidden between the intake manifold and the engine of an F150, with another secret compartment packed with one hundred bags of cocaine that could not be found by x-ray. The compartment could be opened by two people only when the truck was in reverse and the magnetic switch under the hood was connected and a button in the back of the truck bed was pressed simultaneously. He made the delivery through El Porvenir to the Columbian stash house in Tornillo. He drove back to the decimated town a second time later, stopped at the auto shop that evening where Piranha worked. He dropped off The Apple, which was all but falling apart piece by piece, and he asked Piranha if he wanted to hang out and play Call of Duty, but Piranha said that his Play Station and television had been stolen. Manny said that he was sorry, and Piranha said that it was okay, that he'd stolen them himself to begin with, so it was a wash.

The brakes on The Apple were now squealing and one of the dual chrome exhaust pipes, which had once shined, was now dragging on the ground, sparking like a pyrotechnic display of ignited sulfur and oxidized aluminum, and although Piranha had agreed to fix both the exhaust and the dent in the truck, Manny did not know that it would be the last time he'd see Piranha, as he knew Piranha, for a long time. He did not know that while he was being dragged into an organization commanding and lawless and dominant, Piranha was becoming immersed in another group, a vigilante group attempting to govern what the government only pretended to, what the government did not dare to challenge. That corrupt power margin.

Mrs. Torrero was talking about entrepreneurship and target markets and market penetration and supply chains the next day. He rested his head on the desk, fought against sleep to keep his eyes open. He was not thinking about business plans.

He'd gotten home after midnight, after feeling narcoleptic at the wheel, four windows open, blowing patches of desert air cool and dry on his skin to keep him awake. He was driving on Highway 4 last night, and he swerved where he thought an animal was down on the road, obstructing the pavement. Orion's kill beneath stars alight. When he got out, he was alone with the sound of his own footsteps, a faint moaning. His boots scuffed the pavement, slowly, where he approached through the double corona of his headlights illuminating the dessert black and cool. He shined his flashlight along the dashed yellow lines, crouched beside the huge carcass to move it, but it was not an animal and it was not dead.

He rolled the body, female, onto its back. Long hair gnarled like tropical Cyprus creepers, skin cyanic blue, lungs gasping their final breaths, agonal and labored, mouth obstructed with blood and vomitus. He covered his mouth with his sleeve, and he tried to forget the scent and he got back in the car and he drove on, through Juarez, west to the hacienda, and he drove up the hill and he parked the Pontiac he'd borrowed from Piranha's shop on the driveway. He hung the keys on the hooks beside the door and he hung his cap and he turned off the cartoon channel on the television and he slept on the couch beside Elvie, who was lost in a dream, laughing intermittent and softly in her sleep, her crooked smile coiled up at the right side of her lip, arms clutching her unicorn where she lay in pink pajamas. She had her bunny slippers on to keep her feet warm. It was very cold last night. Very cold.

"How do we determine the total addressable market?" Mrs. Torrero's arms were crossed.

"Manny, wake up." Justin poked a sharp elbow into his rib.

"What?" He jerked back in his seat.

The class laughed. He felt his skin rush with pink and he rubbed his eyes and he asked Mrs. Torrero to repeat the question where she hovered over his desk, one arm planted on her hip, the other holding a stick of chalk like she wanted to smoke it. Mrs. Torrero always smelled like smoke and she always had a full pack of cigarettes in her purse, except for the dozen or so times when Piranha had stolen them.

He did not know the answer, had not met with his group in weeks to work on his careers project, in which Justin and Piranha and Aubreanna Zuluetos, the class know-it-all, had to design their own business. They'd decided their company would sell pizza logs at lunchtime, cigar-sized rolls that they made from frozen puff pastry and canned sauce and mozzarella cheese, baked in the oven at 350 degrees, wrapped in white wax paper, sold in packs of three and five.

Mrs. Torrero's eyes narrowed and her mouth scrunched into tight wrinkles, as though she had sucked on a lemon. She sighed, spun away from his desk on her heels, told the class that the total addressable market was an estimate of how much of the market a company might gain if there were no competitors.

It made sense.

That evening, he was at the restaurant, *Casa de Pescado*. There was a mariachi band in black velvet jackets trimmed gold and red, and trumpets playing, and there were four of Luis' men who he did not know, but they seemed to know him, wanted to know him very well, and they welcomed him to sit. One of the men offered him an oversized margarita and another pinched his cheeks and smiled and said that his name, Emmanuel, meant, "God is with us."

He already knew what it meant.

The men looked drunk. He wanted to be drunk. It had been a long day at school and he was very behind and he did not know if he would graduate.

Luis came into the back room where they sat, said that he had an important meeting with the men there. The tall and thin and young man sitting beside Luis had a handlebar mustache; they referred to him only as *Mustacio*. There was Mauricio "G-spot" Guerra, and Paulo "O-Ring" Ortez, whose mouth was always in the shape of an O, blowing out rings of cigar smoke. O-Ring made cars blow up when Luis gave the order.

Until then, he'd thought that maybe, just maybe, he wasn't getting in too deep, thought that maybe it was just a transient nightmare that he could escape from any time, that he'd wake up from it and be at the fish market with Juan, sweeping the innards and washing the floor and feeling the zing down his legs from lifting impossibly weighted crates, setting the shipments out right, minding his own business, under the radar. But that was illusory and this was real; he was already engulfed by this thing, this organization.

His mother had told him, "*Mas vale ser cabeza de raton que cola de leon*"—It's better to be the head of a mouse than the tail of a lion. She made the sign of cross and swore to Mary, when he said he was neither. He said he wasn't hanging by a thread with the big dogs and he said he was still a good kid, that he'd take care of her, the farm, put her and Elvie and Juan and the *estancia* first.

"Family first," he'd said.

He thought Enriqua would like this, thought he'd said the right thing when he was sitting at the table beside her, shoveling rice with cilantro and lime and chicken into his mouth, but she hit him with the slipper.

"God is first," she said.

Once, instead of arguing with his mother, he just kissed her forehead as Juan did, because now he'd grown considerably taller than her. He said nothing but he buried her head against his chest. She looked up with brows that seemed permanently knitted together with worry and she began to cry, and she turned away from her tears, pulled her *rebozo* tighter over her shoulders, and left the room. He watched her go and then finished his chicken, confused because that hug had always seemed to work for Juan. This was harder than listening to her scream at him, so he did not do this again. Instead, he continued to argue with her.

Now in the restaurant, Luis ushered him away from the men and past the lobster tanks, past the illuminated bar and the podium where the hostess, Lydia, stood. She was a young woman with large breasts and very red lipstick who was always dressed in black and wore shoes like spikes. Tonight, she was smiling. She was always smiling.

Luis told him that he needed him to act as a lookout, *el halcone*, and apologized for giving him such a menial job that evening, left him outside at one of the tables on the patio overlooking the *Boulevard Tomas Fernandez*, the stone fountain in the *zocalo*. Luis said that there might be trouble later and that there might be *policia* and to told him to keep his eyes and ears open. There was trouble, alright.

His mother called him on his cell phone, screaming.

"*Usted no va a la escuela. Se llama senora Torrero.*" You do not go to school. Mrs. Torrero called.

"*Juan ha estado muy ocupado.*" Juan has been very busy.

"*Usted no ha estado con Juan. Voy al mercado todos los días.*" You haven't been with Juan. I go to the market every day.

"Ma," he said.

"*¿Así que vas a abandonar la escuela?*" So you're going to leave school?

Enriqua swore to Mary and she began to cry, and she begged him not to drop out of school. She screamed over the line, said she wanted to see him do great things, to live better than she did, longer than his father did. She said she knew who he was with and knew what Luis would do to his life because he was a shark that would tear him apart, to bloody pieces, leave him floating in the ocean. She told him he had to face this shark and he needed to go to church to repent, and she said that now was the time to ask God for forgiveness, not when he was in the belly of a whale, a shark.

He shouldn't have provoked her, should've known how to settle her down like Juan did, but instead he told her that being inside the whale's belly had worked just fine for Jonah. "*Ma, voy a salir. Relajarse.*" I'll leave. Relax.

He disconnected the call, cutting her off. He would deal with her later.

On the *Boulevard,* the lights were starting to come on and there were birds in the eaves of the Spanish-tiled roofs that were starting to roost, cooing softly. The floral smell behind him was sweet, a trellis of pink bougainvillea. A group of boys his age walked past, very loud and probably drunk. They were smoking and one of them was tall with dark skin and hair bleached white in gelled spikes. He looked rough, not a weathered rough like the mountains of Juarez, where the final meniscus of the sun shrank beneath a rounded peak in the distance just then, but jagged rough, like the snow-topped cinder cones, angry *Popocatepetl* and her lesser sibling, *Ixtaccihuatl*. He'd seen those peaks once from Mexico City, as high as a plane flies, linked by their saddle, *Paso de Cortes*, had traveled there with his father as a boy, when Juan was eleven or twelve, but he did not see his father again after this time.

His father spoke in hushed tones then with men he did not know, and he'd waited with Juan, listening, as he listened now. He could not hear what the boys in the *zocalo* were saying. He licked the salt from the rim of his glass.

He got up from the table on the patio and he walked past a couple whose food smelled of lemon and oregano, and he walked beyond the wrought iron railing, tangled with the bougainvillea that bordered the restaurant, past the sign where the menu was posted. He crossed the street and he walked into the *zocalo* and he stood where the boys were talking. One was a thin Mexican with a shaved head, wearing a black shirt and a Kevlar vest beneath it and combat fatigues, who had come to stand beside them. He exchanged a small package of drugs. Both the man's arms were tattooed with crocodiles. On the right, the side Manny could see over his shoulder where he looked on and listened, two reptiles were carved onto the man's skin. They were gray-green and drawn in low water and mangrove trees, overlapping one another with teeth on their bottom jaws that protruded in a crooked grin, bodies scaled and hooked, with tails coiled that crisscrossed, elongated down the length of the man's forearms.

Manny tried to listen, tried to make out the specifics of the deal they were conducting, when his phone rang again.

His mother, again.

He silenced the device. A municipal police car drove by, down the Boulevard, and it circled through the *zocalo,* but it did not stop. He swore, and he walked back to the restaurant and through the kitchen to the back room where Luis and the four men were eating lobster and drinking *cerveza* with lime, where it was very loud through the door with the sounds of the line cooks and the dishes and the orders being called out. He told Luis that he had to get home. Luis raised his glass, chewed, told him he should sit and eat, and Luis ordered the waiter nearby to get him a drink, and Luis told him that they were celebrating an important deal, achieving control over moving drugs through the ports of Cozumel.

He said that he could not stay, that he was needed at home.

"Emmanuel, I insist," Luis stabbed a piece of steak with his fork and chewed it, took a swig of *cerveza*.

"Luis, my teacher, she called home because I have not been to school. She said I may not graduate. She told my mother that I'm falling asleep in class, and that I know nothing, that I'm smart, but that I don't apply myself."

Luis nodded, said, "Who's this teacher who says you know nothing?"

He should've smiled and left it as the rhetorical question it could've been, had he let it stand alone, had he sat down and eaten some lobster and smiled and had a beer with them and then another. He would've enjoyed that, the butter and the lemon and the cold beer, but he said, "Mrs. Abril Torrero."

Luis looked up, looked around at the drunk men, said, "Okay, Dolly, I'll see you tomorrow."

Walking into school the next morning should've been an ill-fated and horrific surprise. It should've made his eyeballs fall out of his head and roll around on the floor when he saw it— Mrs. Torerro's head, sliced where she'd once had a meticulous surgical incision to remove her thyroid from her neck, now dangling from the basketball net of the gymnasium, her brown hair tied in ropy strands to the netting so that her bludgeoned face hung, ashen, three feet below the rim. Above it, fallen from the wall and collapsed in wide streaming ribbons was the gonfalon, the white and red banner announcing the school dance.

It should have shocked him, but this was no hieroglyphic message needing translation, no clandestine act of violence that left him to question who was responsible for the brutal and heathenish profligacy. It was something that he was growing accustomed to and something that he saw repeatedly now and this desensitization, his lack of alarm, was what scared him about himself. It did not surprise him, and he did not question that it was Gusto who had beheaded Mrs. Torerro. He knew by the way the head was sawed off that it was Gusto who had set her corpse on display, and Luis who had ordered it so. He tasted vomit from the pit of his stomach that reached the back of his mouth and he swallowed it down and he turned away, and he left the gymnasium and he left the school, and he did not return on that day or ever again.

11

Things started to happen fast after that.

Three years passed. He ran numerous shipments to the United States, always with someone to meet him on the other side, to connect at the stash house, and always wondering if this was the time that he would not make it, not complete the delivery. The *Federales* and the border guards were only running for their dinner, but he was running for his life. Every time, he was running for his life. It was inevitable that eventually, these foxes would catch him, catch that fat jack rabbit with muscled thighs and pert ears that he was back then.

The situation in Juarez worsened. Every day, the murder rate rose. The bakeries and cafes and fruit vendors, whose carts were once stocked with pyramids of mangos and dragon fruit and kiwis, with *balons de futbol* pink and neon green dangling from their displays, ceased to operate, overnight, it seemed, disappearing fearful into the chaparral and through the Franklin Mountains, only the shopkeepers were not heaved there over millions of years like the majestic peaks of the Sierra Madre; they ghosted overnight like the spirits of the dead that today wandered among them in this perilous, mutinous war.

He walked among the worst of the vile, and each day he dreaded them less and resembled them more. The nativity of the Lord in all antiquity eclipsed in His light somewhere this mired and frail city, Ciudad, a fugitive ember escaped from hell if hell was a city in His grand design, designed to expire in blood and profanities and all things unholy.

He still had a gap in his front teeth, and he had no tattoos and he did not smoke, and he still went to church with his mother. He had grown nearly a foot in those years, and his arms at last matched the length of his body.

They still called him Dolly, because he had never killed anyone.

Over time, though, his waist thickened, his senses dulled, his hearing weakened from the sound of gunfire that he practiced in the desert at close range and far, usually with a Colt pistol, sometimes with an AK-47 with 39mm ammo for fun. He loved the sharp sound of the magazine locking into the weapon. And his vision lost acuity from the fatigue in his eyes and from consecutive nights without restful sleep, and though this did not have the effect of making him less alert, it made him, he felt, punchy and short-fused, always anxious, always ready.

Except when he was with Alena, of course.

She had finished school and was learning English and working at *Canal 44*, cleaning the offices and getting coffee for the anchors and running errands, and he thought that she might like to be a teacher, or a nurse at the *Hospital de la Familia* taking care of newborn babies, but she said that she always felt that she wanted to tell a story, always had something to say. That was the truth—she was never without words.

Sometimes he missed the days when he would sit on the couch and play *Grand Theft Auto* with Piranha, who had very little to say except when Piranha had done a line of coke and his speech got very rushed, fast. Sometimes Manny wasn't sure who talked more, Alena or Gusto, but he liked listening to her, liked what she had to say. He could just listen and say nothing, and she didn't expect him to talk much.

Her skin was soft. Her body was firm, and every time he entered her and touched her flesh and smelled her hair not yet dried after showering, it felt like the first time, and afterward, he could just lay there and listen to her talk. Often, he didn't have to say anything at all, he just listened to her, and he didn't think about anyone else or the things he had done that day or what he had to do the next. She rarely asked; she had her own things to tell him.

One day, they were in her bedroom after he had climbed in through the window of her grandmother's small *estancia* where she lived, after her grandmother had long since fallen asleep. After they had made love several times until he felt emptied out and hollow, he was lying there in her bed beside her, and the night was cool and smelled of dew and the moon had a rim of white around it. He stared out the window at it, his eyes closing, nodding off to sleep. She was wide awake and she said that she would like to go to El Paso to buy *charro* boots and he mumbled that she could buy *charro* boots here in Ciudad but she said *no*, that she wanted American *charro* boots, and she said that she wanted him to get a pair, ones with silver tips, and he said okay, that they would walk over the bridge and go and get some.

Alena was much smarter than he was in school. She had finished *secondaria*, still loved to read. She would read him passages from her volumes of Cervantes and her new favorite, an author from Columbia, and she read him a colorful story of a fallen angel that perhaps should have been revered, should have had a merciful place set at the dinner table in case the angel was Jesus himself—but it was not. Instead, it was poked and prodded as though it was a circus freak. He liked this story very much; he liked the expression in her eyes and the warmth in her tone when she read it aloud.

His mother told him that Alena was too good for him, and inside, he felt this to be true, and his mother said that Alena would tear out his heart and hold it before his face, still beating, but his mother still called him one, two, six times a night when he stayed out with Alena, wanted him home with her and Juan and Elvie, and on days when he had spent the entire night out with Alena and had not returned until morning, his mother shouted and sulked in episodes that waxed and waned for tortured hours that lingered into the evening.

It was spring in Mexico when he awoke one morning in Alena's small bed, and he came to the kitchen and Alena had made *huevos rancheros* and beans and he sat, and he ate them at the wooden table. Her cat was lying there sick on the floor, and she gave it some of her eggs to eat, placed them beside it where it had thrown up near its pillow bed. It was going to die today, she'd said, so it should eat well. Its fur bunched in marmalade clumps and its eyes were dimmed with membranes and pus at the corners and they were injected with threads spidery red and teared up yellow where they should've been white. Alena scratched the pathetic creature's head and wrapped her shawl around her shoulders, and when she saw that Manny was staring at her, she stopped, and she smoothed her cotton dress and painted her lips red and wiped off some of the coal eyeliner from last night, where it was smudged beneath her eyes.

"You look beautiful in the morning," he said, and he imagined that they were married and that the bulge in her abdomen that had grown since they were younger was not the effect of womanhood alone but of his child growing within her, though he did not say this to her then or ever.

Her face made a lovely and furrowed expression as she continued to fix her face and when she stopped, she sighed, said that she didn't have the heart to put the cat back out on the doorstep where she'd found it begging a week ago, even though her grandmother had twice set it back out. It coughed, a moist and air-hungered sound, as if its lungs were suffocated with fluid. Now she looked at it again and she said she was sure that it would be dead before they returned from mass, and even though there wasn't much milk left, she poured some into a saucer for it and she left it beside the animal.

She told him about a dream she'd had the night before as they'd slept.

"It was a terrible dream."

"Tell me," he said.

"I don't want to. It's too terrible."

"Tell me."

She set down the wooden spoon and she sat across from him, wrapped her hands around her cup of coffee. She said that the dream began much like today, that Abuela had already left for mass, and she was hurrying down the Avenieda 16 de Septiembre and through a back alley where men slept in the shade on the faulted cobblestone, breathing in sonorous whoops like those that followed coughing spells of children fallen ill at the orphanage. She came to the Cathedral de Nuestra Senora de Guadalupe and she hurried up the stone steps and she sat down beside her grandmother on the scratched pew. The doors were left wide open but still the air was stagnant and swirling fans blew it upon the congregation and smoking incense masked the smell of a fire burning in the old city somewhere outside the cathedral. The sunlight streamed in prismatic rays through the glass and colored red and majestic purple the face of the little nina in front of her, flickering in roving quadrilaterals that made the nina squint and dance in the aisle until her papa yanked her ear and she was once again seated and still in prayer.

And she said that, in the dream, the old woman in front of her was fanning herself with the missalette. *Abuela* had already nodded off where she sat, and her eyes opened and closed periodically, and she mumbled. Alena nudged her and *Abuela* roused but then, soon after, *Abuela* nodded and mumbled something else that could not be understood.

Then she said that he entered through the back, when mass was almost finished. The priest had covered the Eucharist and locked it in the holy tabernacle and now he turned toward the congregation, walked out into the aisle away from the white marble altar. She described the area beside the altar, the tomb that faced them, enshrined with potted lilies and golden tripods of wreaths of gladiolas and carnations and chrysanthemums tangled with baby's breath.

She said she knew that they called him Dolly because he'd never killed anybody, and in the dream, he was her age at the time, about fourteen, and she'd seen him many times on the street. *Halcone.* The eyes and ears. He reported the activities, the dealings of the *Federales*, the military, and the rival gangs, but soon he would be higher ranking. Soon, he'd be old enough to be a *lugarteniente, a lieutenant,* guarding their *plaza.* And she remembered dreaming this one thing about Manny, that he'd never killed a man. She said that her eyes met his in the church and he smiled, and she looked away and then she looked back at him.

She said that they called him Dolly in her dream, too.

In the dream, he walked up the aisle on the left side of the *Cathedral.* The priest made the sign of the cross and turned and bowed toward the altar. Behind him, another man dressed in a white T-shirt and jeans and black boots walked in, smoking. The congregation turned. The older man took a drag of the cigarette and exhaled and walked forward and she said that everyone could hear the man's boots where he walked. She said that *Abuela* swore to Mary then and another *abuela* fainted and the priest shouted at the men, but she said that her eyes were fixed on Manny.

Then she said that she saw a man in the congregation whose lump in his throat rose and fell and as it did, the man turned from his wife to leave, but the older man with Manny crushed his cigarette and removed a knife from its leather case in his belt and grabbed the nervous man in the congregation with the tense throat.

On the other side of the church, another man strode along the aisle.

The man coming up the other side was eating a bag of Cheetos and holding a *Diete Coke*. He was tall, had a beard. Across this man's chest an automatic hung loosely diagonal. The man put some Cheetos in his mouth and they made a crunching sound and he washed them down with the *Diete Coke* and he put the cap back on it.

She said that this man turned down the aisle and pushed a *nino* out of the way, told him, "*Vamanos*," and the kid ran out the back door. The man coming up the right aisle pushed past the kid's mother and the priest shouted at the men, "*Sali de aqui ahora.*" Leave here now.

The man on the right threw the Cheetos down on the pew and set down the Diete Coke, removed the gun from his chest and shot the priest, who fell to the floor.

She said that in the dream Manny's skin was smooth, his hair as slick as oil. She said that she remembered holding his hand at some point, said it was smooth in the dream, too.

She stood in the pew, frozen, staring at him, while *Abuela* screamed and clutched her cheeks and shook at her breast. She pulled down her dark hair where it was pinned up and it fell beneath her shoulders and buried *Abuela's* face so that she might not see. The congregation was screaming. Some ran, and others crawled on the floor between the pews.

The older man with Manny in her dream clutched the man in the pew and held the knife to the man's throat. It had serrations pointed ragged, each like a tiny tidal wave that once set in motion could not be stopped until they crashed at the shore, and it had an ivory handle with a colorful skeleton commemorating *Dios de los Muertos,* and it had a curved tip like another huge wave.

The older man holding the knife told the one he held to pray to God, and the man kept praying, "*Salvame. Salvame.*" Save me. Save me.

The older man with the knife cut at the other man's throat, sawed at it back and forth several times until all the man's extremities went flaccid. Then he threw the body to the floor, where the dead man's wife dropped to her knees, screaming and praying to Mary and where blood pooled about her on the marble and she held her husband's head.

Alena said that in the dream, the man on the right with the Cheetos crossed the center aisle three times and came to the front of the church. It made little sense. There was dust on his boots, and he stopped and brushed off one and then the other and looked around and he paused and tossed the gun to Manny and told him to finish the job. Alena said that she met Manny's eyes and that he looked for a moment like he would not do it, but he took the gun and aimed it at the screaming widow and fired rounds into her chest.

He listened, took her hand now, asked her what happened next in her dream.

She said that in the dream, outside that cathedral, the remaining family ran, screaming for the police. The uncle, *tio,* ran up to the city police and began to explain the story, telling him about the bloodshed in the church.

Alena stopped and she finished her coffee and by this time, her eyes were growing sad and her smile had weakened to something like worry. It was no longer merely a vision to her.

Manny took her hand. The skeletal cat was still breathing at his feet. He envisioned that he and Gusto would walk out of the back of that imagined church of her dream, past the city police. Gusto would tell him to hold his Cheetos and his *Diete Coke* just like in the dream and he would light a cigarette, right there on Sunday, smoke right there in church while the city policemen they knew well searched the family, confiscated a pistol from *el tio*. He figured the police would put the family up against the police car and frisk them, maybe arrest them for possession of illegal weapons, and the murder in Alena's dream would go uninvestigated, because the city police did not work for the people; they did not work for that *tio,* not that *familia*.

That's how it would go outside of this dream. One way of putting it would be that the *policia* would do nothing to catch the criminals. And another way would be that the *policia* would do nothing because they were paid to do nothing. And still another would be that they would do nothing because they were paid by the criminals to do nothing.

He was still staring down at the cat, only one of the numerous animals she sheltered from time to time. She had gotten up and knotted her *rebozo* over her shoulders and she was waiting at the door for him to walk her to mass when he came out of this daydream with alacrity, rose from the table.

12

The summer passed and it was during the parade in the *zocalo* on the Day of the Dead that year, 2010, when a black Jeep with two men standing on the back with their faces covered in black cloths, their heads covered with black ball caps, and their chests crossed with automatic rifles, AK-47s and M16s, tore down the *Avenue 16 Septiembre*, mowing down the umbrella-covered carts in the *Juarez Market* and the *Mercado del Mundo*, killing four people with the mud-covered vehicle before they even began shooting.

Alena was on her first real assignment as a reporter for *Canal 49*, the television station, covering the parade and the celebration in the *zocalo*. She had cut her hair page-boy short for her job and it fell just below her ears, framing her face in crisp and pointed waves like the fins of a shark. For nearly a week, residents had been preparing for the November First celebration, shaping floral crowns that streamed with bright purple and yellow and red ribbons, and the stench of marigolds and holy rosewater saturated the air.

There was a girl beside him whose hair curled at the ends like Elvie's did, sitting on her father's shoulders, eating the sweet bread of the dead, shaped of crosses and skulls and long bones. The girl's face iced with white sugar that fell from her lips and covered her father in a fine powdery cloud, as she stuffed the twisted piece of *pan de muerto* into her mouth, filling out both of her painted cheeks.

There was a huge float blanketed in the Aztec marigolds, the *cempasuchil*, flower of the dead, and gerbera daisies and white and red carnations, a machine on its platform emitting dry ice, and a woman who came out from sheer draped curtain into the wisps of sublimed carbon dioxide fumes, dressed like *Calavera de Catrina*, and there were impossibly loud drums and a mariachi band next behind this float in the parade, so that the screams were not heard until the Sinaloa's truck was very close.

Earlier that morning, his mother had completed her *ofrenda*, the sacred altar commemorating Gustavo, his father. She had been constructing it all week, draping the revered table with silk organza cloth from a high point like a castellated tower which she claimed would keep away the bats, soricine and diabolical night creatures that could drain the blood and the vigor of the sacred spirits and prevent their return, and she had gotten up early to rearrange the flowers and the fruit, which she had been arranging all morning, all week, and she asked him if he had moved the orange marigolds out of place, which he had not. She had made dozens of sugared churros and a pitcher of hibiscus tea, and she had made tamales and fried plantains, and that morning she had made Juan French toast with cinnamon and powdered sugar.

After breakfast, she sat by the table, praying, inviting the presence of Gustavo, his father, and Juan's father, and apparently Luis' father, too, who had all been ripped from their lives by death like some huge celestial vacuum. Manny knew without speaking to her that she thought Papa could be put back, if only for one day, and he kissed her as if to tell her that he could not, but he did not say this. She sighed and she did not say much but she got up from the altar and he saw her standing at the window when he left.

The music continued through the shooting, the sounds of the accordion and the horns and the vihuela and the bass guitar loud on the *Avenue*, where the floats made up like *ofrendas,* lit with arches of candles, wobbled steadily on their platforms draped in crepe paper and flowers, until the music was overtaken by screaming and shouting and the popping of the automatic rifles, and the engine of the truck ripping in the opposite direction of the parade, the tires peeling as the truck swerved through the *zocalo*, delivering the message of the Sinaloas.

This message was never spoken nor was it written, but it was intelligible and elucidated unquestionable and immediate in rounds fired at the men and women on the patio of the *Casa de Pescado,* who were sipping tequila and margaritas and smoking behind the iron rails. The message was made clear to the man who walked each day to and from the square with the Alder wood cane and rickets that had made his legs misshapen and his gait wide and impassable, who took one of the tissue-shattering bullets to his chest. It was made clear to the women that clutched their babies to their breasts in a rictus of terror before falling dead.

The message was that the Sinaloas, not the Gulf Cartel, not the Juarez Cartel, would now giveth.

And taketh away.

And this message was that the Sinaloas, and their *patron*, would unleash their hellish mechanism, the cogs and spokes of their new machine. Its entrepreneurial authority would be obtained by any ill-fated and violent means necessary, with their swelling criminality in its grand order designed to monopolize, control the *plaza*, the routes, by ordering tortured executions and beheadings and massacres by street gangs that murdered for hire. It would be obtained by their own *sicarios*, carrying out the shooting that now raged on the *Dios de los Muertos*, to drive the Juarez Cartel, Luis' business, off the coveted routes, out of the territory bordering El Paso, the terrain that trailed out into the Chihuahuan desert, a priceless commodity because of its proximity to the United States; this part of that two thousand mile border.

If the businesses paid their *piso,* their fee, to Luis for protection, they would be driven out; he was no longer protecting anything.

Luis no longer owned anything.

It was theirs now. That was their message.

Except that of course, Luis did not see it that way.

For the next few months, every murder was answered with another.

The body count for that year had already approached 3,000. Every lost shipment had to be answered for, usually with blood, and every relationship with every municipal policeman and *Federale* had to be reevaluated. The bribes, the *morditas,* had to be upped. Every *mordidita.*

Every nibble.

The Sinaloas would use their resources, the murderous gangs they subcontracted, the Barrios Aztecans. The Juarez Cartel would use theirs, the Zetas. Both would use the incalculable cash, millions of U.S. dollars collected every week in laundered revenue, to drive out the businesses, drive up the *mordita,* the bite, the bribe, to the *Federales* they owned, and the ones that they intended to buy. These corrupt officials, whom the government pretended to pay, would then pretend to work for the government. They would look the other way, offer their loyalty to the masters they feared, the hands that fed.

This bloody determination to define power was war.

Manny carried a Colt that day. He carried it Mexican-style down the back of his jeans, where his belt held it tight against his skin. He was seated on the patio, eating salted chips with lime and watching Alena from afar, because she had told him that he made her nervous, when he heard the screams and the shooting.

He dove onto the concrete, rolled with his head in his hands, taking brief cover from the automatic rounds. Then he stood, ran, without his own life in mind, only hers, across the square where *Canal 44* was broadcasting.

The station had done a story that afternoon about the murder of the chief of police, suggesting that the Sinaloas had to be stopped, and they'd used some colorful language regarding the Sinaloa's newfound presence in Juarez.

Alena was not part of the story, hadn't spoken to any sources. She worked on writing pieces about restaurants and cinema and theatre and travel. She'd told him she was looking forward to toasting her first assignment with him over her homemade sangria after she worked through her nerves, got through the live broadcast. Sometimes she made white sangria with peaches and oranges and lime, and other times, it was spicy, with red wine and blueberries and apples. The last time she made it for him, he was feeling very tired, and he told her he would prefer a beer. She frowned, but she did not say anything more about it; he did not get to toast her assignment with her that night or any other.

The truck reached the square first. The tires squealed, stopped. There were people dressed as skulls with faces painted, running, screaming, and in parts of the *zocalo*, the music was still playing over all of this. Gasoline shot from the side of the truck, blowing up the open flames into magnificent orange blasts, igniting the floats and filling the air with the smell of torched marigolds. By this time, he could see Luis' *halcones* looking over the parapets of white cracked adobe, nine-year-olds on cell phones. The tone of his own phone rang a birdsong from his pocket. It wouldn't be long before Luis knew of the attack. He'd escape from the back office, order a counter attack like round of margaritas.

The Sinaloa *sicario* had a small patch of beard growing on his chin, dark eyes very close together, a scar across his cheek. The *sicario* ran out of the truck, lunged at Alena, knocked her to the ground. Manny could see the cross he'd given her glinting, silver and turquoise, in the lights as he ran toward her, his legs elongating, arms pulling hard, challenging the limits of his speed as he stretched his gangly limbs. She screamed from the suddenness of the *sicario's* vehement embrace as she fell, the road raking against her bare shoulders where her arms emerged, exposed and graceful, from her sleeveless dress.

The man trained an M-16 on Alena where she lay on the stone ground. Another *sicario* got out and put his gun to the temple of the cameraman, who trembled but did not lower the lens. He stood mumbling in silent prayers until the *sicario* told the cameraman to stay live, keep filming. Then the *sicario* spit tobacco on the ground, said the cameraman was going to be dead if he did not follow instructions carefully. The red light stayed on; the camera kept filming the violence.

The man was going to be dead either way.

But not Alena, not Alena, he swore it as he ran, knocking over *ofrendas* in the market and a food cart of *tamales* steaming with pepper and onions, women in *campesina* dresses with faces painted as white skulls. He pushed through the crowd surrounding the truck. The man was shouting at Alena, down on the ground, shouting with very quick speech. The man's voice was rushed, as though he had done a line of cocaine, or like he was the one with the gun to his head, telling her what she was going to say. He ordered her to get up, send the message.

All Manny had was a goddamned Colt, a damn Colt.

Alena rose from the ground, shaking, her eyes timid and round and wet, and the cameraman dressed in black, stood, the camera wobbling unstable at his shoulder, and the *sicario* reminded the cameraman to shut up, keep filming.

Alena was there in the *zocalo* and now, with the red light on the video equipment signaling live communication. She was everywhere in homes on televisions, in offices and cantinas and stores, but she was present in none of these places. Standing fawnlike, frozen, absent before the wide lens, prey to the *sicarios*, fearful creature completely hollowed out; her voice cracked, begged them not to shoot her. The *sicario* shouted, pulled at her hair, ordered her to parrot his sick threat, the cartel mission, to repeat it before the camera, before living out the final moments of a fate already delivered.

Alena saw Manny in the crowd, running. She dropped the microphone when she saw him. He crouched behind a marble bench. Delaying, she picked it up, dropped it again.

Between them, the *sicarios* magazines held hundreds of rounds, a thousand maybe, and he only had a pistol.

Damnit.

He'd begged her not to even consider journalism. It was too dangerous. The cartels controlled the information in this way, controlled what they wanted people to know, and the truth was that their message was illusory and whitewashed, and it was not objective. It was painted in false witness by fear. Unholy dreadful law. Broadcasts did not expose violence, they covered it up, embellished the *Narco* cult of personality, its mass threats, the extortion. *Narcos* demanded from the press a blind faith against legitimate observations, from an evil handed up from Satan's own hands filthy and diabolic, and the press manipulated the people, sold them a fictitious brand of reporting, staged an imagined apathy from a bucolic and impoverished country, a Catholic and impossibly optimistic, hopeful country. And the cartels overlooked their own irreverence for human life, expected everyone to overlook it, too; it was nothing more than a matter of doing business and it was everything to be ignored, and everything to be accepted, unpunished.

Or else.

She was only covering the parade, the *Dios de los Muertos*.

"Hurry up," said the *sicario*.

She picked up the microphone, said, "Please, senor, please."

"You will say, 'Today is the last day of my life. Do not—'"

"Please, senor, please. It is only my first day."

With the metal alloy of the rifle barrel against her back, jammed hard into her spine, the *sicario* repeated, "Today is the last day of my life. Do not make my mistakes. Protect your families, your children."

"Please, please don't kill me," was all she could say.

The cameraman began to cry. He sank to his knees and cried without control, begged the *sicario*, incoherent and panicked, "Please, please, senor. She's just a girl. I have three children. They cry for food and they do not have enough to eat, and I do this only to feed their mouths."

The *sicario* who had his automatic trained on the cameraman hit the man over the head with the butt of the AK-47, opening the cameraman's forehead in a wide and linear gash, said, "Get up, pick up your camera, you worthless *soplon*."

Snitch.

Informer.

Manny pulled the Colt from the back of his jeans. His eyes swept the crowd. Gusto was over the parapet now, his AR-15 sighted down into the square. Gusto nodded to him and took the shot first at the *sicario* behind the camera. It missed the hitman, but it shattered the camera, ending the broadcast. Metal shrapnel hit one of the parade mules, who was covered in a red and gold saddle blanket. The abandoned animal moaned, and it fell, braying. Its frayed tail swayed briefly and there were flies buzzing around it that followed the animal to the ground.

Alena screamed. What was left of the crowd was screaming, too, and he took the second shot and it found the shoulder of the *sicario* who was holding Alena, but not before the *sicario* holding her shot the cameraman in the forehead and the man fell forward onto his knees, onto the cobblestones.

Then the *sicario* grabbed Alena, cupped her mouth, threw her into the back of the truck and slammed the door.

Manny clicked the hammer of the Colt, unseen, and shot again, this time at the driver, shattering the windshield, spraying shards of glass, as the *sicario* who had thrown Alena into the truck emptied his magazine out into the crowd.

He ducked now behind the marble balustrades of the fountain in the center of the *zocalo,* but the *sicario* saw him and ran toward him as people scattered, further exposing him.

The *sicario* kept shooting at him.

He reloaded the Colt, but before he could get his aim, Gusto took out the *sicario* while the *sicario* was changing his magazine. It was a single sniper shot from the parapet through the back of the chest. The bullet did not leave the chest, must have been the kind of ammo that stayed within the body, a hollow-point bullet, maybe, destroying and fragmenting tissue, but there was shrapnel and shells from the other rounds on the ground everywhere around the vehicle.

The truck took off, the driver spinning its wheels at first, moving down the narrow street, ripping through the crowd as the truck straightened out, moved back onto the *Avenue,* out of sight.

She was still in the truck that was barreling down the *Avenue*, out of sight.

Everything he loved, thrown in the back of a truck.

13

He'd get her back, he had to get her back. He kept telling himself that the *sicario* would not harm her, would not kill her, but the more he said it, the more he tried to convince himself of this; he knew it to be false. To Luis, the attack was bigger than Alena, one woman. The streets of Juarez were decorated with posters of disappeared women.

But to him, she was the whole world.

To Luis, the attack was about a loss of control of the businesses that Luis took a cut from, the cream off the top, the *piso*. It was about the *Federales* Luis owned. Luis needed all the Juarez men to fight this war now, to stand up for the territory, the right to move product through Ciudad Juarez, the valley, and across the bridges to El Paso, where Luis had relationships with the customs agents. Luis knew their hours, when they came on and when they left. He had lookouts watching their checkpoints.

Luis carefully arranged deliveries from the restaurant and accepted the volumes of cash returning, so much cash that it had to be buried out in the desert. Luis ordered the shipments passing from Mexico to El Paso to the safe house out in *The Middle of Nowhere*, Texas, where Columbians picked up their cocaine to make it into crack in their labs. Sometimes, marijuana and heroin distributors accepted their product. Then it was back on the roads again, heading south, with suitcases or steel drums or garbage cans filled with hundred-dollar bills.

To Luis, the attack was bigger than one woman.

But to him, it was only about Alena.

Nothing summoned a hatred for him in humanity, the consent he gave himself to do harm, the authority for evil, the will to defy a God he was not sure he believed in anymore, the way losing Alena did.

He got behind the wheel of The Apple, an AK-47 riding shotgun on the passenger side seat, He was going to find her, to hunt down that fucker who had taken her and then torture him within an inch of his life until the man defecated, as many of the men that Gusto tortured did, right before they expired, and at that time, he would make that asshole swallow his own shit. And then he and Alena were going to get out of there, he swore. They would get away from Juarez and the valley and the cartels.

They'd leave Mexico altogether.

He would see her round cheekbones shy in crimson lumps when she undressed and smiled, and he'd watch her do this again and again until her skin was red from pores that had grown large with age and from broken capillaries, long after the blush of youth abandoned them. He would see her narrow hips widen, fill with life, and roll to him alone each night with the energy of a beautiful and terrible tempest advancing, discharging, transferring its dynamism into new life until their bodies like one were inextricable.

After he got her back.

He was going to get her back.

After the shooting, it grew silent in the square except that, as he drove down the *Avenue,* he could hear the air move between his clenched teeth and he could hear the water falling from the fountain in the *zocalo,* and he could feel the rage trying to escape from his chest where it pained him, where he felt the pressure, squeezing, where his heart pounded, wrathful and strong.

In the desert, beyond Juarez, thunder tore the air apart in loud cracks.

There were strings of Christmas lights lighting the stores and palms in the street and some of the animals were running around, braying, and there were abandoned stores in the market where music had not stopped playing *corridos* to the deceased. A few chickens were flapping through the streets and a rooster was crowing loudly.

And at that time, he realized that he didn't know his most important, closest remaining friend, the one who would never abandon him, nor deny him—as he had, repeatedly.

Piranha still knew him. He had seen him in the square just before the shooting. Piranha had joined a vigilante group, an *Autodefensa* organization that met in the *zocalo* every few days, rallying to protect the town, the valley, against the Juarez cartel. But he'd learned from Gusto and Mustacio that many of the members were Sinaloas, Trojan horses. Piranha had begged him to join the group, which he said was composed of angry Juaranese, fish sellers like Juan and bakers and grocers and mechanics and cab drivers who were tired of the extortion, the false promise of protection that offered no protection, that protected nothing, that had destroyed their middle class and did not guarantee even survival. But the group included the Sinaloas, forming a presence with the townspeople, pushing their way into the daily life of the people, and onto the Juarez turf.

"Únete a nosotros, Manny," Piranha had said, when he had seen him sitting outside the restaurant, sipping tequila. Join us. Piranha was still skinny with his pants bunching in ribbons where his belt coursed through the loops, but his head seemed clearer now, determined, and he did not look like he was on drugs. Manny had felt out of place next to Piranha at that moment, sitting there well-dressed with a pressed shirt that Luis had bought him, wearing expensive leather shoes, dark jeans, a silver belt buckle. Piranha had called him a *Narco* cowboy and they'd laughed about it, but then Piranha asked him again, very somberly, to join the *Autodefensas*. "Help stop them. What they did to my mom has to be avenged."

He didn't disagree.

He sipped the tequila and he looked around and he said, "Just make sure she buys from us."

"Is that a threat?"

"I'd never do anything to hurt you or your family, Josef. You know that."

"But your bosses would."

Piranha's mother was a wasted ghost now, addicted to crack, and meth, barely surviving, getting up every morning solely to seek more crack and meth. Her teeth were blackened, her lungs wheezed, and her muscles were atrophied bands. She wandered the earth like an augury of the valley, her wanton soul already taken, clawed every day closer to hell though even hell had no use for her.

He and Piranha had grown apart. He didn't know what to say to him now except, "Let me get you a drink."

"I've collected an army, Manny. I've collected Colt pistols and ARs and M16s for the civilian *Autodefensa* group. Why should the government be the only ones allowed to carry them when they are part of the problem, aligned corruptly with the cartels? We need to be able to defend ourselves, defend our families against the violence."

God only knew where Piranha had gotten the weapons. Piranha could steal your shadow unnoticed.

Manny should've brought him in then. He should have explained how deeply he was entrenched with the Juarez Cartel at that point, admitting that Luis Barrios was his half-brother. It wasn't fair to Piranha. Piranha was his friend, the one he'd smoked weed with and the one who had fixed up The Apple and the one he'd told about his first night with Alena. Piranha had been with him when his best friend, Ramiro, was killed. God, he missed Ramiro. Maybe, with Piranha, he could've escape where he was then. Maybe he could've erased the disdain he felt for the part of his life that had allowed Ramiro's death, the vulnerability, the hatred he knew, everything about it. He wanted to discharge it from his soul like a high capacity mag, be on the other side of it again. That hungered sinful wish.

Bringing in Piranha would give Piranha a better life, even if there was no hope for Piranha's family. Luis had warned him, though, repeatedly, not to talk to anyone.

Lealtad primera.

Loyalty first.

Firearms were illegal to carry. It was part of the bigger problem of government corruption. He used to think that only the cartels paid the government to get away with the things that they got away with, but now it was becoming clear to him that it was the other way around, too. He had witnessed the influence, the power, and the billions in political collusion going both ways that dwarfed the GDPs of most countries. He didn't know what Piranha thought. Maybe he thought it was going to be like when they were in *secondaria*, skipping class, playing *Call of Duty* or *GTA* where they went out for the bad guys and even after the bloodbath and the decapitations and the thousands of virtual rounds, after all the replays, that it was going to be okay.

There was no replay.

Once you had a price on your head, once your head was offed, game over. Piranha said that he did not think that it was all okay at all, said that there were no bad guys, only worse guys, and that only Satan's will in man was absolute, and that he needed to have the prescience to destroy the lesser evil in order to survive.

Manny didn't disagree.

Shortly after telling Piranha no, that he could not join the *Autodefensas*, without explaining himself further, Piranha had walked away, disappointed, and told him to take care. And then the shooting had started.

He drove on now, taking off in the direction of the truck, but it was lost. He drove to Luis' ranch. It was cooler and it was dark now and there were many hours still before dawn. He had to get her back; he kept swearing to himself that he would, that Luis could somehow do it, get her back with him, so that he could hold her and smell her hair and listen to her stories about the legend of the *Cempasuchil* flower, about the romance of two young Aztecs, *Xochitl* and *Huitzilin*, even listen to her talk in her inflexible Catholic ways.

Gusto was there at the *hacienda* and Luis had a woman there who was barely twenty whom he introduced as his bride to be. The girl was short with pageboy hair brown and shiny eyes that looked Asian, and she was big and round everywhere he liked women to be round, maybe a little too round.

"Sylvia," she said, shook his hand, made a shy glance away.

"Congratulations," he managed, but it did not sound genuine, he knew.

Luis kissed his cheek, slapped his back. "More on Sylvia later. I want you to be my best man, my brother, right after we get your woman back, sort out this attack."

They sat at a square table covered in blue and white tile. Sylvia left them, and Luis poured tequila and Gusto lit a cigarette and held his head at the forehead, shook it.

Mustacio burst open the back the door, dragging the man who'd been driving the truck during the shooting. Gonzalez, one of Luis' men, was there, and Mustacio held the barrel of an AR15 to the man's back as Gonzalez hauled the man across the Talavera tile. The driver was still dressed in his *Dios de los Muertos* costume attire, identified as Paulo Hernandez. Hernandez was one of the Sinaloan *sicarios*, rumored to be gay, a handsome man with a square chin and a wizened mouth and a masculine dorsal hump of a nose that just fit his face. But Paulo's face today, in honor of the holiday, was regaled with theatrical makeup, black stitches painted check to check across his wide grin that smiled something like cocksure hubris.

Or as a failed disguise of his identity.

Or maybe Hernandez just liked to dress in costume. Gusto had told him a story, always liked to tell stories, so it was hard to know if it was the truth. Gusto had told him that Hernandez had been seen out in Juarez dressed in drag, on more than one occasion, making it known that he was going to have his own *plaza,* that the Sinaloan *patron* intended to give him a piece of the pie, make him a *lugarteniente*, put him in charge of Juarez.

A *Narco* in heels, out and about; he'd heard it all.

"Where's the girl?" said Gusto.

"They dumped her off somewhere first, at a stash house somewhere." Gonzalez pushed Hernandez forward with the rifle, onto his knees.

Manny rose from the table. "That girl is Alena. I'm going to marry her."

Gusto looked at Luis, and Luis at Gusto.

Gusto put a hand on his shoulder, the other hand over his own heart; the scar on Gusto's missing finger was shining, twitching, he said, "My apologies, Dolly. I meant no disrespect. We'll get her back. We'll negotiate with this vile carnival reject."

"We must get Alena back, negotiate with them," said Luis, though it sounded as though perhaps Luis was just being respectful.

Hernandez's eyes were blackened flat across the forehead against a palette of white, ghastly and opaque. His lips curled in red paint, almost to the cheek bones in a churlish smile, with the vertically painted stitches crisscrossing them in black, abhorrent, lines, giving the appearance of a mouth sewn shut. The nose, like charcoal, fell away as though it were a hollow opening to the skull, the *calavera*. Red glitter spread over each eyelid.

"Don't make a mess in here. Get him outside," said Luis; he lit a smoke.

With Mustacio's help, Manny had Hernadez handcuffed to the wrought iron gate that curved in twisted whorls and came to sharp spiral pickets along the length of the staircase on the back patio. Manny ripped the duct tape from Hernadez's mouth and began to beat the man. He continued to do so throughout the night out the back of the ranch, looking down over the mountainside. He used a baseball bat across the trunk, the knees. The sound of the ribs breaking was wooden, sharp, and he liked that sound very much. Mustacio told him more than once to ease off, reminding him that they needed information from the little faggot, said that if his head was fucked up and Hernandez couldn't speak, that Luis would not be happy.

He eased off, but it wasn't easy.

Mustacio hugged him, said he'd come a long way, and he said he was proud of him, but Manny did not feel proud of himself, only wanted her back.

Through those days, he maintained an unlikely hope.

Sometime later that night, that long painful night, Luis had The Doctor, Dr. Manuel Kelley, there, a former U.S. Board Certified Surgeon, half Mexican, who Gusto said had had his privileges, his license, revoked when he was found passed out in his office, injecting narcotics into his groin. The operating room nurse who had found him in his shiny, second-floor office in El Paso had assumed he was beating off and had closed the door and walked away. Kelley was found unconscious by his coworker sometime later, after he had sustained a stroke and suffered brain damage that left him with full use of all fine motor and surgical skills that he'd always been proud of, but with a severe impairment in his judgment and capacity for decision-making. Much like a high-functioning autistic, he was unable to empathize with others.

He fit in well there.

When Kelley arrived with his old-school black medical bag, Luis patted the doctor on the back, lit another smoke, and said that he was going back to the restaurant and that he hoped that things went well. He reminded them all again not to make a mess. Luis didn't like to get dirty. He washed his hands with near-psychotic obsession, and he disliked the thought of his ranch being dirty, had cleaning women there twice a day.

The doctor took the needle driver and he loaded it with a suture, and he clamped Hernandez's upper and the lower lips closed with a stainless-steel instrument. Its ends pointed and narrowed to a blunt tip, and its alligator clamps closed the ends of the instrument tightly shut, then more tightly as the teeth paired closed with each successive click of the chilled metal. Kelley drove the needle through the bottom lip and out the lower lip. He held the needle driver and tied four surgical knots. Then Gusto cut each of the ties and Kelley continued down the lips, suturing them shut and tying the stitches with surgical precision, moving the alligator clamp to keep the mouth approximated as Hernandez struggled but could not move during the procedure.

"Are you sure you don't want to talk, *hermano*?"

Manny could not be sure, but it sounded like Hernandez was triying to say, "Fuck you, you, medical fuck up," through the sewn lips, as Kelley continued suturing.

14

After all of this, there was some information obtained, though Hernandez was loyal, not an easy source of information. He was fiercely loyal to the cause, and he was no *soplon*. Luis returned when the interrogation was complete. Gusto loaded Hernadez's body into the back of The Apple, dumped it on the highway.

The Sinaloas apparently did not like the broadcasts that *Canal 44* had made, exposing the violence and the executions and their new corruption in Juarez. To the station, the broadcasts were simply reporting the truth.

"They have something against the obvious?" asked Mustacio.

"Hernandez has been paying the journalists, but the journalists have not accepted the payments. He claims the attack the Sinaloas made was against the station, claims that they would not do such work to us personally, that he knows how things are done," said Gusto.

"Someone ordered an attack on Luis," said Mustacio.

"He claims they did not."

"He's lying. Luis' Porsche 911 exploded outside the back of the restaurant. It was by God's will alone that we got into the Blazer when we left."

Luis raised his glass and made the sign of the cross, said, "God is great, Amen."

"Amen," said Mustacio and Gusto. Manny nodded. The men drank their shots. Luis filled them with another round of *Anejo* tequila.

"As the old saying goes, if someone says you smell like shit, you should take a shower before you argue." Luis was quiet and pensive and wrathful. "Or better yet, clean the whole house. That is what the Sinaloas are trying to do here, clean house."

"By buying out every municipal police officer they can entice, or threaten, and by eliminating our affiliation with the Zetas, La Linea, and by tearing apart our routes, our territory." Gusto examined his nails, looked out the window. "It will not happen, boss."

"They want to replace our connections with the federal and city police with their own. What about Gutierrez? I've suspected trouble with him for some time. Whose side is he on?"

"I'm not sure, and that means I don't trust him," said Gusto.

"Keep an eye on him, a very close eye."

"*Si*, boss," said Gonzalez.

"Pay him a visit."

"*Si.*"

The next day, there was an immediate and violent retaliation from the Juarez Cartel in response to the shooting in the *zocalo*. Two city police officers and a *Federale* suspected of forming ties with the Sinaloas were shot as they left their homes for work. Officer Cordoba, the barrel-chested *Federale* who'd laid him on the ground by the Rio Bravo several years earlier, when he'd first started mule work, had had a son with him when Luis' men shot him. Gusto put a bag over the little boy's head, tied it tightly and left the child there until his mother came out onto the front porch. She'd heard the gunshots and found her son screaming, gasping, seconds from death. When the boy's breathing returned to normal, she found Cordoba, her husband, dead on the driveway.

Luis called upon La Linea during this uncertain time, the corrupt arm of the city police that took the offerings, or bribes, to supplement their modest salary and provide payouts to their families if they were injured or killed in the line of duty.

But the Sinaloas had infiltrated them, too. They had already brought some of them over to their side, and it was getting impossible to tell who was affiliated with who and what he knew for sure at this time was that he could trust no one.

There had to be traitors among them, too, but he did not yet know who they were. He slept with one eye open and he looked over his shoulder often and he had a remote starter installed in The Apple, always started it before getting in; he became used to checking beneath it for signs of a charge.

Two days after the attack, the *patron,* from prison, ordered an attack on the poppy fields in Jalisco. Luis communicated daily with the *chapo*, also known as *El Gato*, through coded messages where every fifth word of the message was the actual content of the note—or, more commonly, by simply presenting a lump of cash that was as much a threat as it was a gift. The recipient guard or policeman or division chief of the prison could accept the offering, or he could be shot, beheaded, tortured. So usually, the benevolence of the monetary guise was respected.

The order to attack the poppy fields came in response to the loss of influence in Juarez, a necessary attempt to remain in control of their territory. If the Juarez cartel could not guarantee the same revenue from the Columbian cocaine routes through Mexico, if the Sinaloas had usurped some of that control, then they would go after the Sinaloa's product closer to their rival's home.

The truth was that Luis was losing ground, and the *patron* was not happy.

How much was hard to say, and this made Luis' men guarded. Not only did Luis have to fight a war in Juarez to defend the territory there that was being lost, but the Juarez Cartel needed to regain part of the market elsewhere to pay for that war in bodies and blood and bribes.

The Juarez Cartel needed new routes, new product.

The Sinaloas not only distributed the Columbian cocaine product, which the Columbians were getting punchy about moving by sea to Miami at the increasing risks of seizures. The Sinaloas were better producers, too: better growers of marijuana and opium, superior cooks of methamphetamine. The Columbians were flying in planes with three metric tons per week and moving the cocaine through to the other side, the United States, by way of Mexico, garnering a grand a kilo. The Sinaloas were doing better than the Juarez at growing poppies and marijuana and cooking up heroin and meth out in the fields of the Golden Triangle, cooking up product like a line order diner. The Juarez Cartel was mainly a distributor.

And now the Sinaloas were moving in on their cocaine routes, too.

To the East, the Gulf Cartel had weakened. The area was a bloody power vacuum, too.

Things were going bad, very bad.

Luis said the marijuana was becoming chump change to them, that the product was changing, that the States were demanding heroin, good heroin.

A few days before the attack on the poppy fields, the Sinaloas retaliated in response to the attacks on the police. Four policemen known to be part of La Linea, the Juarez affiliate of the police force, were dumped on the highway, and a tape was delivered to the restaurant.

He wanted to watch it but he could not, and after that day there was no doubt that Alena was dead, but Luis watched it, and Gusto watched it, and Gusto told him the things that happened to her, things that he later wished he could erase from his mind, but after this time there was an anger impossible and unfulfilled in him that would never allow this. She had refused their demands, kept saying, *"De cualquier manera, gano."*

Either way, I win.

Damn them, and damn her faith. Maybe, just maybe, they would've let her go if she had agreed to make a statement.

It was several days before her decapitated head turned up, discarded without remorse. Manny found it floating near the same spot she'd been disappeared from in the *zocalo.* Her scalp had been shaved and her neck sawed high up to the occiput of her skull. A few strands of her newly cut hair hung down over her eyes, wet and matted over the swollen lids, eyes murky and clouded and brown, all their warmth and passion and hope removed. A hole had been drilled in the back of her skull. He lifted her head where it bobbed in the fountain, buoyed up and down under the trickling of the falling water that washed away what was left of the blood that had crusted around her nostrils, her right ear, her severed neck. He held it between both of his hands, stared at the bludgeoned face he loved. Then he dropped it and the water from the fountain splashed his jeans and there was the faint smell of blood ferric and old and he gagged. Gusto came behind him and lifted the head out of the water, began to palpate around the neck, around the base of the skull.

Manny turned and he grabbed his abdomen and he knelt and he vomited.

Gusto placed his hands up inside the cranium.

15

Chickens were still running about the square, pecking at the remains of abandoned food carts. The same rooster he'd seen during the attack crowed loudly, jutting forward its neck and its breast as it circled the fountain. He kicked it, swore to it, and vomited again.

"I know you're not talking to her," he said, staring down the pompous bird. "I heard you. You got no business to say a thing to me. Get out of here."

"Emmanuel," Gusto said, extended his hand, holding two small bones.

The rooster cooed again, this time softly, but it did not strut about anymore. Gusto hadn't called him Dolly; it didn't feel right.

Manny chased the bird and he caught it and he broke its neck and the chickens scattered. He threw the dead rooster at the statue across from the fountain.

"What are these?" he looked at the tiny bones Gusto held before him.

The smell of blood and rotted fruit was still faint on the air where flies buzzed and there was no one shopping at the marketplace. When he looked around at everything, the ghosts he could imagine and those he could not, everything driven away, he smelled something like fear, too. The municipal police had cleared the bodies and turned over the scene to the federal investigators, who were largely on one side or the other, and neither of those sides was the side of the people murdered in Juarez on the Day of the Dead, or those murdered on any other day.

What side he was on, he did not know.

Gusto put an arm on his shoulder. He unfastened Manny's gold chain and took the bones of Alena's cervical spine that each made an oval loop, and Gusto placed them around his neck, refastened the chain. Gusto held one of the bones up from which a tooth-like projection pointed, and he gave the anatomical names for the bones, said, "The Atlas, the Axis. You and I are part of the Axis. We hold up the world, this empire, this business. We're family." Gusto nodded, twisted the bones, and held up the flatter of the two, refusing to dismiss his gaze. That stare wound taught. "This bone is the Atlas. It holds up the head, like Luis holds up our world while the *patron* is away."

"Gusto, you're one sick fuck."

Gusto shrugged, said, "Anyway, your beloved is remembered, kept close to your heart."

Manny did not take them off, did not remove the bones from his chain; he wore her bones around his neck.

For many months, he was sullen, and there was an anger in him that kindled, grew exponential and consuming like gasoline in fire, and there was a part of him broken that could not be made right in his lifetime, and he no longer tried to tease that evil apart from his soul, he just let it fester in those days after she was murdered, and that part did very well without her love or His, he thought.

That night, he thought about those first runs he'd made. He called Juan, wanted to know how Juan had been right there when Gutierrez and Cordoba had seized the cocaine. With Gutierrez's rifle in his face, he'd never felt closer to death than that day in the desert, even during the shooting in the *zocalo* with the shrapnel flying and the screaming and the barreling truck plowing down the *ofrendas* and the parade and the people.

Juan refused to talk, ended the call immediately.

Things settled; the violence abated for a short while, but the routes, their plaza, was still under attack. Before they made the trip to Jalisco to light up the Sinaloan poppy fields, there was a meeting, orchestrated by Luis to work out the clandestine details of the operation. The location was at a warehouse somewhere in the *Valle de Juarez*, and Manny wouldn't have been able to find it again if he'd tried. Shipments that were supposed to be smooth and efficient were being seized, thousands of kilos of cocaine, millions in revenue, was lost. Luis had grown paranoid that the restaurant and his home and his vehicles had been bugged.

"Gutierrez is becoming a poppy thorn in my ass," said Gusto.

"Poppies don't have thorns," Luis said.

"Those spiny things, at the top, near the seed pods. They look sharp."

"Those are the crown."

"They look like thorns."

"They're not thorns. And they're not sharp at all. Gusto, have you ever seen one? Stopped to smell the roses, as they say?" Luis rubbed his brow where it was developing grooves like the coarse wrinkles of Asian dogs.

"I don't stop to smell them before I torch the fields. He's a pain in the ass. You get the point."

"Why is he suddenly interested in the fish trade and what's in my trucks?"

"He's suddenly interested in distribution rights. He doesn't care about fish."

"He wants to sell out, or maybe he already has, to the Sinaloas. He was slighted by what we paid him on an old run to Tornillo," Manny said.

"Dolly, come here, brother." Luis kissed his cheek. "It's nice to see you speaking up, I love it. But fuck the Sinaloas. He needs to get over it. It was one run."

"When have you known a slighted Mexican to let go of anything?" He smiled wide, self-conscious of the space in his teeth.

Luis shrugged. "*Si*, Dolly. You're right. I knew we would be close. Our brother Juan, he is a good man—but you and I are alike. How do they say in English, two peas?"

"The weight of that chip on Gutierrez's shoulder would've crushed him by now. There has to be something more," Gusto said.

"He's suddenly interested in the value of cocaine once it hits the States," he said. "That's what I hear on the street."

"He never cared about that before. There has to be more," said Luis.

Gusto clipped the end of a cigar. "We never moved much cocaine before. We were moving mostly marijuana, some brown heroin. It isn't Mexican cocaine. It's Columbian."

"And the Sinaloa's comes from fucking Disney World? They are moving the same shit. No different. Why does he want to destroy my route from Jalisco?"

"Too close to Culiacan?"

"We're going around Culiacan, away from the Sinaloas."

"They want the central territory."

Luis exhaled cigarette smoke, said, "They want the moon, but it's untouchable—and if it were reachable, it would be mine., too."

"The Sinaloas wanted to give Hernandez his own plaza, maybe Gutierrez now. There's still the demand for cocaine, to make crack over there, but the real money is moving into heroin, good heroin."

"You can't suck and blow. Well, I've had some whores who can, but Gutierrez, you know, he can't keep his position as a *Federale* and have his own plaza, too. What does he think this place is coming to? There are still rules, still empires, your side of the street, my side of the street. We cannot exist without them, nor them without us."

"Maybe he wants to give up on the *Federales*."

"Impossible. The power makes that narrow-waisted prick hard as the rock they make with it."

"There's talk of the politicians disarming the law enforcement here, because of corruption."

Luis laughed. "Then they want us to pay them more, too. Unbelievable."

"Fuck that, and fuck him, Luis."

"I agree, fuck Gutierrez."

And that day, Luis laid the price of Gutierrez's head: five hundred thousand dollars, and he laid out the details of the operation in Jalisco, said they would start a little fire to send a message.

They plan was to demolish acres of poppy fields, and the plan was to blow up a few meth operations, and it was to catch a few of the Sinaloa's allies used for enforcement and to execute them. Luis said that heads were going to roll, and this statement was not a figurative when Luis said it on that night or any time thereafter. Luis said the *capo* wouldn't be happy until his orders were carried out, said that since the *capo* remained behind bars, it would be a full-fledged, all-out blood bath in Juarez, a dirty war fought devoid of honor.

Gusto thought that it would be good for Manny to get away from Juarez, told him his mood was sulky and assured him his sorrow for Alena would pass. Mustacio and Gonzalez were going to light the largest poppy fields of the Sinaloas with grenade launchers, eliminate the peasant farmers. They would scare out the locals, chase them out of the mountains, bring in their own, and start from scratch. Then they would helicopter out, and maybe shoot up a few of the Sinaloa's meth labs the following week.

Manny shot down his third round of tequila now. A nervous sigh fell away from his breath with the smell of the alcohol. Luis sensed his apprehension, turned; he'd never shot another man.

And always, they called him Dolly.

"Dolly, what's the matter."

"Nothing."

"You okay?" Luis smiled.

"Yeah, I'm okay."

Luis leaned over and slapped Manny's back, kissed his cheek, patted it. "Okay."

There was only so much they could do by taking out their men because there were always new recruits to fill the shoes, new warm bodies to place on the front lines, to fill in the scars of those who'd preceded their infantry. There seemed no end to the war, to the violence.

It seemed everyone was expendable.

And it was at this time, after Alena was murdered, that he embraced it.

Luis intended to take down production, establish new relationships with the suppliers by any means necessary. Luis wanted the war now, and Manny, too, had developed a penchant for it, had tasted revenge cold and savage, and craved its satisfaction. At times, he felt his body mimicking the body language of the *sicarios,* which at first gave him pause. His arms crossed as theirs did and his mouth remained expressionless and he leaned back, allowed his eyes to squint into amaurotic discs like Gusto's as he began to perform interrogations, breaking the bones of infidels with bats and scalding men's skin with rods of heated iron. He carved up the anatomy with Dr. Kelley and grew numb to the way Gusto clung to the demented remnants of bones and eyes and ears, without thinking to define this surreal taste for butchering as anything atypical.

Juan had become distant in those months, but he was still allowing him to drive The Apple he'd been driving when Ramiro was shot, knowing he clung to the memory of The Terminator and that night through that truck, which now had brakes that made a metal-on-metal squeal that screamed at him in protest, needed rotors and pads. He tried calling Juan twice that evening, but Juan said that he could not talk at that time, and he thought that Juan was angry with him again, though as usual, he did not know for what, so he stayed at Luis' ranch more often than he should have.

When he woke the next morning, his phone was blowing up with text messages from his mother, and from Juan, too. He wandered out onto the patio where two doves had just begun to stir, and where the air smelled of aloe and bougainvillea and it was very humid. He was wearing black jeans and a clean white undershirt and combat boots. He sat beside Sylvia, overlooking the desert, and he and drank some cactus juice and some coffee and he ate some mango that Sylvia was peeling and cutting into wedges.

"Your eyes are sad," Sylvia said as she cut the fruit with a very sharp and large knife that looked like a machete, slicing carefully so that she would not cut herself. "Like a lost boy."

She was childlike and timid and still learning customs, yet she was older than him by maybe only a year or two, and much younger than Luis. Luis had likely arranged the marriage with her parents in some business deal shrewd and calculated, purchasing her virginal beauty. Just before the shooting in the *zocalo*, something like mid-life anxiety in Luis had been set into motion and he now seemed preoccupied that his time was nearing an end. Luis said that he needed to marry, and he said often that he loved his brothers and he said that he loved his family and that he wanted a son. Luis had spoken about Sylvia coming for some time, about how he needed a queen whose character was unmarred by the lifestyle he led, talked about how lovely she would be, how he couldn't wait to meet her.

There was no sophistication about her, as he would've expected from Luis, although he did not know this brother well. He knew that Luis often had women. He'd seen them at the restaurant with white-tipped fingernails and long stem legs and skin like honey that smelled floral like a trellis of pink dahlias until after the women had been intimate with Luis. He thought that perhaps Luis sought worldly traits in these adorned women, and it seemed a beautiful and hypocritical and privileged thing that Luis could also appreciate Sylvia's *campesina* innocence, the long eyelashes that fell closed in soft and delicate and destructive flirtation. Manny was careful not to look too long at her. A brief flush of crimson came into his face, a shameful heat that reminded him of the little flames he created when he and Juan were younger, when they would strike matches just to watch them burn down to ash. Something was burning in him, too, but he could not say what then and when she asked him again why he looked sad, he rose from the table, stepped away from Sylvia in a necessary gesture of obeisance. He stood beside the bougainvillea looking out at the desert, and Sylvia rose, too, and where Luis' blue parrot was perched on its stand, she gave it a slice of mango and it said, "*rojo.*"

"*No, anaranjado,*" she said.

He sat again and there was a long pause while he chewed his fruit, sipped some coffee, and set it down, said, "I don't think I was ever a child. Children don't exist here. Not for long, anyway."

"I would like to have many children." It was awkward, her conversation, the way she tried to hold his eyes. She sat beside him again. Then Gusto and Mustacio came out onto the lanai, smoking, and said it was time to go, that they were bringing around the Jeep. She smiled and she pinned her barrette in her hair and smoothed her dress and she looked over the side of the mountain and back at him.

"You're looking for yourself," she said.

He sipped the coffee, bit the mango, chewed, said, "Don't know what I'd do if I found me. Never felt like I had much of a choice anyway. I've thought about that, thought about what I'm looking for. Thought that at some point there was probably some decision that I made that took me on some twisted path that got me right here sitting beside you having breakfast—but probably it was somebody else's choice, much farther back than me, ancestors that date back way beyond me."

She smiled, cut some apples into wedges and she set them out before him.

Gusto's wife, Anna, came and sat at the table and lit a cigarette. Her leathered skin made a sharp contrast next to Sylvia. Anna crossed her legs and uncrossed them beneath the table. The spicy tones of her perfume ripened the air around them that morning and she fanned herself heavily with the placement and her sweat beaded on her forehead, though the heat of the day was not yet soupy, and it was early still, and to him the sun did not feel intolerable above them in its arc.

Gusto returned to the patio and he kissed her cheek, told her that they would return in a few days. On a perch beside Manny, the McCaw parrot dropped the mango from its claw, and said, "Few days." Anna shrugged and exhaled her cigarette and looked out at the mountains of Juarez, but she did not reply.

Luis was in his office, cleaning the money, accounting for the millions of U.S. dollars that came this way after the drugs went up that way. By now, Luis owned six restaurants, two in Juarez and two in Nuevo Laredo, an Italian one in Piedras Negras that served a diablo sauce that invariably gave him heartburn, and one in Matamoros on the Gulf Coast that had twice been remodeled after shootings from the CDG, the Gulf Cartel.

The CDG was a bitter rival, though they both had allies in the Zetas. It was hard work making all the cash disappear, but it had to be accounted for, and somebody had to make that money look clean—because Luis did not seem to like to get his hands dirty, not only figuratively, but literally—he washed his hands obsessively with grainy sink cleansers and antibacterial soaps so much that the skin had worn away it eczematous patches that blistered red and white on the palms. That's what Luis did.

Luis kept it clean.

Luis not only managed restaurants, but he now owned a fleet of trucks, a shipping company. He also had heavy investments in oil in Brazilian and Venezuelan developing companies, and he had his hand out to the politicians of both PAN and the PRI parties in Mexico City. He had his own fleet of DC-8 places, offshore accounts in the Cayman Islands that seemed only vested in protecting clients' security and cared nothing for the source of the funds, which were largely deposited in suitcases full of hundreds of thousands of dollars in cash. What Manny found most impressive was Luis' access to the American banking system with millions invested in mutual funds. Luis said that he and Sylvia planned to start a family right away, and that he wanted his children to go to college in the United States.

During the rainy season there were often men that came and went from Luis' ranch. These men came to pay Luis the fee for running drugs through the Juarez *plaza*, giving Luis a minimum of ten percent of everything that passed through his territory, and sometimes they came to explain why they could not pay Luis the fee, either because the drugs were seized or the money was seized on the way back to Mexico or they did not receive the planned amount at the time of delivery. It was at these moments that Luis' eyes appeared to detach from his soul entirely, and it was always then that Gusto and Mustacio entered the room, and when the afternoon thunder clouds seemed to heat up the worst.

This morning Luis was standing inside, dressed in black, and gazing out through the glass wall, at him, as though he saw something in Manny that perhaps he could not see himself or behold in mirrors. The night before, Luis had played Uno cards with him until they were drunk on *anejo* tequila and Manny's mind was removed from Alena and he could sleep heavily and immediately without thinking about her as he drifted, a somnolent and tortured prisoner in bed.

He had sobered up somewhat when a coyote woke him at an hour when the moon was full and bright, but his thoughts did not return to Alena; he thought of his father, tried to remember the last time he saw his father, or the funeral, but he could not, and he imagined his father looking back at him through the glass now where Luis stood. He did not notice Luis' chiseled jaw or the cleft chin that his brother, Luis, also shared with Papa, the silver strings appearing at the temples, the sun damage around the corners of the eyes; he looked past these. His father had disappeared from his life too long ago to remember such details. What he saw staring back through the glass was something like approval, or retribution.

Gusto whistled then. Manny rose and they left the *estancia* and drove in the Jeep to a small airstrip not one thousand yards long. A pilot flew them hopscotch in a DC-8 to their final stop on the west coast, where they landed in Jalisco on an even shorter airstrip near the city inland of *Ixtapa,* among the mountains of tropical trees and hardwoods and *oyamel* firs in the *Sierra Madre del Sur.* In the deep canyons of the range, he imagined the deaths of many souls concealed beneath banana trees and palm-thatched huts. A swallow began hard on his lips and passed down his throat.

There was a resurgence of fear within him now, one he'd always had, a fear of heights. On one side of the driver was the mountain, and on the other side was a cliff, and he could not see the ground below it. Twice on the ride his is voice squeaked avian like his mother's old Quaker parrot when the ragged bird had flown, frightened up into the papaya tree in the yard, and it had taken all afternoon to get it down. Gusto teased him today, asked him if he was ready. As they passed the last gas station before the climb up the mountain to the poppy fields, his heart thumped. Mustacio parked the Jeep.

"Are we riding up?"

Mustacio laughed but did not answer. He only said, "Dolly," slapped his back, and started the truck belonging to the Mexican army men who were accompanying them.

They drove in a yellow Mercedes Benz Unimog with a raised chassis and extra wide tires designed for military use, filled with ten former Mexican military who wore the attire of the *gendarmerie* and were facilitating their operation. These soldiers, former veterans trained in special ops, were now affiliated with the Juarez Cartel. Behind them followed a convoy of three more trucks equipped with rocket-propelled grenade launchers and automatic rifles, rounds, old carbines, M1s, reloaders, gasoline, and explosives.

Using drones, they'd found the location of a large field where trees had been burned out or sawed off to clear away room to cultivate the acres of opium-producing poppies.

They rode a mountainside perilous and green of hairpin turns and narrow dirt from which vehicles fallen lay in ruin below on a hillside cliff. He held metal bars beneath the covered roof of the vehicle riding open air, bouncing around over subtropical terrain uneven and jagged, of rocky formations with outgrowths of oak and pine. Later, farther up the mountain, they passed enormous stretches of scrub and thickets of *Dyewood* and *Tampiciran* and *Parotas*, and they stopped near a tributary that snaked in high-pitched trickles toward the *Canopy River* below them.

They listened for the bird calls, the doves, the yellow-headed Amazons that perched and sipped on the droplets of condensation. Where they heard the subtle leak of water near irrigation systems, they found the rolls of black rubber tubing, followed the irrigation hoses climbing the hillside. They stopped the convoy to scope the area where the air smelled of orchids and smoke, but there were no poppies and the convoy moved again until they reached the first poppy field on the leeward side of the mountain.

Abandoned villages were interspersed with the mountain at breaks where the road widened, growing flat and dusty. The local farmers had been driven out by the militant organizations that the Sinaloas used to oversee their poppy production. The criminal groups had *halcones*, digital surveillance, and he suspected they'd been seen. Gusto stopped and glassed the area with binoculars, looked back, went ahead.

It was not only the poppy fields they were after today. Their objective was to fragment the allies supplying the opium paste to the cooks, thereby cutting off a major supply of product and toppling the heads of the gang distributing it to their competitors, the Sinaloas.

The militant arms of the Sinaloa were spidery and far-reaching. They had their hands into everything from farming to distribution, extortion, arms sales and kidnappings, and the groups had loose alliances—friends of their enemies, he could say—with the Rojos, the Guerreros Unidos and the Ardillos, remnants of the Beltran Leyva Cartel, which had largely fallen apart. These factions were warring in Jalisco and Guerrero to oversee poppy production from the Sinaloas, making sure the farmers were using the land to grow their cash crop.

This crop was not peppers or mangos or cantaloupe—it was opium poppies with razored seed pods seeping brown paste that they cultivated for heroin, commanding a grand per kilo. In many areas, they drove the farmers out and down the mountain into refugee camps along the coastal plain and the highway beside the tourist town of Puerto Vallarta.

Today, they were after those militant governing arms of the Sinaloa; he planned to send them a message.

Mustacio rubbed the tip of his handlebar mustache where it greased to a point and he checked his reflection in the glass of the Unimog, snapped his suspenders over his lean frame. Gusto was eating potato chips, licking his calloused fingers; he offered Manny the last one, crinkled the bag into a ball and threw it at him. Gonzalez lifted the RPG-7 from the truck and handed it to Mustacio, who rested it on his shoulder; he advanced. Their helicopter overhead was spraying flammable herbicide, flying low. It took rifle fire from the farmers below, battering its side, but it did not crash. The chopper gusted winds downward that blew through him, blew his hair, his skin back, and he could not hear again until the pilot raised the rotorcraft out of sight.

Gonzalez settled his grenade launcher and looked behind him, told Manny he'd better get out of the way. Gonzalez sighted the RPG, activated the fuse. He moved ahead, and behind Gonzalez, there was a cloud of scorching exhaust. The high-explosive grenade had shot out faster than he could see it and it whizzed into the field and ignited its target terrain into an orange fireball.

"What do I do?" Manny asked.

"Go," Mustacio screamed, and after that he did not stay in one place long while using the rocket-propelled grenade launcher, because it made his location entirely transparent, made enemy reconnaissance a no-brainer.

There was rifle fire from behind him now, coming from the farms, and Manny ran out around the blaze, breathing dust suspended in a wet and heavy air where carbon specks and embers flared and floated softly, like fireflies. The dense smoke that rose from the torched flowers hovered low, but he had to stay down there where it seemed he was drowning in soot and he could not inhale a clean breath. The gangs and peasant farmers retaliated by setting fire to the Mercedes Unimogs. The trucks squelched in an orange blaze, and there were rogue peasants shooting with old rifles and bandoleers like some mid-century war of Crusaders scorned.

There were very young boys returning rifle fire and only moments of quiet came between the shooting and there were shells flying in all directions. After what seemed like an endless pause, the peasants who had flung themselves out of the line of fire and onto the ground of the jungle, slowly, began to retreat. Mustacio and the army men stormed the fields, advancing from the spot where they had parked the convoy. Mustacio detonated explosives and lit the remaining acres of poppies, ignited the red petals, the green-gray pods. The blaze ascended high into the wind, glowing like a signal flare, a squelching wildfire that spread, wave-like and terrible, high up the mountain.

He lifted a mini-Uzi from the stock pile of guns in the back of the last Unimog in the train and shot several rounds at one of the Ardillos dressed in green fatigues. Then, as he ran between trees to conceal his frame, one of the Ardillos knocked him in the temple with the butt of his rifle and he fell to the ground. Now the man was close enough to shoot him, held an MP5. Manny's eyes burned, emblazoned and wide; the gang member hovered over him where he lay on the ground. The Ardillo aimed his MP5 at Manny's head as Manny looked up from the grass at this man with a crooked and sinister scowl, but another shot—from somewhere he did not see—took the man out, and the man's body crumpled its sac-like mass forward so that it fell onto him.

He shoved the body off him and laid it beside him where poppies grew, untouched by the intensifying hellfire, their petals mature and red and velvety, their ellipsoid seedpods bursting.

He panted heavy, carbon-flecked breath and coughed, his pulse racing and his thoughts contesting a close second. He took a particulate-filled gasp of air, saw moments of his life in

Mexico City with his father holding him high on his shoulders and the Mexican National Anthem playing loud around him, around Juan, from the taverns and street musicians and this vision warmed his thoughts now. The cartel had hardened him in many ways, but he could still recall a few memories occasional and soft. An image came to him of his mother, younger, pregnant with Elvie, standing beside the ranch in the arroyo near the stream as he led the goats, the cows, around the farm, where from the pasture he could hear Enriqua speaking to the unborn girl, pointing, naming the animals, *vaca*, *oveja*, *cabra*—cow, chicken, goat. The adrenaline pounded within him as it had with Piranha and Ramiro and Justin Vazquez playing paintball, only this game was real. It was war, though the stakes were higher and again, he was surviving, but he did not understand why and this time it did not seem like it was by much. A bird called, and he turned; twigs broke; the roar of the fire spread.

Around him there were bodies littering the burning field, and as in paintball, he was one of the last ones standing, though he still did not see where the shot that took out the Ardillo with the MP5 had come from. He thought it may have been meant for him. He proceeded on the ground, slowly.

Across the burning field, his men were retreating to the remaining trucks.

He looked left and right at the dead that lay in the field and he rose from his feet and stood forward and he ran, ran out of the field where shells were still flying and where the engines of the convoy of Mercedes trucks burned. He did not see Mustacio or Gusto. He kept running, ran at least a mile, taking cover behind huge Parota trees every fifty feet or so, as he had in paintball, until his breath was dry and tight in his lungs and he could no longer smell the smoke, and no longer see the fire. He ran toward a tin-roofed shanty whose side of jungle wood was burned away and open to the pine forest now, where he stood at 10,000 feet, with perplexed clouds twisting low and grey and almost in reach, and where the smell of orchids grew stronger, and where only the loud calls of macaws and smaller parrots among the tamarinds and the crack of the twigs under his feet could be heard. There was a footpath ahead of him, where at some time men had entered the brush, cutting back scrub and fallen palms and high grass.

His pace slowed, exhausted, and he walked into the forest, down dusted paths forked thrice, crinkling grass soft beneath his boots. He entered the shanty. He was not sure he wanted to see what was inside, realizing that there were innumerate things in his imagination that could not be removed from his head and nearly as many now that had been removed from his material world that he wanted put back, but which could not be.

Alena, Ramiro, Papa, he remembered at this time, though the memories could not soften his anxiety now or ever again when he thought of Alena. Rage seethed and built within him something terrible.

He stepped over the threshold of the shanty, over the creaking door frame, with a hand on his pistol, that lethal weight of it in his hand pumping its own adrenaline through him. The Uzi was slung across his chest and he had at least thirty rounds and another magazine in his belt. He'd taken the MP5 from the fallen Ardillo soldier, but there was nothing in the magazine and he suspected this was why the Ardillo had hit him with it instead of shooting him. He rubbed his temple where a lump from the butt of the gun had formed.

16

He understood that the *sicarios* believed in their version of order over the people, derived their power from them, and so loved the people for this power, gruesome and sick. The *sicario* who did not take the ultimate prize, the lives of others, at least from time to time, lost authority, because there existed no other hand, no jurisdiction, to enforce their variety of power, that sacrifice terminal and bereaved. Their brand was fear and intimidation and menace.

It was death.

Death was God; and Mustacio and Gusto and Gonzalez were his preachers. Impenitent evangelists unhinged.

The *sicarios* were not *Federales* nor police officers nor soldiers, though they could subjugate these men. Like officers of law, Gusto, Mustacio, and Gonzalez risked life, fortune, family. A vile power, their retribution.

He came to understand that he was falling into this role that he had at first resisted, but he was not sure if it could satisfy the thing in him that had been created at Ramiro's death, that had fed itself on Alena's death, and now needed no worldly thing to kindle itself.

Halcone.

Sicario.

Lugartieniente.

There was a coveting gustatory and insatiable for violence, perhaps so that he might be removed from the victimization of it, a desire to sit aloft from its vulnerability. He wanted his own piece, to please his brother, to face these great giants, and with this he wrestled with his desire to see the Truth and to sit again with Alena, though today he could not.

Today, he wanted to sit beside Luis, and he wanted to return to Juarez, and to tell Luis that they had done what they had set out to do, that they had sent the message.

Duplicitous ministry delivered.

Inside the dwelling, his heart settled; his breathing slowed. Beside cinders and earth smoked a dying fire where two barefoot peasants poked at it with gnarled sticks, a young woman and an old man with an excrescence pendulous and membranous and pink, hanging from his face where one eye should have been and extending down below his chin. The man's other eye was clouded white with a hazy and confused and membrane of cataract, and the young woman was his age with knotty hair hung like vines and a dirty face. She was dressed in a *hiupil* of wrinkled and torn cotton.

Behind the shanty, a gathering of multicolored goats stood with horns asymmetric and stubbed and coiled, with mangy fur clumped in gluey chunks. The blind man with the monstrous weeping tumor sat milking one of the goats. The meat of another charred over the fire. The blind man rose, and with his head pointed aloft to better utilize the auditory sense, he approached. The tumor ballooned over the man's lip, draped loose and tuberous and wet.

Manny's hands shook, He took the pistol and he shot the blind man in the foot and the man fell to the floor, screaming.

"¿Por qué hiciste eso?" the girl said. Why did you do that?

"¿Qué es?" What is it?

"No es nada. Algún tipo de tumor." It's nothing. Some type of tumor.

"We're going back down the mountain. Wasn't running away." She was unconvincing. "Was going to see about maybe a doctor that might come up here to help him."

"A doctor, up here?"

"Yes, sir. Wasn't running away. We'll have paste for you to pick up next week. I'll radio you myself."

He looked at the rucksack on the ground, stuffed full, and a canteen, and a picnic cooler.

"If you weren't running away, you'd better not run away a lot faster, because we're about to light up another field, scorch it until it's no good for growing nothing at all."

She said, "Why are you telling me? You mean to kill me. I know you do! So just do it. Please, do it now."

He lowered the weapon. "What's in the cooler?"

"Just a few kilos. We can scrape more tomorrow. The seed pods are not all ready to cut. We'll go back on up there, get back to work."

"But you're not running away with it."

"No, senor."

He didn't have the heart to tell her that there was no pod left to scrape, nothing left to make this living of hers, and he felt a look a pity befall his face for these *rayadores,* scratchers, peasant farmers who cut the milky paste from the poppy plants, who spread out the product, the *Papaverum somniferum,* compressed it into plastic-wrapped bricks to be manufactured into heroin.

Gusto had intercepted a radio signal about a pick-up last week while they were playing cards at a high-end brothel, and Gusto had all but thrown the naked woman dancing and grinding on his lap off of him at that time when he'd heard the call about the Jalisco pickup of two thousand hooded sweatshirts, and they'd closed in aerially on the location of the 200-acre field with the help of their pilot runners.

He opened the cooler. It was packed full of opium paste, pressed into patties the size of hamburgers, wrapped tightly in clear plastic.

"You're running."

"We're not."

"Who owns this field?" He grabbed the canteen and he drank from it, drank all the water.

"That's him right there, the one you shot. He owns it."

The old man had not stopped groaning on the ground, holding the foot with firm pressure. The excrescence lay on the dust where the man lay on his side, on the floor, holding the foot with both hands, squeezing, pleading for mercy, and the tumor seemed to throb, pulsing with vessels prominent through the mucosa.

"I mean, who do you report to?" He asked them who forced them to grow poppies on their land, who oversaw their production and who came to pick up the opium paste.

"I don't know their names," said the man.

"I need a name, *senor*. You can give me a name and we can find you a doctor in Puerto Vallarta, or I can make this a lot harder for you right here." He clicked the hammer of the pistol and he aimed it and a lump rose in his throat and could see one rising in the man's throat, too.

The man said, "There's one they call Changa."

The girl said that there was no way that the man would be able to get down the mountain, blind, with his foot shattered. She said that even if he led the man, surely they would fall into one of the valleys or rock pits or plunge off the side of the mountain, and she said that the roads were narrow and sparse.

"What makes you think that I couldn't get him out of here?"

"What makes you think you can?"

"Do you know a way down the other side of the mountain? The road I came from is blocked, lit up with explosive charges that burned out the fields."

"Suppose I might." She was curt, frowned her big lower lip in a pout that, for an instant, was reminiscent of Alena.

"Suppose you tell me."

"I might. You wouldn't be able to find your way down the other side safely without me."

"With all respect, you both look like you wouldn't be able to find your way out of a paper bag. We're going to find Changa."

"You want me to take you down the other side. You want to find Changa."

"Yes."

She said the paths were labyrinthine and infested with snakes and jaguars, ocelot and other cats with gnashing teeth that could, in an instant, grind a man into a paste just like the brown opium that was spread into the bags in the cooler, and that the animals would leave their remnants for scavengers, predatory birds that called like Indians and whose speed rivaled that of trucks.

He said that she was lucky he hadn't killed her.

"You are lost. You will not find your way down safely."

"I'm not arguing that, Miss."

He looked over his back, out of the shanty, and then back at the girl and at the man who was fading on the ground. The only unburned truck in the convoy had left, driving further up the mountain in hopes of getting down the other side. He'd have to catch it to get down. Gusto would be looking for him.

He drew the machete from the old man's belt, put it in his own.

"Do it," said the old man.

"He wants you to shoot him."

He looked at the girl; she did not protest, and although her eyes were dampening, she said nothing.

He shot the man in the chest; he felt a disdain for the man, for the excrescence. He looked at him a while, lying there; then he stepped over him and he stood and looked out at the back of the hut, where the smell of wood smoke was fading. He waited. He did not think that the first man he killed would be so weak, so vulnerable, but it did not shock him, and he felt no remorse.

A short time later, he sat among poppies outside the shanty and he looked at them and he took out a cigarette and lit it from the dying fire and he smoked and he recalled learning something about Mr. Charles Darwin and natural selection from *secondaria*. He sat and he looked at the flowers bloomed red, high and stiff, and the seed pods, and the ones scratched with razors by the peasants, their brown paste seeping out, dripping down the stems, and he thought that if he could look at that little red flower and think somehow it had something in its grand design that, over millions of years, had evolved to let mankind destroy itself, then that flower was genius. And the coca plant was genius, too. The marijuana leaf, almost as smart.

He looked at the girl, who was watching him, said, "Human beings think we have everything figured out, where mankind came from, how to make it better, if there is such a thing. We've got artificial intelligence. What we don't have is real intelligence. I think we don't know anything more than when we crawled out of the sea. If we did, we'd crawl right away from all of this and right back in it."

With narrowed eyes, she said, "I smell smoke. We need to move."

He pulled a stray poppy from the earth, crushed the creped petals, the olive interior, between his thumb and fingers. "Somewhere, some night, some guys, some guys are going to have a great night. They're going to think they're having maybe the best night of their lives, like they're racing cars, or they just met some great girls that are really into them and they're on top of the world, and they're going think, let's get some heroin, and then they go and get it. Maybe one of them's never done it, or maybe one of them does it all the time and is going to do too much, or maybe he just does the usual hit, but maybe it's laced with fentanyl. There'll be an overdose and cell phone calls that can't get through fast enough to 911 and to friends who've overdosed before, asking, *What the fuck do we do? What the fuck do we do?* And there might even be an ambulance ride and an injection of Narcan or epinephrine, if things get really ugly and then in that someplace, somewhere, that guy is going to die and the whole world surrounding the one he lives in is going to die, too."

"I just grow the poppies," she said. "I'm not the one using the drugs."

"Some people say we should torch these poppy fields all over Mexico, all over Afghanistan, and the marijuana grow ops, too. But I say that shooting the messenger never solved anything. Even if it is Satan's messenger. That little red flower never did nothing to nobody on its own. What's it say about mankind if it takes tearing up a field of God's green earth and red poppy plants to put an end to the way we destroy our own mothers bearing a flower?"

"Don't be an ass. You contradict yourself, your whole kind. Do you want to find the men that run the fields or don't you?"

17

He drew the Colt and pointed it at her head, clicked the hammer. She did not move and her eyes shined mercurial and unwavering, holding her gaze as though she feared nothing. He lowered the gun slowly.

There were parrots quivering above them that whistled premonitory and the sun had fallen beneath the treetop *brise soleil* and many rows of cumulus clouds piled in the sky in the west. There was an eerie quiet where the birds roosted, cooing softly. The days had seemed longer with Alena and they had revolved bluer beneath the sun in cloudless skies.

The girl said again that they needed to get going; she got up, walked over cracking branches and into the open beneath a sky that cracked thunder intermittent and loud. The rain began to fall, musical, on the tin roof and on the ground where the old man's blood dripped away from the hut and where it mixed with the droplets and the dust and the smell of the slaughtered goat. She brushed back hanging palm fronds in the thicket as she left, walked on without him.

He got up and followed, said nothing.

They left the hut under a leaden sky that rolled suddenly, bringing a coldness to his skin that he could not shake, and he was covered in the man's blood and confused about the girl, whose dispassion seemed to him a privileged curse. There was a weakness in him for purity, and he was not sure if she was innocent, but he allowed himself to be led by her an hour away from the hut where thunder shuddered the forest and the rain began to soak the jungle, dripped down upon him in continuous rivulets.

Her name was Pilar. She led two goats and stopped where the path ended in a dust trail and where an area fenced with spirals of barbed wire surrounded a chapel of broken stucco. She wore a scapular laminated in plastic and she said that the man with the tumor had been her father. He asked why she had not been angered to see him shot, and she looked back at him as they walked toward the crumbled foundation and she looked away and then she looked at her abdomen where it was swollen, and she did not say.

He saw a shadow pass among the lattice of the balustrade behind the chapel and he stopped, and he settled a consternation within him and ignored his conscience so that he could exist as a killer of men, allowed his wrath for the wrongs done to him to overtake it. He walked beside the trail and into the thicket. She asked him what he was doing. He said that he needed to urinate, and he walked out further beneath hanging vines where she could not see into the canopy, and he looked back at her through the jungle. She was tying up the brown and white goat. The black and white one was bleating.

He radioed Gusto, who demanded to know where he was. Gusto said that largest acres of fields were ablaze and that they had taken out a good portion of the gang. Mustacio had taken a few hostages he could use. Gusto went on about the condition of the field and began to explain in detail how, with a grapefruit spork, he had enucleated the eyes of the Ardillo leader who reported to the Sinaloas.

At that point, Mustacio grabbed the phone, said, "Dolly," and he heard Mustacio say to Gusto that there was no time for stories, and Mustacio told him now that there would be a helicopter to lift them out and that it would be landing in the clearing and that he needed to get there.

"Get where? Where are you?" He could not hear over the sounds of the rotors, and the rifle fire, Gusto's voice.

"Manny," Mustacio said, breaking up.

He said that he had found a dwelling in the valley that seemed from the outside an incongruous and malefic hideaway where the leaders of the Sinaloas—ones with prices on their heads—were likely to hide. He said that there was a girl leading him who he did not trust entirely and that he wanted them to check out the building, said it looked like a chapel or a prayer grotto, with a crumbled fountain and a statue of Mary outside and a satellite dish on the roof. It was just the sort of place that wanted men would retreat, remain hidden.

He wandered into the jungle, into palm leaves tapered and spidery like fingers and others broad like the fans of pharaohs. Trunks crosshatched like pineapples, wide on some trees, thin and colored white and tan up along their length on others. Ropy trunks intertwined fat and narrow and intermediate in girth, all intermingled, tangling with moss hanging like the hair of witches.

He was urinating as he spoke. He heard a cacophony of low-pitched frogs croaking and looked over his shoulder but did not see the girl. He put the phone in his jeans and shook himself off and began to zip his pants when from behind, a male's hand covered his mouth, held a knife to his throat. He kicked, and he reached for his neck with clenched teeth.

Another man pushed him forward to the ground and jammed a boot heavy with its sole mapped in rubber cleats, into his back, his ribs. His cheek was wet now where it rubbed the ground where he had urinated, where the rain had pooled. He looked up, staring at another man's bare feet, thick and dirty. This man tore the Uzi and the MP5 from his chest and placed it across his own chest over a white *guayabera* shirt. The other man pulled him up, grabbed his pistol from his back, grabbed the machete.

"I go in peace," he said. "I'm just helping the girl."

The man mocked him, laughed. "He goes in peace. That's cute. I've never made peace with a submachine gun. Have you, Changa?"

"No, no, I have not," said the man in the *guayabera*. The man had a bushy mustache that disappeared into a badly cleft lip. It gave him a lisp when he spoke, but this did not seem to bother him, and he licked his lips often where the lip was split in two. It was something like a nervous tic the way the tongue slid wormlike through the skin, though he looked very comfortable wearing linen pants and a Panama fedora hat, and he smelled of expensive cigars.

The other two were dressed in fatigues and had faces covered in black sackcloth, cartridge belts coursing their abdomens, revolvers hung at their middles. They dragged him into the demolished chapel. The men in fatigues tied him to one of the support beams riddled with crumbling stucco, while the other took the girl, Pilar, who was screaming. *Guayabera* gagged her mouth with cloth, and he pulled and tied the restraint, encircling her reddish hair, which was cut into chunky points and sun-streaked blond where it hung about her neck. They bound her wrists and ankles, threw her onto a soaked mattress in the corner.

There was a corpse there, headless and rotted, with flies buzzing about it, and there were weapons on a wooden table and a box radio and communication equipment that alternated between popcorn static and sour notes in high-pitched, discordant squeals. Wires snaked across the length of the floor in thick bundles. The stain on the wooden table had faded away long ago, and now a Connect Four game was set up on it next to a cup of coffee.

The men took the cooler she'd been pulling along in a cart beside the goats, opened it.

"Stealing?" *Guayaera* slapped her; she held her cheek. "You filthy whore. There's enough opium paste in here for you to live off for a year."

"I wasn't."

"Lying, too. We'll see how you like it when people take what isn't theirs, you worthless gypsy." *Guayabera* knelt on the floor and he pulled up Pilar's dress and, with a thrusting motion, he pulled her hips toward his once. Then he pushed her forward, throwing her against the wall so that her head hit the plaster hard, made a cracking sound.

She screamed, "Please, not again."

"She brought you to us, handsome."

"He said he wanted to find Changa."

"You found me—or I found you. Though it's unwise for a rabbit to hunt a tiger."

"I see two useful goats, two donkeys, and a black bean monkey. What tiger?" Manny moaned as this man, called Changa, kneed his scrotum and unbuttoned the top buttons of the *guayabera* shirt and loosened the collar. Then he stepped back and kneed him again, harder.

Now he remembered Juan's words most where his balls ached: *Labios sueltos hunden barcos.*

Loose lips sink ships.

He repeated it to himself, told himself to shut up. He'd grown more than a foot since he'd first met Luis, Gusto, and Mustacio, and his confidence had grown at least three feet, made him his own Goliath, this insurrectionary establisher of his foulest adversary, himself, Emmanuel Ayala.

He told himself not to say another word and he did not just then.

The black goat bleated, louder. A layer of smoke was wafting into the clearing outside the crumbled structure, like the horn of an anvil, rolling in like the flanking line of some great storm; the fields were still burning. Changa stood before him, looking half African, black, and part Mexican. The fedora hat fell away from Changa's eyes at a curious angle as he smiled, and he drew his fingernails jagged and long across Manny's cheek and yelped with pleasant exasperation, danced about the room. Manny suspected he was the leader who ran the paste out of the hills to the Sinaloas, but he was not certain that Changa was one of the Ardillos until Changa took off his shirt and screamed, bestial and loud and raw, pounded his chest. Smiling, he revealed the tattoo of a Narco squirrel across his bicep.

Changa handed Manny the phone. His two men were obedient, standing planks of strident posture, poised, giving the impression that they'd been trained in special ops.

"You call your compadres. We wait, ready for them."

"Fuck off." He spat at Changa's feet and then he wished he hadn't. With his right hand covered in brass knuckles, Changa punched him square in the nose. His blood splayed against the white stucco where it crumbled at his neck, his feet.

"Changa, the fields," shouted one of the men in fatigues. His face was still covered with a black balaclava.

The fire was spreading quickly in the direction of the wind. The rain had stopped, but parts of the remaining poppy fields still smoldered, and patches of the blaze had not been extinguished. Those patches now licked the waxy leaves of the avocado trees and the White Sapote and the thin trunks of high-reaching Canistel trees. The men began to scramble, reaching for the irrigation tubing, began making a fruitless effort to put out the approaching forest fire with garden hoses.

From the floor where he lay bound, he saw the Unimog tear up the path through an untouched area just clear of the flames, huge tires barreling through the mud, leaving prints that he thought might one day look like trace fossils of some antediluvian beast, when those perilous mountains of the *Sierra Madre del Sur* became once again deserted. But all he saw now, through the semicircular, barred window of the chapel, was the approaching Mercedes symbol. The engine roared something terrible and the shocks creaked fearlessly as it emerged through the jungle, raced toward the crumbled foundation. The men inside held the bars above them as they were tossed about the interior. The truck climbed over the pits of mud, navigating the rocks, and the uneven terrain.

Changa said, "*Vamanos, Gutillo.*"

Gutillo, one of Changa's men, pulled the sackcloth up over his face, where it had slid down, covering a fish hook scar up the side of the cheek. Gutillo took the Uzi, checked the long magazine, and pulled back the slide. It slid forward, and Gutillo pointed the barrel out the metal barred window of the chapel and aimed it against his cheek and pressed the safety and shot at the Unimog. The driver slumped forward, causing the truck to veer off into the trees, tilting sideward so that it looked as though it would tumble off the side of the mountain but it did not. Six men jumped out and charged the entrance. Their bullets whizzed through the metal bars. The man who had dragged him in was taken out, fell to the ground. They missed Gutillo, who emptied out the magazine of his Uzi but hit no more of the men in the Juarez convoy.

The girl, Pilar, still lay on the ground. She snaked toward him in a commando crawl, arms and ankles bound. She wriggled them free, and she loosened the tape from behind the wall and she freed his fingers. Then she sat up and she grabbed the machete from the table, and she sawed through the rope that tied him to the beam, and he stood. Changa aimed, fired a shot out the window, killing one of the army men. He emptied the magazine, killing another, and he dropped the magazine and he clipped in another.

Manny grabbed the pistol from the table, and he tackled Changa, placed the gun to Changa's temple. Before he could pull back the hammer, Changa rolled on top of him and pinned him, slapped the gun from his hands. It slid across the dusty floor where a cat cachectic and white tread across the floor to the corner of the room and it hit the cat and the animal howled and its fur bristled.

Mustacio entered the chapel and he shot the masked Ardillo with an AR15 and the Ardillo fell to the floor and Mustacio placed the bolt and fired again at the other masked Ardillo, but the round failed. Mustacio tried to adjust the bolt and shook the magazine and jammed it up hard, but it did not clear the round. He took cover, ducked beneath the window outside the chapel where the foundation fell away in large pieces of debris, and he pulled out the magazine and jammed it in and the double-fed rounds fell out.

It was him and the girl and Changa and Gutillo in the chapel now. He dove for the pistol and he rolled over the skeletal cat and it hissed and when he was on his feet again, squatting, he aimed at Gutillo and he shot the gun, but he missed. Pilar grabbed the knife. Changa,was out of ammo for the Uzi, ran out the back, leaving him with the girl and Gutillo. She came at Gutillo with the knife but Gutillo caught her wrist, twisted it, and brought her to the floor. Manny kicked Gutillo in the chest, just beneath the shoulder; Gutillo released the knife.

From outside, the men called to them, "Get out!"

The air was thickening to a low, carbonaceous cloud. He coughed on the black smoke, he smelled his singed nasal hair, and he held his hand over his mouth and he grabbed Pilar's hand and he ran out the back.

The Unimog was too wide to go any further down the mountain trail. Its breaks squealed. It stopped.

"Don't lose him, he knows the terrain," Mustacio called to the men, pointing at Changa, who ran into the canopy under broad-leafed tress, slipping across mossed rocks and ferns at his feet.

Manny was close behind, holding the girl's hand; he did not stop to look for the men behind him. Ahead, Changa and Gutillo leaped over a short foot bridge. They crossed a crevasse of faulted rock, came to a zip line cable tethered across a 1,200 meter valley green with the foliage of great trees beneath them. It was impossible to say if it was designed as an escape route or was part of a tourist attraction in the town of Nuevo Vallarta, but he suspected the latter.

Mustacio had informed him of an operation bringing drugs to the clubs of Puerto Vallarta, where the tourists went out into the *Bahia de Banderas* on the speed boats in groups of twenty or so. While the group hiked, ate lunch on the beach, and enjoyed the jungle scenery, the Ardillos organizing the tour made a pickup, loaded the boats with the heroin paste from the mountain, and brought the cellophane-wrapped bricks back across the bay, where the same buses that took the tourists back to their hotels were ready to pick them up, delivering the bricks to the cooks with a generous tip in hand.

Gutillo tore away the bridge now, breaking the suspension planks behind him after he crossed. He ripped the planks and their supporting structure away so that Manny would have to jump at least five feet above a great depth beneath to reach the other side, where there was nothing to grab, nothing to secure his arms so he could pull up his body.

He was suddenly conscious of his fear of heights. His heart thumped; it muscled the breath out of him within his chest, against his ribs, pulsing adrenaline, drying his mouth, tightening his lungs. He looked down and then he wished that he had not, and he looked up again, across the ravine. He looked over his shoulder, where Mustacio's long limbs were moving closer to the men, carrying the RPG launcher on his shoulder, the AR15 across his chest.

The galvanized steel cable was looped double over an eye clamp and attached to a saddle clamp, and a steel pulley wobbled from it. The cable connected to a chain link wrapping the tree with an easy link clamp, and the galvanized line was pulled taut. There were harnesses at the base of the line, on a wooden platform, and Changa began to pull it over his hips, his shoulders. He tightened the harness and he pulled down the pulley, where the steel slide attached to the steel cable, and he fastened a latch onto the cable and he double-fastened the safety clip. Then he sat back, dropped down, and coursed across the line without breaking. The pulley made a grating sound on the metal cable and it looked like it would snap as it dipped down parabolic and low above the canopy, but it did not break. Changa reached the other side, laughing, yelping, as the fedora flew from his head and his salt and pepper hair blew back wild, taunting. Looking back, Changa landed on the platform on the other side of the cable and waited for Gutillo, who was dressing in the harness.

"No brakes, no brakes," shouted Changa from the other side.

There were no gloves to brake with. Gutillo began to reel back the pulley.

"What?" Gutillo repeated, over the rifle fire echoing through the valley, the sounds of the gendarmerie that had reached the cliff side. Gutillo clipped in double to the pulley and to the line and seated backward in the five-point rope harness and took off down the line as Manny leaped across the cliff onto the platform, toward the top of the zip line.

"Shit," Manny said, losing his footing. Loose rock slid down the ravine. He pulled himself up by his fingernails, examined the valley.

18

He reached out for the girl and extended his hand and she jumped the ravine, fluid and cat-like, and he looked down over the jungle lush and green, clutched his chest where a series of palpitations fluttered in him. His fear of heights gripped him. His fingers were trembling. His knees, too, and he had to settle them before he pulled the pistol and he shot it from the hip, missing the line and missing Gutillo. But the shot caused Gutillo to brake with his hand naked and raw and ungloved, against the front of the line. The pulley tore over Gutillo's fingers, and he pulled them back. Then Gutillo lifted the hand and tried to brake by holding the line behind the pulley as it careened over the valley. At the low point of the arc, Gutillo slowed to a stop, spun 360 degrees, and hung in a perpetual dangling motion over the acres of jungle 200 feet below the line.

Mustacio was just behind him.

From the opposite platform, Changa was shouting, "*Vamanos*," but Gutillo torqued his body in an awkward set of maneuvers that did not propel him forward on the line. Gutillo jerked forward and backward but did not slide much on the line.

Changa immediately clipped his safety onto the line and threw his legs over it with crossed ankles. Changa leaned back supine, hanging beneath the line, and then, simian and agile, went hand over hand, climbing out to the point where Gutillo hung, started to pull him back.

"It was him, he made me like this," Pilar said, pointed to her abdomen, swollen with child. "Changa, the one with the broken lip."

He took the RPG-7 from Mustacio, set it on the hollow inside his shoulder and felt its weight settle upon his balance, wrestling with fear at the edge of the cliff where his nerves twitched and pebbles and plates of igneous tumbled. The propelling charge was screwed into the warhead, a stabilizing pipe of nitroglycerin and primer, and now he lined up the trigger mechanism with the tree platform on the other side, propelled the charge along its trajectory terrible and predetermined and violent, and he blew the supporting tree apart into splintered and charred wood.

He saw Changa's eyes widen before the line. The two men plummeted beneath the trees to their deaths.

To his left, at least 100 feet below the platform where they stood, there was another zip line over the valley, but the fire was spreading, encroaching on the area near the cable. Above them, he could see the rescue helicopter, as Gusto had promised, looking for a flat place to land. Its rotors chopped at the wind, gusting down near the approaching smoke. Gusto was in the cockpit, pointing, screaming something that he could not hear. Below the chopper, peasants with rifles stormed the area, but the fire engulfed them from three sides.

One of the Mexican army men, Tomas, removed a pair of binoculars from his canvas vest, glassed the area, said, "*Vamanos*"

Mustacio jumped back over the ravine where the footbridge had stood and Pilar followed, grabbing her abdomen as she jumped, with the gusts from the helicopter whipping her fiery hair into angry strings that obstructed her vision.

Manny swallowed, jumped with his eyes half-closed. He planted the boot of his bent left knee on the rock on the other side of the ravine, kneeling forward, touching his right hand to the ground as a knight would, head bowed. When he had his foot firmly rooted on the ground, he straightened at once, kept running.

They followed a trail down, away from the smoke, where ten saddled mules were tethered, and where a crumbled stone foundation of an old grocery store stood with an aged woman cooking tamales and quesadillas over a metal grill. Beside this was a Pepsi machine and a group of tourists rigged on a clear platform rectangular and plastic. Over the counter of the store were drink boxes of coconut water and real coconuts for sale, cut open with straws, and some cigarettes, but he could not see beyond that.

The tourists were clipping together harnesses with the tour guide, getting ready to rappel a waterfall, a 100-foot bridal veil of white spray slicking polygonal rock, and with large droplets splaying outward and seeming to free fall from its mass entire below them into the green-blue pool of water mossy and cool.

When the men charged toward the group, some of the tourists began to scream, panicking chaotic expostulations like the speech of starved parrots. Manny ordered them to remove the harnesses. He held his pistol to the temple of the guide, a young man, freshly shaved and clean-cut, dressed in a blue Lycra top and khakis and a white helmet.

"*Yo no quiero problemas, Yo no quiero problemas*," said the guide, throwing up both arms where he stood on the platform. I don't want problems.

He handed the RPG to Tomas. Mustacio was behind him. The other men in their convoy ordered the tourists to remove their harnesses, told them to sit on the ground. Luis was going to be *pissed*, he knew, because messing with tourists, was *fuera de sus limites*.

Off-limits.

Tourists bought their product, marijuana and meth and heroin, while enjoying a weekend bender, a honeymoon or spring break vacation. Some of them found that first taste of their inner wild child in Mexico, land of *no ver ningún mal no oír ningún mal,* see no evil and hear no evil. Some found that first hit that might or might not suck them into a chemical void of dependency, a grace-fallen and abusive reliance culminating in innumerable dollars funneling through Luis' pockets.

Tourists were off-limits because messing with tourists was bad for business, and Luis was a businessman.

Now the women in the group—American women wearing shorts cut short and water shoes and sun-bleached hair—were screaming louder. The old woman with her gray wires of hair pulled into a bun, who was cooking the quesadillas, ushered the tourists behind the crumbled concrete near the grill where steam rose, behind the Pepsi machine. Manny stood there on the translucent platform of scratched Plexiglass as Mustacio rushed to clip his harness to the rappel line, exposed on three sides and looking back over his shoulder below at the fall.

Below them, another tour guide. Though he trusted no one, least of all himself at times, he had to then, and this came with difficulty, summoned in him a disparate hesitation that Mustacio did not allow, not even for a moment.

"Am I clipped into this right? How do I—?"

Mustacio's shouted, "Go," and shoved him off the platform where he was seated in the harness. He was rappelling the waterfall using the belay device, bouncing his feet off the rock where it faulted out in crusts slippery and jagged, abseiling vertically downward. The bight of rope passed through the metal sticht plate and back out to the locking carabiner that was clipped to him and as he moved down, down toward the plunge pool below, it was not the frightening experience that he had expected.

He felt his gap-toothed smile widening and he looked up at Mustacio, laughing at his fear.

Then as his body cut the surface of the cool water, his skin rose with gooseflesh and he heard Mustacio from above ordering the guide beside him to unharness him, and as the rope was pulleyed up again quickly, Mustacio clipped in the first army guard. The tourists were still shouting. Mustacio fired off a round with a Colt, and that pretty much ended the commotion from the tourists.

The girl, Pilar, was the last to rappel, her dress billowing in cotton clouds at her sides like a parachute until she plunged into the pool, soaked. She did not know how to swim, and she thrashed about in the deepest area directly beneath the falls until Manny dove in where she struggled, spitting and coughing water. He slung her arms around his neck and kicked hard, frog-leg style, until they were safely at the edge of the blackish water. Then he climbed out of the water, set her down, and ran on toward the other men.

They descended the other side of the mountain, running down a hill parched with grass dried white where it looked like it had not rained in weeks there. He found his cell phone had remained in his pocket and as they ran, he was phoning Gusto, yelling, "*Donde estas? Donde estas?*" Where are you?

He did not see the helicopter overhead. The guns and all the equipment the men carried had been soaked and the radio did not work and soon the phone shorted out from the water damage.

Where the side of the mountain grew steep again was a water slide at least 150 feet that must have been part of the tourist attractions. It seemed the fastest way to get down to the bottom. He saw helicopters circling, but they were not theirs, said *Policia* on the sides of their cabins were circling now, too.

He called to the others, seven of them now, "*Vamanos,*" Let's go.

One by one, the men threw their legs over the top of the slide, not waiting more than a few seconds between each of them before launching into the half pipe streaming cold water, whizzing past branches of almond trees and tamarinds and orchids that hung low into the concavity of the slide. They rode slick and fast, and the foliage battered their faces where it dangled from the obstructing umbrellas of green.

They had ignored the helmets that sat at the wooden deck at the top of the waterslide entirely, riding bareback toward the bottom. Tomas, who had been holding an AR15, had the gun thrown from his arms as it hit the branch of an orchid tree, and the AR15 flew backwards and hit the last man to get on the slide, DiSalvo, one of the army men with a bushy mustache and a proud smile who was donned in an army green cap and combat boots that like the others', were soaked. The magazine of the AR bludgeoned DiSalvo's face first, and the barrel of the rifle that impacted horizontal at his neck decapitated DiSalvo's head from his spine, sending the head barreling parabolic off the edge of the pipe. The crystal water rushing down the slide at once became thick and red and warm as his body slumped forward, continued to fall toward the end of the slide. It smelled heavily of orchids there where the body lay severed from its head, and above them a howler monkey was running across Parota tree branches, screeching loud and intermittent in the trees.

At the bottom of the slide, Manny pushed DiSalvo's body onto its back, swallowed.

Mustacio grabbed his arm, pulled him from the body, said, "*Por ahi! Es Gusto!*" Over there, it's Gusto!

The other men were running toward a black Ford Expedition labeled *Policia Federales* in white on its side, with its blue and red and white lights flashing and its siren blaring. The Ford pulled up closer toward the base of the slide, where the mountain flattened to a shallow plain, past a wooden building with a huge sign on the roof that read *Vallarta Tours*, where tourists had gathered, screaming, some sheltering in place with their heads in their hands and some crawling on the ground for cover.

The body of a tour guide lay on the ground near the slide and Manny did not stop to look at it; he ran over it, followed Mustacio, and climbed into the truck, crammed in the back with the other six men. A man lay on the seat, his mouth duct taped, and his arms and legs tied. The Gypsy Kings were playing on the radio and it was a song his mother liked to sing to Elvie, *Volare*, and Gusto was singing to the music. Gusto pulled a sharp right and Mustacio held the grab bars on the interior of the roof as the Ford sped off down the dirt trail and onto the closest highway, passing cars at top speed. When Gusto was certain that they were no longer being followed, he turned off the siren and moved into the right lane and lit a cigar.

"What do you plan to do with the Ardillo?" he asked, looked at the bound man.

"What do you plan to do with the girl?"

"I don't know," Manny said, and he looked back at the pregnant peasant, Pilar, who was sitting with her head to her knees, soaking wet, in the back of the Expedition. "Pull over, let her out."

"She might be useful," said Mustacio.

"She looks useful—like tits on a nun," said Tomas, who was sitting next to Pilar. Tomas was the youngest there, looked barely fifteen. "Pull over. I'll shoot her and dump her."

"No," Pilar screamed from the back. She began to cry and to rock in place with her head to her knees.

Gusto ashed out the window, checked the rearview. "Dolly could use a woman, even if she's a nun. All he does is sulk over Alena."

"Watch it," he said.

"Dolly, why don't we go to the club when we get back to Juarez? Luis will get you some young women to take your mind off Alena, only for the night."

"I said, watch it." He pulled the Colt and he clicked the hammer, and Gusto backed down immediately and laughed, exhaled cigar smoke.

"Easy, easy, Dolly," said Gusto. "No disrespect."

"Gusto should not have said that." Mustacio backhanded his arm and there was a quick snap on Gusto's flesh where it rested on the gear shift.

"Of course not, I wasn't thinking, Dolly." Gusto turned up the music.

The rumba *Gitano* was now strumming flamenco guitars and playing the blare of trumpets, but in his mind, he did not hear this; in his mind he was playing out something of a plan for the rest of his life, how it would go. Expiring a stagnant, brutal end. Or rising, fleeing a hopeless raw demise. That bane of hellish lure. The architect of his profligate divination was not revealed and this burden devoid of proof and this doubting still vexed him and made guilty his numbered days.

"Turn it down. Call Luis, Dolly," said Mustacio, handing him a cell phone. "We need a flight out of here, fast."

Mustacio argued back and forth with Gusto. The discussion grew heated when Mustacio hung up with Luis and said, *"No le gusto el resultado. Esta hecho un aji."* You won't like the results. This was a mistake.

"You didn't tell him about the tourists, did you? How was I supposed to know this poppy field was on the other side of a resort excursion? The whole mountain was on fire. It was the only way out," Gusto said.

"Are we getting out of here or what?" Manny asked.

Mustacio said, "Yeah, he said he's sending a plane."

"Good. The peasants shot at the helicopter. It didn't go down, but it's in no shape to fly. Then I had to take this truck from the *Policia*." Gusto looked in the rearview, his glaucous eyes flashing with sudden pity and something close to warmth. "Dolly, you look so down. I simply want to see the fire in your eyes like when we met. Do you remember? I told you that I had no son, but that I would like to love you like my own son."

Gusto pulled two marble-sized masses from his pocket.

"I remember." He bit his fingernail, spat it out the window of the back seat.

"For you, Dolly." Gusto passed the two masses back to him, the eyeballs of the Ardillo he'd killed in the field, the brown corneas, and black pupils, wet and empty and cold.

"I love you, too, man, but you have to stop giving me body parts."

"I'll put them on a necklace for you. Here, in my pocket, there's a sewing kit, the little kind from hotels, you know."

"*No es el tipo de hotels en los que te alojas,*" said Mustacio. Not the kind of hotels you stay in.

Gusto reached in his pocket and pulled the thick needle from the rectangular cardboard and put the needle between his teeth and the car swerved off onto the shoulder, kicking up a dust cloud. "Yes, Mustacio—those fancy hotel rooms! You know, where they have little bottles of mouth wash and cans of shoe shiner and tubes of mint toothpaste in the bathroom."

"I've never seen him stay in any kind of hotel like that. He goes to the ones you rent by the hour," Mustacio said, grabbing the wheel to straighten the path of the truck. "Watch what you're doing."

Gusto took back the wheel, and Mustacio took the needle, doubled the black thread and passed it through the eye of the needle. Then Mustacio took the eyeballs of the Ardillo, and passed the needle through them, too, tying the string in a long loop.

Mustacio put the necklace on over his black shirt where silver dog tags hung beside suspenders that attached to his beige tactical pants and he looked in the mirror and he nodded.

The red, white, and blue Beechcraft King Air 200 prop plane landed thirty miles away on a short strip between the mountains, only about a mile from the poppy field. Smoke from the blaze made the air particulate, and dense, almost too thick to fly. The dust made it difficult for the pilot to navigate the skies out of the region at dusk and the flight was turbulent at the low altitude and twice Pilar hit her head on the roof of the cabin, but after another hour, they were headed back to Juarez, landing just after nightfall on an airstrip in the desert.

19

Luis called a meeting two nights later.

Manny sat at the table in the back of Luis' restaurant next to Luis, and there was boiled lobster with butter and sea bass served with a relish of finely chopped tomatoes and mango and cilantro with lemon, but he was not hungry; he ate very little.

Gonzalez offered him a cigarette.

"I don't smoke," he said, although at rare times he had taken to lighting up, when his nerves got the better of him, like Tuesday, hearing the creaking shocks and the squeal of the brakes of the Unimog riding the hairpin turns up the Jalisco mountain, or after rappelling cliffs to escape vigilante heroin guerillas. It had been a long week. "On second thought," he said. Then he took the cigarette and he lit it from Gusto's, and he inhaled.

Mustacio poured tequila and cut up a lime and there was a white wine opened that he tasted. It was cold and made his glass sweat and he enjoyed several glasses, but still he did not eat much.

Luis began by saying that he was pleased at the demolition of the poppy field, hundreds of acres, millions in Sinaloa revenue. Then, with a sharp thump of his hand on the table that bounced the dishes in an unmelodious crash of porcelain and stainless-steel angst, he made clear that involving tourists was "*desaconsejable*." Inadvisable. His voice rose as he paced the room and he hurled a water decanter at the wall that shattered into a crystal explosion of sharp fragments. After some time screaming and pacing, Luis regained his composure. He sat down and he regarded each of the men with those obsidian, probing eyes that threatened men without speaking.

"There is a *soplon* among us," Luis said. "I've always preached, above all else, loyalty. Yet someone here denies me—despite my pledge of friendship and love to the families of each of the men who work for me, for the patron. This cannot be."

Gusto said, "How do you know this?"

"Cordoba, Gutierrez and the whole lazy bunch of incompetent *Federales* have information they cannot possibly come to know, doing the half-assed job they do. Flies do not enter a closed mouth."

Gusto was the first to protest. Though it could not be Gusto who would betray Luis, his words sounded defensive. They reeked of the tiniest guilt, but Gusto's words always sounded a little corny, a little fishy, like the spiced and cured miniature smelt in the salad dressing before him, so Luis did not seem suspicious of Gusto.

"Luis, you worry too much. We've lost some ground with the police, La Linea, but we've sent a powerful message. Now they know we have the manpower to fight, to maintain our territory." Gusto crunched the salad and he sipped his tequila and he wiped his lip with the stump of his severed finger.

Luis' eyes narrowed; he said, "My deliveries once went smoothly, without hesitation, without having to check that they were, in fact, delivered to their destination. I've lost shipment after shipment—five this week alone, to be exact. That's millions in cocaine and meth. I've lost track of the weed, it's gotten so sloppy."

Around the table, the men's eyes fell away from the feast, and all forks were set down, and some heads were bowed.

Luis continued. "Someone is informing police, Gutierrez, the Chief of the *Antidroga* Division, of my shipments, the date, time, product, route of delivery, even the street value of the deliveries. There is no other explanation. I wish this wasn't so, but it is."

Mustacio rose and he knelt before Luis. "My honor is to you—and to the *patron*, though *El Gato* is away—and to the Juarez Cartel, Luis. I assure you, it is not me."

Gusto did the same, knelt and swore his allegiance.

"Enough," said Luis. He got up and washed his hands and dried them, and then he began to pick at the skin of the palms where the dried white and pink dried patches bubbled eczematous and raw. "My trust is shaken, and so I've made a choice. While I'm in charge, in the absence of *El Gato*, I must consider what would happen if I should fall from this tenuous position of power I'm in, if something were to happen to me."

Gusto looked attentive, returned to the wooden chair, and when seated, took a sip of tequila, began a toast. "To Luis—"

"Stop," Luis said, staring, harsh and cold. "Because I cannot be sure who is my friend and who is my enemy, or the friend of my enemy, I've decided that should something happen to me, I must trust in blood."

"God is great," said Gusto, raising his glass of red wine.

Luis' said, "I am not talking about the blood of Jesus Christ, Gusto, my friend, although God is great and his blood flows through all of our veins. My blood sits beside me, Emmanuel. Manny, Dolly, shall preside as lieutenant of this territory, my plaza, if I should die in this line of work."

"But, I'm—" Manny started to say.

"Dolly?" Mustacio protested, while the others spoke in hushed tones. "He's so young. He's not ready."

"Dolly has come of age. He's been tried, and despite losing his love, he remains loyal. He requires no further initiation."

Luis placed a hand on Manny's shoulder, and he felt this weight as though it were the world and he were tasked with holding it up. He remembered the bones of Alena that Gusto had scooped from her severed skull, fragments that still hung around his neck on a linked chain, and he pulled at them. "I had hoped that Juan would be my first consideration as my successor, but though Juan is steady like the tide, like his fishing boats that come in and out, Juan chooses to come and go. He pays his fair *piso* to carry on his business, for my respected protection. I had hoped that Juan would learn the ways of this business, one that affords him less labor, with greater reward, without tax. It would have been smart of him to do so. But Juan does not anchor here as Dolly does. I don't see his face out in the *zocalo*, reporting the comings and goings as Dolly does, nor at the hacienda, nor at our meetings, though he is welcome. I don't see the same in my oldest brother as I do in Dolly. I see hesitation. While I respect Juan, and will allow him to continue his operation, I've chosen Dolly."

He felt he should smile, but he did not. He felt the truculence upon him in the room, the skepticism of an ambitious goal unrealized by Gusto, and he felt some vague severance, though none was explicit. In that glimpse of his life, from where he stood, he was looking in at some boy he did not know. When he examined this thing he was becoming then, he would've liked to have said that he felt like he was lost on one of the casual fishing expeditions that he'd taken with Juan and his father, one that ended fruitless after magnificent anticipation, with its lines cast in expectations enthusiastic and far-reaching, expectations of reeling in a massive marlin after an indelible struggle. *Nada ganado, nada perdido.* Nothing gained, nothing lost. But that moment predetermined and vile was worse than losing a prized catch. It was as though his ship was not returning in vain, but rather, set loose in a sea of unyielding momentum, among the unmerciful beasts of the ocean and waves of concussive force; it was not returning at all.

"But the *patron*, he is—"

"The *patron* is aware," said Luis. "Any questions?"

"With all due respect, just because Juan is not interested, that does not mean Dolly is ready for such an undertaking, should it come to that," Gonzalez said.

"He'll need to be, and I'll be sure he is, when the time comes. And though I'll expect much more from Dolly in the days to come, God willing, I pray I won't be going anywhere soon," said Luis. Turning to Manny now, he said, "*Mi hermano*, do you accept me as your brother?"

"*Si.*"

"Do you trust me?"

"*Si.*"

"Do you accept this responsibility?"

"I do," he said.

"Then this meeting is done."

Lights dimmed to candlelit calm. Vaporous air. Smoke and melancholy thoughts. Did devils conspire to drive his fate? He finished his wine, the last to leave the table. The remaining guests lingered in the restaurant. It was late and balmy and humid that night when he walked out into the *zocalo*, alone, adrift. Thick heat weighed on his chest, made it hard to breathe.

He had not been home in five nights and he had not spoken to his mother in two. There were two shipments to deliver tomorrow, one through El Porvenir and another across the bridge to El Paso—a truckload of cocaine outfitted beneath the hull of an eighteen-wheeler and a shipment of automatic rifles and submachine guns to pick up on the way back from the States.

Gonzalez was waiting in the truck with the doctor. There was unfinished business to take care of with the girl, Pilar, and the Ardillo they had brought back with them from Jalisco. The interrogation was incomplete, but the two of them remained in a warehouse in *Valle de Juarez*, chained to a boat trailer.

On Thursday, he was sitting beside the pool looking over the cliff at the caramel mountains of Juarez and the saguaro cacti where clouds rolled slowly in the afternoon. The storminess of last week had passed, and Sylvia and Luis and Gusto and Mustacio were beside him, drinking *cervezas*. He wore the gold cross around his neck that his much huskier father had been wearing when he was shot, and his neck was still so thin that the braided chain pooled in a ropey loop about his clavicle. Juan had left the chain on his dresser that morning and left him a note in an envelope that he had not read yet but placed in his pocket. Luis' parrot was on a perch of driftwood and Manny was feeding it peanuts. He had started to feel the *cervezas* that he was drinking when they got word that another shipment had been lost.

Luis said that the poppy field wasn't enough.

Gusto was cleaning his revolver, but now he set it down. It had a gun metal barrel, shiny and long, and he reserved its use for times when he did want any shells left behind.

"Blow up another one of their meth labs," Luis' said; his resolve was flat and unquestionable, the light in his eyes lurid, immitigable. "Today."

"You're crazy," Gusto said. "That's what you are. You've gone mad."

Mustacio put his hands to his head, ran his fingers through his slicked hair. Then Mustacio placed his elbows on the table and he twisted his mustache, and he sighed heavily, but nothing else was said.

Sylvia got up from the table and picked up some glasses and a pitcher of cactus juice and she went into the house, closed the glass door.

After some time, Luis repeated himself, said, "That's an order, from the *patron*."

Manny rose, stood beside his brother, and he looked at Mustacio and he looked at Gusto and he swallowed, and he said, "*Vamanos*."

It was an uncertain experiment that made his palms sweat, and it convoluted his guts, and it could've ended in comedy or disrespect or death, but with Luis standing beside him it was none of those things and soon after he claimed this authority, they were on Highway 2, heading east to Juarez Valley.

They had only been on the road a few miles and he was behind the wheel of The Apple when, without warning, Gusto grabbed him by the collar. "Who do you think you are?"

"Your son," he said. "Or was that all just bullshit?"

Manny kept driving.

Mustacio held a Colt pistol to Gusto's temple, said, "*Hermano*."

Gusto loosened his grip, the amputated finger a nascent stub that brushed his wrist and chilled his skin to gooseflesh, its mica-colored scar reflecting sunlight, primitive and Devonian, like a scaled fish. Did the missing digit drape, prized, from the neck of another, or hang victorious from the rear-view mirror of a truck? Manny wondered, swallowed.

Gusto said, "I've worked my good years for Luis. You think this is all yours."

"I didn't ask for any of this," He said; he stopped the truck and got out and said to Mustacio, "Maybe you should drive."

The location of the meth labs in Sinaloa was unclear, but he'd heard on the street about an explosion recently in a gas station bathroom. And nothing screamed 'meth lab' like a random explosion in an Oxxo bathroom, except maybe random acts of cartel violence, but Gusto said he was sure it was a meth lab. Mustacio drove them over and parked in front and Gusto said that the week had been exhausting, and that he wanted to sit outside and smoke, said that it was time for Dolly to step up. That skeptic wounded pride. Gusto faced him cynical and narrowed-eyed and thin-lipped, lit a smoke.

Manny put his Colt down the back of his pants.

He still walked with the confidence of Luis' endorsement when he got out of the car and walked up to the counter and put his pistol up to the cashier's head.

"I want to talk to the pharmacist."

Shaking, the man, said, "This location has no pharmacy, sir."

"The pharmacist who does his business here in the bathroom, sometimes—and not the kind of business everybody else does in the bathroom. His *business*." Click of the hammer.

And just like that, he had the name, and afterwards, Gusto picked up some jalapeno-flavored almonds and a *Diete Coke* at the Oxxo, and Manny paid for them. Gusto got back in the truck and was shaking the almonds in his hand and throwing them back against his palate, washing them down with the *Diete Coke* soon after that, and they were driving along Highway 4, all of them smoking. Mustacio was driving and singing to a Spice Girls song on the radio when they pulled up to the cookhouse in the Valley.

The house was pale pink with two square windows out front and a door barred with iron, and Manny walked through a gnarled garden of weeds around the back where browned cheesecloth and crumpled aluminum foil and two-liter plastic bottles, capped and filled with coffee-ground murk, were discarded about the lawn. He clutched the Colt and he peered in through a window. There were plastic pitchers and measuring cups and wooden spoons and a large-size operation built across tables in the kitchen, where pots vented steam, soured and pungent, that settled an acerbity like ammonia on his tongue and burned his nostrils.

Beyond the kitchen was a purgatory salad of slurred words, coming at him in garbled sound-bytes over the sound of a television, a radio, too. The putrefaction in process seeped its reaction hot in bubbling pitchers and aluminum cans corroded black across their rims, debasing precursors of ephedrine and salts and lye. He covered his mouth and listened, but he could not make out the language of the cooks who awaited the steamed reactants.

He stepped into the kitchen where on the counter there was a stack of bills, which he stuffed into the pocket of his jeans. An aged pit bull rested on an old rug colored and braided; its eye was mangled pink and globular and a patch of its coat was scarred away where the black pigment of its hair had been lost. It rose, and it sniffed the air and it coughed and it limped on past his feet, but it did not bark, and he suspected that the dog could not see him.

He crept forward, standing at the threshold of the living room.

He recognized the sound of the voices, the successive tapping of plastic buttons, the sounds of the video game *Grand Theft Auto*. The man in the game wore black sunglasses and a gray suit, and the town was San Andreas. He'd played that scene before. He clutched the Colt in his hand now.

Three men pockmarked with skin burned away in scarred, leathery patches gathered in the house like modern alchemists. One had a proboscidean nose, and all of them had teeth blackened like anthracite and their clothes were mired in filth. They looked vagabond and indistinguishable, except for the youngest in the center.

Piranha.

20

His heart fell twice, the first time because he'd hoped his once friend was on a better path than he was, and a second time knowing that he was now on a search and destroy mission. Piranha was a target who he could not harm; not ever, and this weakness in him created a surety of stubborn disquiet that brooded, emerging in terrible and subtle grace. It settled an examination of his conscience that felt like redemption was still possible. Gusto was right about him not being ready.

And he knew then, that he would not ever be.

The three men slumped on a ragged couch with their backs turned and spines kyphotic, looking invertebrate, with limbs like jellied tentacles, their faces garish with sunken eyes. Piranha's muscles were atrophied, and he was wearing Kevlar like some armored and bottom-dwelling placoderm, inhabiting this world like a ghost walking, unconscious through time.

It occurred to him that the men were fragmented from reality, stoned figures wandering adrift, ruinous, playing in a fictional underworld of sirens and shootings and criminal consumption. Automatic rifles were piled in the corner of the room—AR's and MP5 and AK47's, along with tackle boxes filled with ammunition and crates of rounds stacked beneath the windows.

Piranha turned from the screen.

Manny put his finger to his lips, backed out of the room.

Piranha turned back to the television and continued the game, soulless, his eyes leaden and misplaced and automatic. The pit bull coughed something hoarse and wet from its throat. In the game, yellow caution signs and red biohazard posters decorated the brick walls of an alley. The meth cooks played on, inexpressive and wasted. The man Piranha played wore a suit and dark sunglasses, and the man got out of his car and went into a warehouse and shot open doors with a sniper rifle and ran back outside into the dust and cars with sirens raced toward the scene and choppers swarmed overhead. It had never been Piranha's game.

Ramiro would've beaten him with his eyes closed.

As Manny left the kitchen, he fired two rounds with his Colt at the larger methamphetamine apparatus that was cooking anhydrous chemicals and steaming foul, bitter reagent from glass beakers with long pipes. It exploded, deafening and sonic, sending fragmented, splintered beams and debris in all directions that kindled a fire. He ran out the back of the knotty yard, away from the clanging of metal pots and the tumult of the disturbance, ducking beneath a prickly pear tree, hopping the dilapidated fence. He got in the car and ordered Mustacio to gas the truck and he said that there was no one in the house, but in the rear view, he could see Piranha's gangly leg, his black boots, crawling from the window.

Before he went home that night, he drove The Apple to the warehouse and he untied the girl, Pilar. He put the Colt to her head and told her she could go with him, and then he tied the rope to her neck and he said that if she tried anything, he would not hesitate to shoot her. Her wrists were chafed and her face bruised across both cheeks. She nodded, looked back at the other prisoner and then at him.

The Ardillo was still there on the floor of the basement, the squirrel tattoo on his upper arm partly skinned off, with a deadened flap of inked skin hanging loose. The man had not been given anything to eat or drink in days. He lay with his skin tenting and his lips pale, parched, and he did not move or struggle much about the floor as he had the previous day. The strung necklace of the Ardillo leader's eyes had been placed by Mustacio around the man's neck and the eyeballs were dehydrated now, too, no longer glassy and wet, but lying shrunken, flat, and puckered on the man's bare chest. The doctor had not obtained any further information during the interrogations. That was ill-fated, but how those things went—misperceptions of truth and lies, expletives, force.

The ending for the Ardillo was close, and when he thought of the ways it would end for him, none was noble. Unfortunate curses profane, in blood and death and prayer, to tarnished gods below.

As he removed the girl from the basement, he saw that she dripped blood. He assumed her body had rid itself of the child, but it had not.

She got in the truck and the lights on the clock were flashing and he thought that the alternator of The Apple was dying. He got out and looked beneath it before he started the engine, but there was nothing there but dust and gravel and a spiders' nest in some tumbleweed of amaranth and dried Russian thistle. There could have been a bomb or a body or a hitman but there were none of those things. The Apple merely seemed a wasted thing now, not the shiny prize Juan had brought home, but it chugged off and he looked in the rearview mirror where The Terminator's crucifix from his first Communion hung, the one Ramiro's mother had insisted he take, and he looked at the dashboard where he had superglued a statue of St. Christopher that Alena had bought at the flea market in El Paso when they had walked across the border to buy American *charro* boots. She'd said that if he was going to drive every vehicle like he'd stolen it, he'd better have the protection of the patron saint of travelers behind him.

The muffler made an awful scraping against the pavement and the temperature gauge was running hot after driving only a few blocks. The truck smelled something like burning oil, but he did not stop to check it; he drove on toward his home.

When he came up the drive past the wooden fence of the ranch, he removed the rope from her neck. She began crying and he told her to stop and she wiped her eyes and asked where they were going. He said it was his home and that he was not going to hurt her if she didn't give him any trouble and she asked if she might have a glass of water. Her lips were peeling in sheets, parched dry, and she was still wearing the scapular around her neck. Her hair had been half shaved off by Dr. Kelley, but her skin, although it was bruised purple over the prominence of her cheekbones, glowed vigorous as though she were seeing something beautiful for the first time.

They walked through the kitchen, where the door had been left wide open and there were beans on the stove. They walked across the terra cotta-colored tile and past hanging pots and a wall where spoons hung, and Talavera pottery of moons colored midnight blue and yellow from the *Mercado de Artesenias* in *San Miguel de Allende*. He ducked beneath hanging chiles, red and dried, and walked past open windows with boxes of flowers with hanging Alyssum and honeysuckle spilling beneath their ledges.

He called for his mother and he called for Elvie, but no one answered. He walked under the arch through the hall, past hanging crosses covered with silver Milagros charms of pigs and bulls and stars and eyes fixed to them with tiny nails, and into the courtyard of the *estancia* where there was a wooden-backed bench of teakwood with a rosemary plant set on it and a round fountain in the center, but the trickle of the water steady in the fountain was all he heard.

In the yard, the sheep was wandering lost, butting its head in the parched grass and chaparral beyond the fence. He ran to bring it back, past his mother, Enriqua, who was lying in the hammock. He saw that her face had browned, and the sun had spotted melasma across her cheeks and above her lip. Her breath smelled of alcohol where she lay, inebriated, along the horizon of a sunset soporific and red, beneath the leaves of the desert willow.

She hadn't had success in raising livestock since Papa died. The animals looked malnourished and the sheep's coat was barren in patches and the alpaca, too, was mangy, and wandering, completely without direction. She'd been helping the women at the *Parroquia San Mateo* Catholic church by working as a seamstress, even though there was plenty of money, but she'd taken to making wines and drinking them to excess. The needlepoint that she had fallen asleep with in the hammock—a beige linen pillow embroidered with a peacock and an oversized flower blossoming with red petals that she was working on for *Sor Maria Magdalena* of the *Hermanas de Nuestra Senora de la Caridad*—reflected sloppy cross stitching as a result of her frequent intoxication, that the nun had twice mentioned to him.

The horse was circling, nervous, swishing its tail and lifting its front legs, running about the perimeter of the fence. It was neighing a whimpering sound, pinning its ears, and he tried to settle it, but it rose up, snorted, and carried its head high. It tensed its mouth and nostrils and circled again. He ran his fingers along its back where a lump was forming and he checked the cinch and the saddle and he loosened it, rubbed the animal's nose, but the horse was still anxious, throwing its head back and pitching and whinnying, snorting short and vexing puffs of air. Pilar was still by his side.

He called to Enriqua, "*Madre! Madre! Levantate!*"

She lay in the hammock, opened her eyes, looking around at the yard, and she rolled from the hammock and onto her feet stiffly.

"Elvie," she said, running toward the river. "*Quien eres tu*?" Who are you?

Pilar looked at Manny, but she did not answer.

"*Quien eres tu?*" his mother repeated.

"*No hay tiempo. Revisa la casa.*" There is no time. Look in the house.

He held the reins of the horse and gathered its mane. The animal swung away from him as he got on it and he turned the stirrup, sat in the saddle. He steered the reins and he coaxed the horse to move, steadied it, kicked its ribs, and rode off along the river. The girl stood watching him against a strong wind, her remaining strings of red hair whipping like flames Pentecostal, her cheeks red, too, like little burning fires. She stared without purpose and the bulge of her abdomen protruded when the wind blew against her dress.

Then the girl and his mother ran toward the house, and he heard his mother calling, "*Elvie,*" as he rode off along the river, out of the fenced yard, where Enriqua's voice faded softer, and the hum of the muddied water and the feet of roadrunners on the rocks of the river bank became the dominant sounds, and the landscape colors paled together, dried and crunchy beneath the mare's hooves. He searched, looking at the desert as though he were colorblind and seeing the agave and the creosote of the bank in only muted browns and yellows.

He had ridden out a mile or so, calling *"Elvie"* and hearing only the whippoorwill return his calls and hearing a scratching that was perhaps the burrowing feet of the prairie dogs, scampering off, as the hooves of the horse approached. He kept calling, *"Elvie, es Manny,"* and he brought the Azteca mare to a stop where he saw a bright object beside the river that stood out among the dowdy colors of the desert scrub.

He took his right foot out of the stirrup and held the reins and the saddle horn, and he dismounted the horse. His boots crunched the dried grass where he walked slowly to the river, picked up the pink object. Elvie's unicorn. It had blue silken hair that was wet from the brook where it was lying beside the stones and its saddle was multicolored, embedded with plastic jewels.

He looked around, beyond a willow tree. As far as he could see, there was no one.

He saddled the white horse and he rode a little further beyond the *estancia*, calling Elvie's name. The horse was athletic and muscled and it crossed the river easily where it shallowed, where it slowed, and the mare came out of the steady current of the water and he rode back, bouncing along the bank, but he did not see Elvie.

He rode back past the *estancia* a while, following the river, past his mother, who was still frantic. The absence of the sun where she had worn her wedding ring for years after *Papa* died had gone now and her doughy fingers were bronzed all over, pointing; she was shouting. He did not see Pilar and he worried that she had absconded, and that Luis would be furious, but he rode on along where a stream branched off and, hearing a soft voice singing, jovial and fluid, he slowed the mare again where the trees near the other side of the ranch shaded the lawn. There the lawn fell graded to the river bank beneath flowering Chilopsis and a desert acacia and a mango tree.

He saw a pink sandal and beyond it another one, and beside the river Elvie's feet were splashing where the stream grew shallow. He heard her singing and he heard the stones clacking together beneath her feet where she stood beside Pilar.

The Azteca squealed and kicked back, and its face made a sour rictus. He stopped and dismounted her and ran to Elvie. The bottom of her dress was soaked, and she was smiling, splashing where she had arranged a house of sticks together crisscross in a square that resembled a log cabin.

Pilar was peeling the skin from a mango. She looked up, said, "*El joven esta aqui.*" Here is the child.

"*Mi unicorno!*" Elvie ran, splashing from the water; she ran to his arms.

"*Podrias haberte ahogado.*" You could have drowned. He knelt and he kissed her forehead, smoothed her hair.

"*No lo hare. Estaba hambriento.*" No, I won't. I was hungry.

"*Podrias haberte ahogado. Mama estaba aterrorizaba.*" You could have drowned. Mama was terrified.

He tried to be stern, but Elvie made a wry smile at his contrived austerity, melting in him everything terrible. "*Mama esta durmiendo. No tengo a nadie con quien jugar.*" Mama is sleeping. I have nobody to play with.

Pilar rose from the bank and she walked barefoot toward Elvie and she handed her a peeled mango. Enriqua was running toward them now, calling. Elvie turned from her and she clung to the girl, Pilar, buried her face at Pilar's knees, and Elvie's face made an angry scowl.

Enriqua began to cry. She scooped up Elvie in her arms, planting kisses on her girl, wetting Elvie's face where her tears mixed with the syrupy fruit of the overripe mango.

When Enriqua set her down, he brushed a curl from Elvie's face and, swallowing down something like pity for his sister, said, "It's time I bought you that Appaloosa I promised you."

Elvie began to jump and clap. She ran to where the water just covered her toes, over weathered stones clinking, challenging her balance, and she threw water up with her hands that covered their faces in tiny splashes expiatory, purifying. Her thin fingers splashed like the ends of the cinnamon stick brush Father Guillermo DeNardin had once used to bless them with when the sterling silver Aspergillum had been stolen from the cathedral, shaking Holy water in renewing droplets that erased in him the venial sins that he would commit again and again, recurrent, repentant.

"She is too young for a pony. Don't say such things."

"Ma, I'm going to buy her a pony tomorrow."

Juan had told him and told Elvie that they shared a father with her, but now he knew this was untrue. Juan had told her that Papa had died when he was six, almost too long ago for him to remember much about Simon Ayala. Looking at Elvie, though, there were uncanny glimpses of his father in her doll eyes and her mischievous nature. He wondered how this could be so, but he did not ask Enriqua, then.

He told his mother that he had brought Pilar to help. It was a sapient lie that, despite Enriqua's independence and pride, seemed an irrefragable solution to his mother's depressive and frequent transgressions into alcoholic languor that left Elvie sulking, neglected, and mischievous. He would have to explain himself to Luis, but for the time, Pilar milled about the *estancia* content. She immediately set to sweeping the floors and scouring the copper pot of beans that had burned on the stove, filling the kitchen with a smell of smoke that lingered for days.

In the mornings, Pilar would dress Elvie in embroidered dresses from the *mercado* made by the *abuela* of *Esteban del Santos,* the boy who was Elvie's age with the club foot, and she would braid Elvie's hair into cornrows and take the girl for walks along the river and around the fenced corral, naming the animals, as Elvie liked her to do. She helped Enriqua with breakfast on lethargic mornings when his responsibilities to Luis, and Juan's absence, enervated his mother entirely, depleting her every ambition to get out of bed.

Over the next month, he noticed that Pilar's waist did not return to a vespine form like he had hoped; it but grew plumper, and her hips widened, and the child that was still within her caused her fits of nausea and audacious paroxysms of hysteria that were boldly impertinent coming from a *campesina* prisoner rescued not long ago from the basement of a stash house. She was, at times, so impudent and demanding and dramatic that Enriqua called Father Guillermo DeNardin and Sister Mary Magdalena Montenesco of the Cathedral to see the girl.

"She is possessed," his mother insisted. But when the nun and the priest, carrying up the graded lawn his thurible of incense and his Bible and a cross, arrived to have a look at Pilar, she behaved perfectly natural, free of even the usual influence of the hormones of pregnancy, save for making complaints about the engorgement of the veins in her legs and the edematous and doughy look of her feet. When Father brandished the cross, and tread reluctant and fearful across the threshold of the *estancia*, Pilar held the scapular up to the light where it was crumpled and wet where it still hung around her neck, encased in a square of clear plastic.

"She has been without God's love for some time," said Father. "There is no demon in her."

21

Sister Mary Magdalena Montenesco stayed for some time after Father Guillermo DeNardin left, praying a novena with his mother which at once brightened Enriqua's rheumy face with a crooked smile that Manny had not seen in some time. Enriqua made the nun *biscochitos* with cinnamon and with large grains of sugar on top, and she made the nun an herbal tea that had a soporific tendency, causing Sister Mary Magdalena Montenesco to fall asleep at the table, her head jerking backward every so often and then straightening out, her eyes opening occasionally to listen to, and to recite, the prayer.

After Sister Mary Montenesco left, Manny approached Pilar on the patio of blue Talavera tile, where the smell of alyssum and honeysuckle tended to induce waves of nausea within her gut, and he asked Pilar if the child in her was still alive. He asked her if she wanted to have it removed by Dr. Manuel Kelley, the doctor, because although during interrogations Dr. Kelley executed macabre acts of plastic surgery, fractured long bones, and upon request, z-lined the pads of criminals' fingertips in a way that the criminals thought that they could not be put back together in latent forensic recreation of their prints, his surgical methods were meticulous, and he had the erudition of a scholar.

"No doctor," Pilar said, without explanation, and she continued making *huevos rancheros* for Elvie, who was seven now, with very white teeth and dark eyes. "It's still alive."

"But—"

She stopped, set down the whisk she was using to beat another batch of eggs, stared with a gaze icy and worn, and he could feel her antipathy toward Dr. Manuel Kelley, for he had felt a repulsion himself toward the doctor, but he did not comprehend the willing provision of her womb, affirming within this temple life unsolicited. It seemed a strange and loathsome compulsion to house this thing growing within her. He wanted very much for her to end it.

Luis answered his decision to house Pilar with imprecations and suspicion and rancor. Luis said that she could be used to body-bag drugs across the border. He had made some runs with mules in this fashion, guiding swallowers through the Franklin Mountains and over the Zaragoza Bridge. Luis said that if the girl was so friendly, she should be walking her pregnant ass over the Friendship Bridge, helping with business.

He considered it.

Then he denied Luis, face-to-face, to Luis' eyes blinding him basilisk and deathly.

Pilar remained at the *estancia* with his mother.

Typically, he and Gusto and Rodriguez recruited kids, sometimes prostitutes, by offering them a few thousand for selling the excreted balloons of swallowed cocaine, heroin, sometimes meth. Sometimes, in the humid warehouse in the Valley, with the industrial fan blades blowing weighty air across the room upon the recruits, boys as young as eight and aged whores sat listening to the directions, tied to straight-back wooden chairs. Gusto stuffed their mouths with rags soaked in gasoline, suffocating them with anesthetic vapors, their sweat beading in salty droplets. Dr. Manuel Kelley would illuminate the darkness by putting up abdominal x-rays on a light board, showing capsules of contraband replete and compact, contained within the bowels, and Kelley explained how the capsules passed unscathed through the mules' internal plumbing, to be eliminated easily, safely. If the money and the x-rays failed to convince the recruits to do the job, then Gusto came out with his famous and final *get paid or get killed* offer.

And they were hired.

He had somehow convinced Luis to hold off on using Pilar, a testament to the soft spot Luis had for him, even though the Ardillo they'd brought home from the poppy field was long since dead and dumped.

Every time his mother brushed past the girl, Enriqua swore to Mary and made the sign of the Cross, prayed for the baby that had made Pilar swollen all over and caused the hormonal and demonic fits of mania. But Enriqua had grown used to her in their home., too. She enjoyed her company, enjoyed the way Pilar made the coffee unbearably strong so that only Enriqua enjoyed it.

It was close to Christmastime and Pilar had strung colored lights all over the *estancia*, and she had stuffed a piñata in the shape of a Christmas star, and she had strung it across the highest doorframe where Elvie could not reach its dangling strings that held back the sweets. Juan came into the courtyard one morning when Enriqua was eating *churros* drizzled with honey, sipping the burnt coffee, and Elvie was drinking from her bowl of Cheerios so that her lip was covered in a mustache of white cream.

"What did you think of the letter?" Juan asked him.

He had not read it.

Elvie set down the bowl and twirled and took up a coloring book and began placing glittered stickers of mythical creatures in it, of golden Tasmanian devils and a Baba Yaga and a Cyclops. She started singing villancicos, Christmas carols, and she asked Juan, "Will you take me to school?"

"Pilar will take you," said Juan.

"I want you to take me."

"It's good when Pilar walks there with you."

"I want my brothers to take me to the school." Elvie took Juan's hand and pulled him to the door, and she took Manny's hand, too.

"*Vamanos,*" he said, offering a weak smile.

He was long overdue for a conversation with Juan. They'd grown apart during the time he'd spent with Luis, and he didn't spend much time helping him at the market anymore—that is, on the rare days when Juan opened his shop for business and there hadn't been some massacre that drove people to their homes for weeks in fear. But beyond that, Juan was subversive, cagey when asked about his business.

He was afraid to read Juan's letter.

At Elvie's school, they were walking in a courtyard like the one he used to walk Alena through, between his shop class and her typing class, where they'd talked about their aspirations, their futures. Around them were jungle geraniums and Azteca fire flowers just like at *Preparatoria 64*, and there were wooden benches, weathered and split. Juan looked over his shoulder and sat down on the bench in the shade of the Spanish-style roof below the overhang of hemi-cylinders of copper that had corroded to pale green patina and soft layers of verdigris, and Juan took out a piece of gum and opened it and chewed it.

"Did you read the letter?" Juan asked.

"No," he admitted. He looked at Juan, and paused, said, "What's your problem with me?"

"*Dime con quien andas, y te dire quien eres,*" Juan said.

"Tell me who your friends are, and I'll tell you who you are?" he repeated the saying, shaking his head. "You think my friends say a lot about who I am. Juan, that's bullshit. You know why? You were the one who told me I could not say no to Luis, that the only reason he didn't want me dead was because we're related by blood. You said I had to be careful in any way that I refused his requests, that he was powerful, and I was nobody. I already felt like nobody. Nobody goes anywhere around here. They're born and what's done to them, and to their families, is done, and you get on a path you never wanted to get on, and only if you're lucky, no one asks you to die for them. You do your deeds and *a lo hecho, pecho*, make your chest full. And you hope that in the face of deeds done, when you present this full chest, you're not going to die for your deeds. At the end of every day, what's done is done, and you're going to face the consequences, whether you like it or not. But you just get up and fight these wars of our imaginary government and the real government of Sinaloas and Juarez and CDG, and in the end, nothing matters because they're all fruitless."

Juan got up, walked past the fountain, along travertine faulted crooked toward an exposed red brick wall abutted to one painted sunflower-yellow, where girls were playing hopscotch on chalk-drawn squares and jumping rope. There was laughter and it was very loud. Juan looked back, said, "Read the letter."

"What the fuck, Juan?"

Manny stood, and there was a hush, and the children turned to him, stopped their skipping and singing and laughing. He grabbed his brother by the collar where it was yellowed, wrinkled. "Luis hasn't been all that bad to me. Where have you been? Where have you *been*?"

"Release me, *hermano*."

He let go, walked out of the school yard, feeling the eyes of the children upon his back.

Weeks passed, and he and Juan said little to each other. His mother cooked an enormous dinner, as she always did on the Feast Day of the Immaculate Conception, a special event with street festivals and food vendors and mariachi music and theatre and children's games in the town of San Juan de los Lagos, Jalisco, where she was born. And on Christmas morning, Elvie ran out to the stables and found a spotted Appaloosa, and a saddle, and tins of sugared marzipan candies made by Pilar.

Gusto returned to his usual garrulous prattle. He was no longer prone to capricious mood swings with him, and though Manny remained guarded, he was glad. He was happy to listen to the story of how Gusto and Anna had met and fallen in love. Anna's face wrinkled into an ugly shape, though, her smile twisting into a tilde of disdain hearing Gusto tell the story, and when Gusto put his arms around her neck and pulled her close to kiss her withered cheek, she withdrew, wrapped her sarong around her thighs, put on her shoes and left the table, joined Sylvia.

"What, you didn't like that story?" Gusto rubbed his amputated digit, and the rest of his earthworm fingers against the stubble of a disheveled beard, following Anna. There was grease under Gusto's fingernails, dust on his pants. "Stacio, remember when we stayed in the United States?" Gusto lit a smoke, began another story. " So we went into this hotel and I don't speak English well like Dolly does. We have to wait for our contact to pick up a big load of coke going to Chicago and the guy is *late,* I mean a whole *day* late. We think we're gonna have to send someone out for him. So we check into this filthy hotel and we don't know it's a brothel and my English, you know, my English is no good. The room's a mess, an absolute mess. The sheets aren't on the bed, there are beer bottles on the nightstand. I tell the maid, or I think I tell her, to clean the room up. She gives me this look like, this *weird* look. Then she goes into the bathroom and starts washing up, painting her lips. She's in there for a full fifteen minutes, except she's not cleaning anything."

Mustacio exhaled. "He told her to clean herself up."

"It was an honest mistake. I don't speak English."

Anna grabbed her purse. "Jesus, did you fuck her?"

Mustacio shrugged. "She sat down on the bed after that."

There was a long pause. Mustacio and Gusto continued to smoke, sipped their *cervezas.*

From across the room, Manny could read Anna's thoughts, though she did not speak until, as she was heading for the glass doors, she said, "I'm leaving to pick up the baby from my mother's house. She needs medicine. She's running a fever. Goodbye, Sylvia."

"Baby." Gusto placed the earthworm fingers, his rough hands, on Anna's face, kissed her lips for a long time.

She pulled away.

Moments later, an explosive noise erupted, came at Manny like a tsunami of pressurized air that ripped through the desert heat, reaching the lanai. His hair blew back, and he took cover, held Sylvia's head under his shoulders where she screamed and shook.

22

Under Anna's white Explorer, a charge had exploded, tearing off the door and part of the rock escarpment, the stone railing bordering Luis' ranch above Juarez. This debris tumbled off the bottom of the cliff into a wide arroyo, burning below.

They ran into the driveway and stared at the edge of the expansive property where the driveway curved, just outside the free-standing five car garage, watching the SUV with Anna's body trapped inside as it roared in squelching flames that twisted the air into ribbons of heat. Gusto's beer was sweating warm beads from the sides of the glass; he dropped it. It splintered glass chards, cracking the travertine walkway. The heat of the burst pressed the dry air to Manny's face. He turned from it.

Gusto offered at once to help clean up the shards of glass, so that none of them got cut or got dirty, and Gusto said that he didn't want any of them to slip. Gusto told them to be careful where the *cerveza*, mixed with oil and dust, slicked the travertine and made slippery the walk down the stone stairs, down into the arroyo, where the air was cool, where they could wait for the fire to subside.

Later that evening, the charred car was still in the drive, and Manny examined remnants of the explosion as he walked around the property. A coyote howled off in the desert beyond where he could see, where night was falling beautiful and savage and lonely. The most notable piece of evidence left behind were not the sharp spears of metal that had thrown from the explosion, nor the way Anna's anatomical remains were set in a terrible rictus of escape. He thought that the most significant finding was a stubbed-out cigar. A brown scorpion scurried over it, where the cigar, an *Aroma De Cuba Mi Amor* brand in a Mexican wrapper, lay in the chaparral.

The cigar was Gusto's brand, though Gusto did not build bombs.

Paulo "O-Ring" Cortez, a bomb artist, made things blow up. And bomb artists took great pride in their incendiary work. Looking at the remnants of the explosion, he did not need to ask who had made the bomb, nor who had arranged for its detonation. Gusto had been saying for a long time that he did not trust Anna, though he loved her very much, and when Luis began to suspect a *soplon*, Luis had said that he did not trust Anna, either.

On Tuesday, when they returned from another search-and-destroy operation—this time a raid on an *Autodefensa* group that returned dozens of automatic weapons and thousands of rounds of ammo—Gusto and Mustacio were sitting at the table on Luis' lanai, drinking *cervezas* again. Lights came on as the sun died away, lights wrapped by sensual, wrought iron spirals that had been bored into the stone pillars of the *estancia*, beside gas-fired bowls that bordered the pool, illuminating the desert enough to dim Virgo and Vega and the twins. Below them, a wolf called to a full moon cratered and low. The horizon scalloped the jagged mountains on a desert shrouding the stories of lives snuffed.

There were prostitutes in the hot tub that night and Luis emptied himself into a woman over the stone seat wall beneath the spirals of wrought iron, where all could see. He pulled the sliding glass closed just outside the bedroom, where Sylvia's crying was soft and muffled by her pillow and by the sound of birds roosting, cooing, outside in the saguaro, and he waited for Luis to finish before he opened the glass, where Gusto sat just beyond it, smoking, talking in hushed tones, and he hung behind the wall where he stepped out onto the patio. Gusto would tell him to take one of the women; he would insist.

He waited, listened.

"We have to teach him a lesson," said Luis.

"Can't I just kill him? I have a taste for it, boss. It's been a long time you've given me anyone good to work on."

"Good, ah?"

"He would be delicious."

"He's family, not a chance."

"You don't owe that family anything. What did they give you, boss? They gave you shit."

"Shut up."

"Abandoned you."

Luis rose, counted bills from his wallet and laid them on the table. The prostitute said she had not been paid enough and he slapped her cheek, pulled his favorite Colt with the gold grip and aimed it, two hands.

"Alright, alright. Easy." Gusto withdrew his wallet and gave it to the woman and told the woman to take the money, all of it, called her a filthy old bird, told her, "Take it, take it," and Gusto pointed his stump of a finger at her, and the woman began to dress very quickly, shimmying her skirt up her wet legs before she ran to the bathroom.

Luis walked naked to the parapet, examined the desert. A whippoorwill was calling its cavernous and nocturnal song that echoed, and the air was cool now and steam rose in a humid little cloud from the pool. Luis wrapped a towel around his waist and turned, sat at the table. "We need the fish market. It's a legitimate business with a good reputation. It keeps the restaurant alive. The restaurant is responsible for 10 million in revenue."

"Every year, *Si*." Gusto frowned, nodded.

"Every week." Luis raised his glass to meet Gusto's in a toast.

"The restaurant is good, boss. What does a fish fry sell for, in America? At most $12.99? And that's with a side of fries and coleslaw. The restaurant cleans ten million a week. That's a good business."

"It's hard work cleaning all this money. Do you know how hard it is to make all this cash disappear?"

"We are also in the fish *selling* business now, the *Mercado* is legitimate. Plus, you have the shell companies in the Caymans, the accounts there, and in Switzerland."

"Then fuck the little connect-the-dots game through Honduras. I pride myself on my Columbian cocaine deals. Bringing in cocaine through all these gatekeepers, because the Columbians can't do it right themselves, because they don't have the same land border we have with the United States. But why do we need Honduras and Nicaragua and El Salvador? We can use my brother's boats to offload the coke. I can bring it in through Cozumel, avoid Colonel Gutierrez altogether."

"Cozumel." Gusto looked surprised.

The tourist cities were largely untouched by the Juarez Cartel. Wars there were kept out of the public eye, by Luis' orders.

Luis asked if he had stuttered.

Gusto swallowed, backed down. "We might have to, for a while. The U.S. is patrolling the boat routes, though, riding the Gulf, Miami, hard, like a whore, Luis. A dirty, stinking, filthy whore with a pussy that smells like rotten tomatillos and with tortilla titties that—"

"Enough, I get the point. I want to know how Gutierrez is getting his information. I've lost three shipments in two months. Big shipments. I'm not talking like baggies of marijuana in a T-shirt cannon. We've lost 200 kilos of coke to that mother fucker. And no matter how much I up the bribe, he still seems bent on destroying my territory."

"He has to have a price."

"He is a little shit turd of brown opium paste worth as much as we're willing to pay him, without the pleasant and euphoric effects."

"The Sinaloas are doing better than brown shit paste. New York wants China White. The East Coast wants it pure. The Sinaloas have been producing white opium, getting over a grand per kilo for the paste."

"Nobody wants better, they want cheaper. If they have to pay five grand for a kilo, then our brown paste is going to look even better. I can't keep up with the demand from the East. I can't sleep thinking about it. Ours reaches a purity of seventy-five percent."

"That's enough to get high."

"Better, it's enough to get hooked."

"Then that's the way of the future. Brown opium, home grown." Gusto toasted, "To our future."

"I'm not giving up my cocaine routes just yet, but I'll toast to the future."

"*Futuro*," said Gusto.

"*Futuro*," said Luis.

With that, Manny stepped back inside, slid the door closed. With his head down as he turned to leave, stepping softly, pressing his feet quietly against the Talavera tile, he bumped into Sylvia who stood at the bedroom door. Her makeup was smeared black on her cheek and her cheek was red and swollen on one side and she was wearing a white *campesina* dress torn at the sleeve. She met his eyes, watched him as he left the *estancia*, and she was still watching him as he looked back, too, but she did not speak as he left.

23

It was early on Monday and the moon was veiled in cirrus and the deliveries were still coming in, freight trucks beeping high pitched, backing over cobblestones. Manny was in the back room of the store reviewing the orders for totoabas on the laptop. He was sipping Mexican coffee with sugar and eating a *churro* stick from Maria Alvarez de Topo's cart when he heard a scooter pull up outside on the *Avenue*, heard Gusto arguing with Juan outside. He closed the laptop and stashed it in the desk drawer with his notes and the names of the customers getting totoaba bladders. The black curtain flew open and chairs scraped, and the men's faces met, gazed abrupt, intense.

Manny rose, told Juan he'd watch the store front, but Gusto said, "No, Dolly, I want to discuss this with you, too. Fish mongering can wait. My business comes first. It's all family business, anyhow." Gusto winked at him, closing the meaty curtain over the cloud of his right eye.

"Luis has new relationships in Cozumel. We're going to load our cocaine from Columbia on a cruise ship. The small planes can't make it all the way to Miami without a refueling stop, which we no longer have, and the waters are too heavily patrolled. The cruise ship is the perfect Trojan horse. It stops on a private island in the Bahamas. You know the one—it used to be an air stop for the cocaine. It's going to be one again. The landing strip is still there."

"You can't fly there."

"I don't have to. You can sail up."

"Onto a private island? Not a chance."

Gusto smiled, shook his head. "They don't own the water. We sail up at night and bring it onto the island right behind the food service trucks, where they cook up the island buffet twice a week. Beside the hot dogs and pineapple cornbread and mahi-mahi topped with chopped tomato and red onion and cilantro. There's only a skeleton crew there, and they're all Bahamians. Bahamians can be bought like everybody else can be bought."

"The employees are owned by that corporation. They'll never risk losing their U.S. dollars being sent home to their twelve children living squalid, palm-thatched huts. There's too much movement among them, too many moving pieces to connect the shipments reliably."

Gusto waved him off. "Everyone has their price. Do you know how much of this business is in payouts? It's sickening. You're going to learn. And they put a customs and immigration officer on the island. A checkpoint, even better. Immigration officers are easily bought, too. This one is well-paid. From there, the ship goes to Port Canaveral."

Juan laughed. "Impossible. You have no access point there. A thousand miles of patrolled waters, around the big cock and balls of the Florida peninsula, or over a U.S. shaved-pussy landing strip you've never set your big ogre feet in."

"Big ogre feet, ah? We don't need to. We're not taking anything off the boat there."

"What?"

"The ship goes back out, Eastern Caribbean, Western Caribbean. It does the same route every week. The next port is Cozumel. Here we offload."

"Who offloads?"

"We've made contacts. The only English they speak is, 'Have a magical day.' Do you follow?"

"You want fucking Mickey Mouse to offload our coke?"

"Sure, if you want to call him Mickey Mouse. Mickey Mouse offloads the coke to the *Alena*. And a few other boats. Hauls 500 kilos of coke every week, takes it right off the *Fantasy of the Seas* with the garbage and the rotten tuna and smoked salmon and little capers those wasteful, overweight, self-indulgent Americans throw from their plates. We avoid all roads through the Yucatan; through Chiapas and Veracruz and Quintana Roo and Oxaca—all the places we're being stopped, all the Sinaloa territories. And we avoid that shit storm Gutierrez and his *antidroga* task force."

"By sailing up the Gulf."

"*Si*. To *Playa Bagdad*. We drive up Route 2 where are road is safe, and it's business as usual over the border through our plaza. If we have any more trouble through our plazas, we find gringos to offload the *Alena* in South Padre Island, and we skip Guitterrez's land seizures altogether."

Juan rose from the table. "Get your own boat. Luis controls most of Juarez. You don't need mine."

"Territories are changing. Your customers are established. Gutierrez and his *Federales* leave you alone. They know you fish. We need you to sail."

"I said no."

Gusto said, "Dolly."

"Don't involve my brother in this," said Juan.

"Your brother is part of the family."

"Gusto," Manny said. "Juan operates his own business. Pays his piece to Luis."

"Be careful, Dolly. Juan, Luis wants a bigger piece."

"I'm not cutting up the pie anymore," Juan said.

"Why do you reject family, Juan?" Gusto ran his fingers over the golden handle of his Colt, those thick sausages circling the engravings on the metal.

"You know why."

Now Gusto pulled the serrated knife from the leather case at his waste, where his abdomen hung pendulous over his belt, and he began to pick his teeth with the sickled tip. "Maybe I can carve it up for you, Juan."

"No."

"Are you hiding something, *hermano*?"

"Gusto, we'll do it," Manny said.

"Emmanuel," Juan objected.

"Juan, I'll help you. You'll be paid well."

He looked at Juan and Juan looked at him and he rose, and he poured Gusto a shot of tequila and he poured some for Juan and for himself and Juan did not object further.

"To brothers," Manny said.

Gusto took a sip, and he put his feet up on a chair, stared anger intense and cold, like he could read Juan's thoughts from across the room. "I'll be honest. Looking into your eyes, I think I don't trust you, Juan."

"That's because they say the eyes are the window to the soul, Gusto, and you don't have one."

"*Si,* I cannot disagree with you. But now it's five a.m. and we're toasting with tequila shots. I'm beginning to love Dolly."

"Then a toast to Dolly." Juan raised his glass to his brother, though his eyes did not move from Gusto's locked gaze. Gusto broke first.

Later, Manny sat alone beside the river eating a piece of the almond torte Pilar had made with his mother. The water was cool, cloudless. It streamed fast and clear there, over his bare feet. The river stones fell out of focus, looking like inexpressive, archetypal eyes. He held the letter in his hand. From the *estancia,* Pilar called in the distance and Elvie was laughing. Then he heard his mother calling louder, but he did call back.

He tore the envelope open and he took out the paper and he looked away at the chaparral and a roadrunner bathing in the stream where it ran over gray river stones, and he looked down and he expected some long letter from Juan; he read:

23.13211N, 82.36749E

It was a geolocation. Havana.

His father's handwriting.

He put the wrinkled paper back in the envelope and folded in and put it in his back pocket.

Later that week, he left for five days with Juan. They sailed from Cozumel on the new boat, the *Alena,* that Juan had bought with his profits from selling totoaba bladders. Each of them now brought their mother bags of money every week, far too many bills to count. Pilar would wrap the stacks of bills tightly around many times in plastic and bury them it in the yard in crates and mark the location in books and with huge granitic boulders outside. Juan brought Enriqua the money from the totoabas and the fish from the *mercado,* Manny brought it home from the runs and the trades that he did for Luis.

Sometimes now, Luis would ask him to disappear someone, but he would create reasons why he could not, and Gusto was beginning to witness this destruction of any loyalty he had ever had to Luis. He could not continue this feigned allegiance indefinitely—not only because he would inevitably die on a rooftop parapet, overlooking the *zocalo,* or in a barren desert arroyo in some mass shooting bloodbath, crumpling quietly into the foundation or into the Samalayuca Dune Fields, but because he was not living. His work with this half-brother was keeping him awake at night, and that was no kind of life, always thinking that the Sinaloas would do to him the same kind of work that he performed—these unholy justice runs, beleaguered mercy.

He did not complete what Luis asked of him half the time now. Instead of following Luis' order to disappear the victims, often entire families, he allowed them to run off; he refused to kill them mercilessly as Gusto did without remorse.

A few times, he cut himself with his own knife, a woolly mammoth tusk Damascus steel three-inch button lock blade covered with a skeleton skin on a blue metal sheath, to make it look like there had been a struggle.

Once he and Gusto went to disappear a coyote who had failed to return a suitcase full of money from a run of cocaine across the Zaragoza Bridge. The kid, not much older than him, had picked up his wife and kid in his home in El Porvenir upon his return and kept driving with Luis' money on Highway 45, forgetting that Luis had *Federales* in his pocket on the roads from Juarez to Costa Rica. Gusto had torched the coyote's car with the young man's wife holding her baby in a rictus of agony, burned them alive. And through the heated stench of seared muscle and gasoline, it was becoming clearer that Gusto smelled Manny's fear, sensed this hesitation in the seconds his gaze held the woman's, just after the match struck, gritty and sulfurous. Her tears pooled glassy like the black, wet eyes of Alena's sick cat, just before it had died, and the instantaneous heat of the blaze where she sat trapped, bound, burning, clutching her infant toward her breast, did not dry them.

24

On the first night out on the *Alena* he awoke in his cabin panting, sweating. He stared at the paneled wall and he rose, and he put on his shorts and he walked barefoot out to the deck, where the sea air blew Juan's hair back in twisted chunks.

Juan's boat was a fifty-three-foot Bertram fishing vessel that Juan lived on for weeks at a time, trolling the Gulf for marlin and yellowfin and the illegal totoabas that each commanded ten thousand dollars. Juan had equipped it with top-of-the-line, stand-up gear, fishing rods and reels, a fighting chair, night lights, a generator. It had bedrooms and an engine room that was powered by two 1000-horsepower diesel engines.

Typically, when they returned to Cozumel, they unloaded their fish. When they returned to Juarez, they unloaded the cash: $1.2 million, mostly in hundreds and fifties of U.S. currency. Sometimes they came into port at Playa Bagdad on the Gulf coast and drove Route 2 west. The Chinese were there to accept the totoabas. Cargo trucks with riveted chassis cabs equipped for towing large loads were always there, waiting. The bladders had made Juan a hidden fortune because Juan had discovered a natural habitat in the Gulf of Mexico for the large, deep-sea fish that had been fished to near extinction on the Baja side, and there were too many ships out there looking for poachers. On this side, no one was concerned about fish bladders or the adorable, hundred-pound *vaquitas*, the tiny porpoises that became ensnared in the wall of gill nets Juan threw out to catch them. Here, the authorities were only concerned about boats moving Columbian cocaine. The DEA agents didn't know the difference between a dolphin and a two-meter totoaba, but they sure knew that white powdery substance when they found it in a fishing boat.

In the moonlight now, out on the water, Juan walked up beside him near the starboard side of the bow. Manny was soaked from the dream he'd had and outside, the air was humid, but it was not soupy like it was inside the cabin where it suffocated him, gave him nightmares.

Lights twinkled in and out of focus on the horizon, dim yellow and pinpoint red and hot white. He made out the *Castillo de Los Tres Reyes del Morro* and the *Fortaleza de San Carlos de la Cabana.* The sea was calm with tiny wavelets not even half a foot high, and the smell of pollution was strong coming from Havana harbor. They were close enough to the shore to hear the squeal of bats and see their polygonal forms working through the sky around them.

Juan put his arm on his shoulders, said, "*Mi hermano.*"

He swallowed.

"I read the coordinates in the letter. Why are we here?"

"Have you noticed Elvie looks just like Papa?"

"Is he alive?"

"No."

"Then I don't understand."

"He was, until recently."

"You didn't tell me."

"I couldn't."

"What the hell?"

"You're too involved with Luis."

"Why didn't you tell me?"

"I couldn't, Manny."

"What happened?"

"I'll explain."

"I had a right to know. You didn't tell me."

"It was for your safety."

"He was my father, too."

"Don't be so selfish."

"Papa was alive … how, where, until when? How could you hide this?"

"I had to protect Ma and Elvie. Luis is dangerous."

"Luis is his son, too," he shouted.

"Manny, you're still a kid."

"I was never a kid!" He grabbed Juan by the neck and he pushed Juan to the side of the boat and he held his brother so that Juan's torso bent as a fulcrum over the side of the *Alena*, and he stared precarious danger into his brother's eyes, as though he might toss Juan overboard where the lights of Havana and the moon reflected silvery on the ocean.

Then he pulled back his fist and it snapped forward hard and he split open Juan's lip.

Juan threw him off, down on the deck. They rolled hard where it was wet on the deck and Juan was on top of him, straddling him. Juan put his arms around Manny's neck, choking him, and told him that he loved him, said he didn't want to see them end up like Papa, and Juan said that he wanted to tell him everything, but he didn't like the direction he was headed. Juan asked him, screaming, if he had done a line of coke just then, said that, more than anything, he just wanted them all alive.

"Damnit, Manny," Juan said, choking him, and Juan said that he wanted them all to leave Juarez, to get out of Mexico, but he didn't know how.

"I can't breathe." Manny gasped, breathed whoops of stridor through Juan's hands crushing him thick and vicious and strong.

Juan released his grasp, stood up, and wiped his lip where it bled, swollen. He pushed his hair back where it hung forward over his eyes. "Jesus, Manny."

He hugged Juan tightly, so hard around his chest, like he could take the air out of it, as though he would never let go. With his arms around him, Juan slapped him hard on his back and he pulled him close, grabbed a chunk of his hair and told him he loved him again, and Juan messed his hair and pushed him off his balance, until he slipped on the deck.

Then Juan said that the boat needed to come into the harbor through a narrow channel, and he needed help maneuvering it.

"Okay," Manny said, and he stepped up onto the stern where it was painted with something like sandpaper so that bare feet would not slip.

Juan steered them toward the channel where alongside the *Alena* there were large fish swimming close to the surface, dolphins and garfish sleek and light. They approached the dock portside and judged the wind and the current, and then Juan told him to deploy the fenders. When they were docked, Juan began to tie up the boat.

Juan steadied the boat beneath a moon that was very high and full, where the lights put out the stars and there was a yellow glare all around them. They sat in the kitchen of the *Alena,* and Juan opened a beer for him and one for himself.

"I couldn't tell you this back home," Juan said. "Luis has every phone and car and place in Juarez bugged."

"The letter told me nothing. It made me think Papa was here in Havana when I opened it. I looked up the coordinates, and when I woke up and saw the lights of Havana in brazen halos, I was certain of it. He always loved Havana. Do you remember? Tell me he's here, Juan. Living in exile."

"I can't, Manny."

"He's here. I know he is."

"I'm sorry."

"Then you stole him from me twice now."

"I want you to know him, to understand things, but I can't bring him back. I wasn't trying to."

"I've thought of leaving Mexico myself, and I know you have, too. Every time you leave on the sea, I can see it in you, and I can see it out here in the brine-filled air when it's balmy and the palms blow like there might be a storm somewhere a few days off, some beast of a storm calling you, challenging you, *come get me.* The winds blow back your hair and you smell it, freedom. I can see the way the troubles fall from your chest here. You want to go. You want to go and to never return."

"Manny," Juan said; he took a long sip of a stale beer and he sliced a lime with a very sharp knife, and he squeezed it into his beer. "There was a chase in Mexico City when we were very young, when we were there with Papa. Papa was shot."

"You said he lived."

"He did, for a while. He ran through the streets. That day, he pushed me into the home of a seamstress to watch over us while he ran. I don't remember everything. He didn't want us killed. I guess he figured he was going to die."

"He's here, Juan. Tell me he's here in Havana."

"He ran with his leg bleeding, looking for help. The streets were full of artisans and the bar at the corner was playing a salsa with guitar and cymbals. Papa knocked over a young girl dancing. Then I saw him disappear. There were men grilling fish on the corner. The steam was hot. It blurred his image where he disappeared around the corner. The grill was sizzling, and the salsa music was playing loud. I couldn't hear what he said, calling back to me. He ran into the brothel down the alley."

"But he was bleeding. The men who shot him—*sicarios*—would've followed the trail, followed the scent of it like wild, rabid dogs."

"They did. Papa told me that when he entered the brothel—"

"When? When did he tell you all this? How long have you known?"

"Papa told me there was a man in the brothel who had been recently shot by one of the pimps. The man was lying face-down on the ground. From the window of the seamstress, across the street, I saw the man who shot the john. He left the brothel. I heard the gunshot just before he left. I saw the man put his gun in his holster. I remember how dry my mouth felt, how the seamstress tried to claw me back from the window. I saw this man come out of the brothel, and he had massive arms like barbells and a barrel chest, and he wore a leather vest and he had almost no neck between his chest and his round head. His skin folded in the back of his scalp like a bulldog's, and his hair was coarse. Papa said that, by the time the *sicario* chasing him burst through the door, that he and the whores of the brothel had shoved the killed man face down beneath the table, where blood ran in a river from his chest and his legs toward the door. He said the *sicario* grabbed one of the whores, put his pistol to her temple. He said he threw her to the mattress in the corner, where a little candle was burning with the scent of cinnamon all around them. And Papa said the *sicario* lifted her *campesina* night dress and pointed the barrel up her vagina and demanded, '*What happened? Where is he?*' and Papa said that the whore trembled and that it was almost possible to hear the thumping of her heart. She told the *sicario* that she didn't know, that a man had burst through the door and collapsed on the floor. Papa told me later that it was impossible to know if the whore was protecting him because he was her customer or if she was protecting her pimp who had just left, but that her voice squeaked soprano when she spoke. Papa said that then the *sicario* threw her legs closed and clicked back the hammer of his Colt and he turned, and he put another bullet through the chest of the man dead on the floor. I could hear the gunshot and the screams of the whores from the brothel all the way across the street, like barn owls, Manny, where I sheltered with the seamstress. She covered my ears, and when the shooting and screams were over, she went back to running the sewing machine. The needle kept pounding up and down above me where I hid below the table. It hissed mechanical, unstopping, sealing everything in place."

Juan said that Papa had escaped through the back window and she said that he fell, broke both bones of his right ankle near the place where it had been shot. There was shrapnel in it that Juan could see when he came back to find him in the seamstress shop. Juan said that Papa had already tied a tourniquet around the ankle, but that it was still bleeding unstoppable streamlets of blood. And Juan said that Papa had begged the seamstress to take his boys back to their mother. Juan described her doughy hands, said that they were cracked fingers bent permanently at their last joints, rheumatoid and misshapen and dried. Juan said that Papa gave her all the coins he had in his pockets and that he wrote the address of the *estancia* for her on a piece of scrap cloth.

25

Manny opened another beer, paced around the kitchen inside the *Alena*, where the Havana lights dirty and hot glowered in through the windows of the cabin.

He took a swig and he ran his hand through his hair, and he sat down again, faced Juan. "He's here. tell me he's here."

"Papa wanted more for us. He wanted an honest life. He was pulled into this empire, too. He was trying to get away, get out of it all, and then he was shot."

"But you said that's impossible, that they would kill us first. You said I had to be careful not to refuse Luis, his entire machine, this whole establishment."

"I did."

"Then what? What can be said? There is nothing else to do."

"I've been thinking of ways to escape it."

"I was just beginning to see your point—that we couldn't. That this was it, this was my life in this war and that it would go on like this until someday, suddenly, one day it would end like Papa's."

"I know you don't think so, but I've been looking out for you, Manny."

"The day Gutierrez stopped me—"

"Yes."

They talked until the sun rose over Havana, extinguishing the yellow halos of the streetlights. The porpoises were still beside the *Alena* in the harbor and they had finished all the beer. When Juan secured the boat, he said, "Let's walk," and they left the dock and walked down the pier and they got *huevos habaneros* with peppers and onions and beans for breakfast in the city. The food was very hot. Manny burned his tongue and he drank some juice and looked out over the stone sea wall that was intended to keep the ocean out. They walked past curio shops and cafes and through an area of homes in the Spanish art deco style, and they walked past a concrete wall embedded with huge stones asymmetric and cold. They passed under crumbling arches and walked by many buildings badly in need of repair and they passed a yellow punch bug and a Ford Fairlane with whitewashed tires.

They kept walking until they reached the end of a long row of homes, a way away from *Calle Obispo,* and they entered the last home. It was painted salmon pink and had a rotting porch and was surrounded by iron gates.

He followed Juan, went in.

There was a woman inside cooking a white liquid over the stove and there were burned planks of wood on the floor and quilts of patchwork in turquoise and reds and yellows covering the table and chairs and couches. The woman smiled when she saw Juan. Juan nodded.

"*Buenos dias,* Juan."

The woman told him to sit.

Juan told him that the woman was the seamstress, Adelia de Rosco, the woman who had hidden them from the Sinaloa *sicario* in Mexico City that day, many years ago, and Juan said that in Mexico City, the cartel had begun to ask questions, and that people on the street had started to talk, so Papa had come here to hide after he was shot.

"Is Papa here?" He saw Adelia de Rosco look at Juan, saw Juan look at her.

"No, Manny. *Tu papa no esta aqui,*" the woman said, pulling him close. Her hands were spotted brown and rough with thick calluses. Her fingers bent like gnarled twigs of acacia branches, ending in fingernails yellow and brittle and split.

He pulled away.

She returned to the stove and she poured the white liquid into a soup bowl and she set it beside him, smiled. He waited for the steam to cool and he sipped the white liquid. Juan said it was *ayahuasca* from the *caapi* vines of the Amazon and that it was hallucinogenic, and Juan told him to be careful not to drink too much at once.

It was warm, sweet, and it filled him with soporific memories.

After a while, his father appeared in the doorway where a velvet curtain with glass beads hung. His father took his hand and walked gently around the garden with him where pessaries were rooting in mud beside trampled weeds of saw grass and straw. They sat in the garden where the deepest red Barbados lilies tangled among Anthurium and where jasmine bells crept along the fence.

Papa had a prosthesis and it thrummed a metal creak, making his movements mechanical and careful and slow. Papa had lost the leg much higher up than where it had been shot, and Papa spoke to Manny from a distance, told him that it had become amputated and infected, gangrenous. Manny watched Papa then, struggling, his labored movements. Manny wanted to run with him, embrace him, but his imagination lulled behind his intentions, kept him somnolent and dreamy. After a while, Papa sat on an iron bench.

Manny sipped more of the ayahuasca brew. On the other side of the fence, a pit bull cruel and beautiful began to bark through the chain links.

He sat with Juan and Adelia de Rosco and his father, who told him how much he enjoyed sitting with his sons there. Papa told him the story of how he'd sustained the gunshot in Mexico City, escaped the Sinaloas, and lived in exile there in Havana for twelve years, telling the story very much like Juan had told it. His father told him he'd been back only one night in twelve years to see Enriqua and that this was the night that Elvie was conceived. And Papa told him that he'd escaped back to Havana through the United States, through the Franklin Mountains, almost dying there on the trails, without food or water for two days, before he hitched a ride to the coast and returned to Cuba by boat.

At the end of Papa's story, Manny couldn't tell who was speaking; the colors before him seemed kaleidoscopic. The sun was already lower on the horizon than when he'd arrived, and his father's words had grown slow. Juan's words grew slow, too, and Juan said that Luis would sit with him like family in a garden like this one, and Luis would kiss him and then allow him to be led off to avenge his father's death.

"Luis wants you to avenge Papa's death," said Juan.

"How?"

"He wants you to take out the Sinaloan *capo*."

"The *capo*."

"He's growing your influence, your skill, and your anger. It would provide redemption for Papa's death."

His father told him, in dreams, "At some point, he'll say to you, Manny, I give you this amount of money, to do this job. Or perhaps he'll say to you, I'll make you my right hand, give you my territory, if you'll prove this loyalty to me."

Manny swallowed.

Luis had already said those things.

His father's face fell, he said, "My death need not be avenged. I've found redemption."

Manny wiped sweat from his brow where it beaded. The hallucinogenic effects of the *ayahuasca* was wearing off, his mind returning to clarity.

Luis' offers were non-negotiable. There was the money. He'd already received plenty of money from Luis, more than he could ever legally account for in any fish selling business, so much that he'd had to bury it. In Luis' offers, there were choices.

There were suitcases of silver, or there were ounces of lead.

If he'd been asked a month earlier to take on the Sinaloan *capo*, he would have been honored. He would have taken on the assignment with a full heart. He'd embraced his half-brother, kissed his cheek, and been led away by his deception. He'd even shut out Juan.

The implications became obvious.

If he proceeded in the direction he was going, he would rise to the top of Luis' empire, but he'd always be a target—not the desert fox running for his meal, but the rabbit running for its life. Every day. Every hour. To survive, he would have to be more than good, he would have to be lucky. Alena would've smiled and told him there was no such thing as luck, only God's love. God, he missed her.

The Juarez Cartel was his only protection here and outside of it, he was a dead man. Even with their protection, his death would come like all the others—young. The Sinaloas would only have to get lucky one day to end him, and he'd have to get lucky every day to cheat death. In the end, it could not be done. He asked himself why he was caught up in the worst of this life in Juarez and how it had come to be. But he knew it was something that had started even before his time, since before his father's time. This ministry of Satan could not be stopped by Juan, the politician, trying to keep him on the fringes of it; Juan could not stop this creature from growing in him with its own intensity, consuming him.

Beneath a jacaranda tree, he sipped more of the *ayahuasca* brew and ate some of the fruit in the garden—apples and some unripe mango and papaya. His vision blurred, and the white drink recycled his thoughts, repeating the unresolved reasoning in his mind.

He chewed the apple, thought *yes*, his life had grown into the life of a rabbit.

And what he'd learned in all of this was the life dinner principle. He learned that a coyote is only running for its dinner, but a rabbit, a rabbit, every time, is running for its life. When he watched the jackals out in the chaparral run, he saw Manny, Dolly, he saw himself—whoever this boy was now—and he did not like it; he could not be this man. Yet any betrayal against Luis, against the cartel, would end the same way, only his death would come at the hands of Luis.

The *ayahuasca* drink was working its way out of his blood again. The lilies and the tendrils of vine creepers came into view now, and Papa disappeared. Manny's mind deepened. The way that Juan and Luis were similar in all their Spanish idioms forced a troubled and crooked smile onto his lips that he resisted. Juan and Luis were always trying to outwit the other in sharp words, their bitter subtexts.

"*Zapatero a tus zapatos*," Luis said to Juan once, when Juan refuted his requests. Shoemaker, to your shoes, then.

"*Gata con guantes no caza ratones*," Juan had warned Manny, about Luis. A cat with gloves can't catch mice. Juan had been telling him to be prepared to get his hands dirty to do the jobs right, mostly to scare him, to caution him. It was clear now that Juan wanted his association with Luis to be a close one— not as friends are kept close, but as enemies are.

The two of them weren't so different.

After all, they were blood.

But the rift between Luis and Juan was deepening; he could only remain loyal to one of them.

There in the garden, his greatest clarity came after this obscure, disappointing fall from reality lifted. His worries melted like the dense fog they'd passed through not long ago on the water: Clouds of soupy gray sat on the ocean, fixing the *Alena* in place. On their last trip to Cozumel, two months ago, they'd picked up loads of cocaine from the cruise ship, which had been loaded by Columbians on the Bahamian island. They'd sailed back through the Gulf of Mexico on this run, and Juan had worried that the shipment would be confiscated, his totoabas found, the *Alena* searched, impounded. But the dense blanket of fog had melted into thinned layers with the sunrise, and they'd come into port without guidance.

He thought it was Juan's voice he heard in his head now, or Papa's, but it was his own thoughts and he did not trust them, did not trust anyone.

Más vale ser cabeza de ratón que cola de león. **Better to be the head of a mouse than the tail of a lion.**

He could no longer hang by a thread with the big dogs. It was better for him to be with Juan, with his family.

Luis was his brother, but he wasn't family.

In the garden, among the twisted mustard weeds, Adelia de Rosco approached. She set a Talavera plate of some fried plantains and beans on the white bench, and a rooster ran through the garden crowing loudly.

Crrrruuuhk Crrruuuhk Crrrrruuuuuuuuuuuuhhhhh.

The pessaries were still rooting in the mud, snorting, and the western sun was bending rays through the fence where it set and dimmed. Juan was ready to go, was thanking Adelia de Rosco.

Papa was gone.

Only the aftertaste of the *ayahuasca* brew remained in Manny.

Four more officers who were not on the side of the Sinaloas—two that were loyal to Luis and two that protected neither cartel—were murdered that week. Their bodies turned up in steel drums like the ones he used to hide cocaine in during his runs over the border. They'd been wounded by gunfire and burned, still alive, in gasoline-filled steel cans. All of them had spoken to journalists, and the journalists had been tortured, too.

In response to the violence, the *Autodefensas* rallied in the *zocalo* twice that week.

It was a small group of men the first time, and some women, too, who met by the stone fountain where he'd found Alena's head. The second time they met, a few days later, the group had doubled in size. Many of them covered their faces with balaclavas, revealing only their eyes. Some of the women did not have their faces covered but were there to hear the chanting, to join in the protest. One woman, who had very short arms and legs and who was thick in the middle, had her hair pulled tightly away, revealing linear notches scarred into the skin of her face that were not darkened by the sun. She shouted that her baby had been killed by the cartel. Another woman beside her had a black *Autodefensa* shirt on and a red bandana tied tightly around her head, not unlike a like a pirate. She shouted that her sister had been disappeared, demanded an end to the murders in Juarez.

It was illegal to carry firearms for protection, but the officers of law were not protecting anything.

The leaders of the *Autodefensa* rolled down the *Avenue* just as the municipal and the federal police did, wearing Kevlar, standing on the backs of trucks. Many of them were known to be previous distributors or drug mules or *halcones,* swearing in false witness that they had changed, that they were not involved with any cartel now, nor any of the cartels' violent and rivaling gangs like *La Linea* or the *Zetas* or the *Barrio Azteca*, groups who subcontracted to carry out the murders, the executions, as a profession.

Changed, my ass, he thought.

Both the Sinaloa and the Juarez cartels were aware of the demonstrations, had their eyes and ears out on the eyes and ears, and on anyone suspected of being a rat—and now, even on ones who weren't. Wire taps and cell taps were routine then, and anyone important was certain that they were having their whereabouts tracked.

Manny was sitting outside the restaurant with Juan when the shouting got loud. He'd just gotten his food from the half-gringo waitress that liked him too much, the one who hovered over him when he came into the restaurant. She always kept his glass full and brought him grilled shrimp skewers and crab cakes even when he did not order them—except the few times when he'd come in with Alena, when she'd ignored him. She set down Juan's drink now and Juan ordered a drink for Luis, thanked her.

She was pretty with plump skin and a delicate chin, and her black apron was tied tightly and smelled like the grill in the back kitchen, and she seemed to live in the same pair of platform heels that made her almost five–foot-five. He'd asked her a few times already what she was doing there, why she was in Juarez. It didn't make sense. But her eyes always twitched, and she came up with a different story each time he'd asked, so today he left it alone. Luis was pleased with the catch they'd brought back from the Gulf, said he wanted to celebrate with them, but he was late.

"He's not late," said Juan. "He's chicken shit."

26

"He'll be here," Manny said.

"He knows about the *Autodefensas*. He's getting jumpy, Manny. When's the last time he threw a party? He's been keeping a low profile now, doesn't want to be out in public."

"Luis loves to be seen."

"But he hasn't been."

The sea bass he ordered was served whole; the head was not removed. It looked up at him from the plate with leaden eyes and fins crisped on either side. The waitress set beside it a smooth tequila in a thin glass and a side of rice. He cut the head off the fish. Inside it was stuffed with bread crumbs, peppers, crab. He chewed the flesh and he scooped up a bit of rice, and he sipped his tequila and he looked to the *zocalo,* where the shouting was intensifying.

The rally didn't last long before the *Federales* rolled in. Black helmets, boots. Automatics. Standing on the backs of their trucks. One of them got down off the back of their truck and told one of the men to hand over his weapon or he'd face arrest, and the *Federale* collected the weapons from several others at the rally. Then the one who was driving an Explorer behind him got out and he gave a long speech and said that everything was under control, said that the men and women would not be arrested if they handed over their guns peacefully.

Most of the *Federales* had their faces covered, too. They carried MP5s and AR15s, and after they had collected the weapons, they did something strange.

They gave them back to three of the *Autodefensas*, the three leaders in the front of the crowd. Manny knew then that the Sinaloas that had infiltrated the *Autodefensa* group, too, because those men weren't with Luis.

And the Sinaloas weren't hurting for guns, either. He'd even heard that they had enough money to manufacture their own. Maybe they already were.

One of the *Federales* stood on the back of the truck, and began shouting into the crowd with a megaphone, said that they would allow the leaders to keep the guns if they remained peaceful. The men receiving the redistributed AR15's and Uzis and MP5s and a few Colt pistols, had somehow bought two truckloads of *Federales* along with the small arsenal of automatic rifles and pistols, just like everything and everybody else in Juarez was bought.

These purchases meant that things were getting worse for Luis.

Another one of the *Federales* got out of his truck and began collecting weapons from the back of the group. Some of the women tried to hide pistols in their clothing, but the *Federale* patted them down front and back, grabbing them in lewd handfuls. Then the *Federale* searched their bags, taking all the money he found inside. The *Federale's* face was not covered, and in the evening, when the lights shined on the fountain and reflected brightly in the center of the *zocalo*—where the fountain drowned out the shouting and violent chanting with an innocent, mellifluous rushing, trickling sound—this *Federale* was easily recognizable.

He was thick in the chest and short and he was the man who had stopped him a few years ago near El Porvenir, made him crawl on the ground with the scorpions. This *Federale*—Cordoba was his name—gave three Colt pistols and an AR to a man on one the side of the gathering.

Manny recognized the man who received the guns—he was a police officer known to be on *La Linea*, the police arm that took side with the Juarez Cartel, and Manny had seen his doughy face in the restaurant more than a few times, but not lately.

Luis had still not arrived when the sun sank beneath the horizon and still, he and Juan waited for him on the patio. He sipped the tequila and he scooped a larger mouthful of the rice. Juan was saying something about Pilar, asking him what he was planning to do with the peasant girl after her baby came, said that she was already getting tired and lazy and that their mother would be taking care of her rather than Pilar taking care of them, and Juan said that Pilar would be exhausted and in no shape to work with an infant.

"Where did you find that woman anyway?" Juan asked.

"Jalisco."

"When were you in Jalisco?"

"Juan, in the last two months, I've been places in this country I didn't even know existed." He rubbed his brow where it tensed in ropy bands.

"You love her."

"No, nothing like that."

"What, then?"

He looked out into the *zocalo* and back at Juan. "I feel sorry for her."

"She should feel sorry for you, *mi hermano*." Juan was laughing. "You're a sad story, Manny."

"I am not."

"You are. You're sad. Pathetic, brother."

"I'm not sad."

"And what are you going to do with the baby? Ma is in no shape to hear a baby crying all night. She already stays up worrying about you. She'll never sleep."

Juan kept talking, but Manny was closely watching the confrontation across the street, realizing how close it was to the end of Luis' control of the plaza, and that turned his stomach. The sea bass that was still looking up at him lifeless and flaccid from the plate.

He finished a pitcher of sangria, toasted to the fishing business. Juan teased him, toasted to his newborn baby, and Manny got up and took Juan in a chokehold, but they were both drunk at this time and both were laughing.

When the stars finally popped in the sky, Luis had not arrived.

Juan said, "I told you he wasn't coming. Not with that rally over there. We should get home, too. Ma's probably blowing up your phone."

He checked his phone, but their mother hadn't called once. "I've got a lot to do tonight."

Across the *Avenue*, in the *zocalo*, the *Federales* were still making the rounds. Cordoba spoke in husky gestures and in words that could not be heard over the fountain but he did not see Colonel Gutierrez of the *Division of Antidrogas*; he was not there tonight, not part of this corrupt little banana republic exaltation, but the *Federales* he could see had their uniform decorated in the same gaudy way that resembled Gutierrez's, with all the stars, and the same cheap little fish that Colonel Gutierrez had worn on his uniform the day he was stopped.

"Juan," he said, and he pushed the seabass away, finished his tequila, and finished Luis', too.

The rally was breaking up, but there were dissenting voices growing into a cacophony of blurred noise now.

"Juan," he said again.

"Rally's over." Juan's attention returned to the table. He cut more of his steak and he took a piece and he bit it and he chewed it like it was very tough.

"Juan, what did he look like?"

"What did who look like?"

"The guy who shot Papa. Who was he?"

Juan chewed, shrugged. "Sinaloa. He had crocodile tattoos all over his arms, and he was Mexican, but his hair was bleached out white like some kind of weird freak."

"Crocodiles."

"Yeah, crocodiles."

"Did he live here?"

"Manny, we were in Mexico City at the time. I don't think so. I don't know."

"But he had crocodile ink."

"Yeah, all over."

"You're sure."

"I don't remember a lot about that day. There are bits and pieces lost, I don't even know if my memory is loyal to me half the time, with all the shit we see, everything I wanna put out of my mind. But I remember the crocodiles."

"A lot of people out there probably have crocodile tattoos."

"Yeah, probably."

"I've seen them."

"Where are you going?"

"I have something I have to finish."

"How about dinner? I'm not waiting around for Luis."

"You don't have to, Juan. I'm not waiting around, either."

In the *zocalo,* the crowd dispersed. The *Federales* rolled down the *Avenue* with two of them standing on each of the backs of their three trucks, faces covered, black helmets, chests slung diagonal with rifles. Manny hurried away from the table. He opened the gate at the edge of the patio, and he thanked the hostess, and he told her that Luis would take care of their check and she said, "Of course," and she kissed his cheek and he looked back and he winked at her.

Juan was wiping his mouth with the white napkin; he called, "Manny, wait."

27

That night, he did not go home. He drove The Apple over to Piranha's, all the way out to El Porvenir. He wasn't even sure Piranha still lived there, and if Manny had been driving anything else, he might have been shot pulling up the drive. He walked through a bed of weeds and burned thistle brush, around to the back of the house, and he opened the door. The screen door hinges creaked, and the door slammed against the frame, and Piranha's mom jumped up from the sofa when she heard his footsteps, screamed, "*Ayuadamde! Ayuadame!*" Help me!

When Piranha's mom, Dell, realized it was him, she grabbed him, and she hugged him. Tears came to her eyes. She sniffled away something melancholy and torpid and coughed a hungered rasp. She wore narrow jeans with a belt made of a metal chain and her eyes were rimmed with coal and her smile broke toward her cheek in crooked red lipstick. Her lungs resounded their beautiful destruction from years of smoking, and her teeth were like dried black corn under her lips. From her mouth, cocaine wheezed, faint and breathy.

"Where's Josef?" he asked.

She said it was good to see him, said that she wished he would come around more like when he and Piranha were boys. She pointed to the room off the kitchen. He knocked on the door once, entered.

Piranha lay on the bed, staring away minutes, hours, lying in some outer darkness on a ruined mattress soiled and misshapen. On his nightstand was a candle. Lighters. Spoons. Glass pipes, their burned ashes. A tiny statue of Mary, with a serpent at her feet and her arms outstretched, stood on the night table. A pizza crust lay beside it and a clock radio with digital red lights, sounding a constant nasal blare. There were needles used and long, and thin ones yet unwrapped, and a powdered layer dusting the tables like the fouled remains of some toxic alchemy.

The skin of Piranha's arms, where the sleeves of his t-shirt ended, was covered in blisters, purulent and sour-smelling. They bubbled in semicircular boils where leathery lumps, resembling the skin of reptiles, rose from the flesh, wet where they wept, and flaky, desiccated, at the bases of the wounds.

He shook him. "We gotta do something."

Piranha stared blankly, and unregistered, said, "Manny," when he regarded him.

"Come on, get up." He lifted Piranha under the armpit, where puss drained warm through the black cotton.

Piranha groaned, gripping the hollow of his axilla where another abscess eroded his flesh.

"Jesus, we gotta get you straight. What are you shooting?"

Piranha didn't speak.

"What are you using, Piranha?"

"Heroin."

"Heroin doesn't do this shit to you on its own. What kind of crap are you getting?"

"Heroin. Been getting a real good deal on it. I help this guy, he helps me."

"I need your help, too, man. Get up."

"I don't want to go anywhere. Hey, where have you been, man? I haven't seen you in months. You don't want to help defend the guys like me getting shot up. I mean, I ask you to help— we got a shit ton of guns—big guns—like the *Federales* use— AK47s and AR15s and, and a bunch of guys who can stand up, and—you turn your back. And now you're here. You're in with your brother and his men. Somebody said to me Luis is your real brother. And now you're here asking me for something— what are you asking me for? You know I'd do anything for you, Manny. I'd do anything. But what do you want? What is it now?"

"You're doing coke, too. Jesus. You're talking a mile a minute. We're going to find somebody. Somebody I need to take care of."

"Take care of."

"Yeah."

"Oh, you mean like that."

"Yeah."

Piranha got up, ran his fingers through his hair. Eyes drunken, falling into his skull where the lids draped heavy, deep. Then Piranha put on a black and silver cap and began to pick at one of the infected boils on his forearm and he took a roll of medical gauze and began to wrap it around the blister where it seeped sanguineous fluid, thin, dripping.

Piranha said, "I got a temperature."

"You're gonna die if you keep this up." Manny hugged him, slapped him hard on the back and pulled him tight. His frame seemed to melt, rachitic and weak, against Manny's grip. Then Manny told him they were taking a ride.

"What the hell happened to this truck, Manny?" Piranha asked about The Apple when they were on the highway back to Juarez.

"I was wondering the same thing about you. If you got a fever, you gotta see a doctor. Maybe you need medicine, antibiotics. Come on."

"You know doctors, too, now, Manny?"

"Yeah."

"Okay."

The engine of The Apple had a knock that could not be ignored. The belts whinnied like an Azteca mare muscled and wild, and the breaks screamed a fearful, metal shearing. The hood was dirtied with mud, had not been washed in months, and he hadn't waxed it again once after the night with Ramiro. From the rearview mirror hung Alena's scapular and the two delicate bones of her neck, clicking against one another, clacking louder together each time The Apple rumbled over a pothole. He was a playing a *narcocorrido* on the radio, *El Senor de los Cielos*. Piranha called him out on it, called him a *Narco* cowboy, mentioned his charro boots.

He told Piranha never to bring up his boots again.

"Easy, Manny." Piranha picked at his arm. "I was just teasing you. You know how you used to go back and forth with Ramiro, calling him a fat fuck. I miss that."

"I miss him, too."

"Yeah, I miss him."

He flipped the station. The mountains appeared sandy in the distance where the firefly rows of city lights came on, and he lit a cigarette, drove west very fast. The air conditioner was broken and blowing only suffocating hot air out of the vents. He opened the window all the way so that he felt the warm air on his skin, cooling his sweat, his nerves, and he offered Piranha a cigarette.

"I thought you don't smoke in here."

"I only smoke before I have to do a job." When he turned the station again, his wrist shook.

"How many jobs you done?"

"Not many."

"Not many."

"Yeah, not too many."

"What kind of jobs you do?" Piranha took the cigarette and he removed a lighter buried deep in the pockets of his canvas pants where they bunched loose on his gaunt frame, but he did not light the smoke then. He took out an army knife and he made an incision across a large pustule on his forearm and another incision perpendicular to it like a cross, did the same against a boil on the inside of his left upper arm. Pus seeped from the boil and he took a gauze pad from his pants pocket and he applied pressure, said, "Fuck, this shit hurts. Where the hell are we going, Manny?"

"Piranha, that's disgusting. That's disgusting." He covered his mouth with his right arm and drove on with his left.

"Smells like almonds, Manny. You know what that means? That means it's infected. Where are we going? I don't got no gun, no money, nothing to keep me high. You wanna tell me where it is you're taking me?"

"Piranha, that day I saw you in the *zocalo*—the day of the shooting, when Alena was killed—there were some guys."

"There were a lot of guys, Manny." Piranha put the cigarette between his teeth now and he covered it where the wind from

Manny's window blew upon him, clearing the stench a little, and he lit it. "Is this about your girl?"

"There was a guy there. He was with a bunch of kids—like kids our age when our lives started to, you know, when they started to go down, or up, however you wanna look at it. You know, when we were young. They were like fourteen and he was like twenty or thirty maybe. He was rough looking and had yellow hair like a big gringo, but he had dark skin."

"Dark-skin gringo? I know a lot of everybody, but I don't know any dark-skinned gringos, and no light-skinned ones, either. Not on this side. Not in Juarez."

"Not a gringo. I said he had hair like a gringo. It was dyed blonde and done like a pretty boy in crusty little spikes. And his arms were covered in tattoos of crocodiles. All over his arms, he was inked up with crocodiles."

"Why didn't you say the part about the crocodiles in the first place?"

"I don't know. You know the guy I'm talking about?"

"He's a dealer."

"Your dealer?"

Piranha shrugged. "One of 'em."

"Where does he live?"

"You want me to tell you where one of the guys who gets my heroin lives so you can go and pop him off. You really are crazy, Manny."

"Where is he?"

"Manny."

"He shot my father."

Piranha laughed. "He didn't kill your Papa, Manny. That's impossible. You said your father was shot in Mexico City."

"He had tattoos, just like what I told you."

"A lot of people have tattoos. A lot of people probably have tattoos of crocodiles."

"Where is he?"

"You know what? You never killed anybody, so you're not killing Berto. I never knew you to kill a lizard, or a man inked up with lizards. You're full of shit. I need to see him, though."

"Whatever you're doing, you need to get off of it."

"You think I know where he lives. A guy like that doesn't tell you where he lives. I know where he does business. Get off here."

By then, they were in Fabens in a neighborhood not as bad as Piranha's, but still part of Murder Valley. The truck was rattling something he couldn't understand, a warning language or some ancient premonition, where they rolled down 43d Street. The oil was low, but there was enough to make it back to the *estancia* without stalling. Piranha told him to turn left twice and then right. He pulled The Apple to a stop and from under the seat, he removed his Colt, and he shoved it Mexican-carry style down the back of his pants. He told Piranha to take the other one that was in the glove box. Then he laughed.

"What?" said Piranha.

"You tried to shoot those Columbians with a damned paintball gun."

"I saved your life, man. I got us out of there."

"I'm gonna save yours."

"You're not killing anybody, Manny. Let's talk to him. I need to talk to him."

"We'll talk."

"Manny, you're crazy. Only people like me who want drugs, something to pick them up out of this life, go looking for Berto. Otherwise, you don't go looking for a guy like him. He goes looking for you."

"He should know I'm untouchable then, who my brother is."

Piranha laughed. "You really believe some shit, don't you, Manny. You may be dead right, but that's still dead."

"I'm not dying tonight."

"Does he owe you money?"

He parked The Apple in front of the house in the valley where a black Maserati was shining moonlit fenders. He pulled up close to it on the lawn, past cement drainage pipes, and went around to the back of the house. He assumed the front door had cameras on it at every angle, and he looked for cameras at the back door, too, but there were none. He shot the lock off the door, stepped inside.

Techno music was vibrating the drywall where it was crumbled away, and when he burst open the door, the shrill crescendo of some woman's scream rose over it from the front of the house, and the sound of a man's heavy feet, creaking the floor boards, came toward him. Manny went immediately through the kitchen to the front of the small house, toward the living room, where the walls were covered in a green and yellow floral paper split linear in many places, torn away in some patches and burned brownish yellow in others. He was wearing the cowboy boots he'd bought in El Paso with Alena. There was a fine spray of clear, broken glass on the floor and it crunched, grinding beneath the boots.

He saw Berto before he saw the naked woman run screaming into the kitchen and out of it again. She had large breasts and short hair, a bottom shaped like an apple, and her flesh bounced lightly where it was tight. Manny pulled the Colt out and clicked back the hammer.

Berto was naked, too, and he covered his front side with a blanket that looked used often but not washed once. The blanket did not cover the tattoos. Manny saw the crocodiles drawn across the inside of Berto's chest and across his abdomen, his groin, extending down into his skin mural of a mangrove, this muscular and reptilian swamp that crossed his midline.

"You shot my father, in Mexico City. Ayala was his name. Jorge Ayala."

Berto's head shook furiously; he said to Piranha, "What's the meaning of all this, kid?" To Manny, he insisted, "I haven't been to Mexico City since I was a boy."

"Neither have I." His hand was trembling now, and the techno music was pounding a cacophony of evil, premeditated and virile, full of testosterone, in both of his ears. "The last time was with my father."

Berto ran for the end table, reached to open the drawer.

Manny swept Berto's ankle, knocking him to the floor. Berto crawled, snaking toward the end table again where a round lamp sat, white and cracked like a prehistoric egg. Berto knocked it over, clumsily groping for a gun.

"You're that *pendejo* kid that works the restaurant, sometimes the fish market, with your brother."

"You know those places well."

"You know, the one Juan, the fishmonger owns. And Luis' restaurant. Don't tell me you don't know who Luis Barrios is. Everybody knows Luis."

"Yeah, that's me. He's my brother."

Berto swallowed. "This is a mistake. Tell him, Josef. I never killed nobody in Mexico City. Never. Never."

Piranha shrugged. "I tried to tell him. Sometimes my friend doesn't listen to me."

The woman was still screaming, "Berto," and her hands and her sides quivered like the wings of hummingbirds. Her breathing was sucking gasps of air, rapid, unable to settle. Tears ruined her eyes black and smeared diluted makeup down both of her cheeks.

28

Berto's head turned, serpentine, observing as an iguana does the heated desert, and his neck wrinkled like an iguana, too, like the one Juan had as a pet whose skin Manny would peel off in thin sheets as it molted. Berto was groping for his clothes, the gun, any weapon to defend himself, but Manny was cold then, an unyielding machine. Before Berto could pick up the bat, he fired a shot, but he did not hit Berto. He stared at Berto writhing, without empathy. Then his ears settled from the noise and he paused. On the wall his reflection faced him in a dim mirror hung crooked and fingerprinted and coated, dusty. He fired another shot and it hit Berto's shoulder and Berto screamed out, and Manny regarded his trembling hand and his reflection and, in his hand, the Colt.

"I didn't kill your father," Berto screamed. "I never been to Mexico City in years, kid."

He could not look away from the mirror at that moment, staring at that other man staring back at him, as if there were some imagined standoff holding his gaze. Piranha said he needed to leave; he kept urging him, insisting, saying that they needed to get the hell out of there fast. He knew that this was true, that he needed to go, but he could not move then. He was paralyzed with some brand of fear in that house. It was the wrong place. It was all wrong. And it was not where he needed to be.

He grabbed the mirror from the wall, and he shattered it at Berto's feet where Berto lay gripping his left shoulder. Berto's arm hung flaccid, lifeless.

Piranha was pulling at his arm, but Manny shook him off. Berto was still screaming on the floor, begging to be shot up with narcotic. He called out, "Elzbeta," to the woman, who had hid in the closet and was still calling for help herself, panicking. Manny opened the closet where she sat with her head to her knees, crouched, and she got up at once and she ran out of the closet, naked and screaming, hitting him, clawing with her fingernails, throwing punches.

"It's okay. Okay. I'm not going to hurt you." He looked around, disbelieving everything around him, his world corrupted and violent and predetermined, a living, breathing thing controlling him.

The woman grabbed her dress from the floor and she ran into the kitchen and then she ran out of the house.

"Berto, where's the stuff you've been selling me?" asked Piranha.

"He fucked you up, Piranha. Are you kidding me?"

Piranha's arms drained red pustules infected and boiled up in lumps that resembled the leathery skin of lizards, or prehistoric crocodiles, even. Manny grabbed the keys to the Maserati where they lay on the end table. He put the gun to Berto's head again and he asked, "What are you selling without my permission?"

"Your permission?" Berto coughed, spit out blood. He was short of breath now, and it was clear that the bullet had hit his lung.

Manny hit him, hard, with the barrel of the Colt backhanded, leaving a wide gash in Berto's forehead where the skin split. "My territory, my permission."

"It's not heroin. Not cocaine. Not weed, you gap-toothed bitch." Berto spit out more blood. "Last time I checked, Luis didn't sell krokodil."

"You don't sell tamales through my brother's plaza without his permission, *bitch*, and you're undercutting us with cheap, knockoff heroin? Did you make it here? With gasoline?" Manny kicked Berto in the ribs and he spat on the floor and he looked around.

Berto had been there, dealing his product before the shooting in the *zocalo*.

There was a Mason jar of caramel colored liquid on the floor in the kitchen, gallons of paint thinner, a red effluvium dusting the table with the phosphorus from the striking strip of a matchbox. A hotplate burner set with a glass vial filled with rancid coffee-colored fluid on its surface, sizzling, stuck up with large-bore needles dipping into the black soup.

He shook his head. "You were there. You were selling in the *zocalo* when she was shot."

"Who was shot?"

A purple and blue afghan draped over the couch and an artist's pottery wheel stood in the corner. The shelves were covered with dozens of trinket mementos with memories, glazed and shiny, remnants of family holidays long past, some other time in the lore of fallen children that could never be returned to their rightful period. The upholstery was torn and popping chunks of yellow foam onto the carpet where it was worn threadbare. A bottle of nasal spray was on the table, a jar of grape jelly, an empty chicken nugget container—and keys.

Maybe this dealer, Berto, didn't kill his father; maybe he'd made a mistake, made some sick and inaccurate justification with the devil, but he'd already forgiven himself for it. Berto was killing his friend, the only one he had left, and Berto might have had something to do with the night Alena died. That was enough for him to kill.

The techno music intensified, louder, thumping in sync with his heart, his heated pulse, the way the sweat beaded at the bulge of his artery in his temple, and he felt the urge to do it.

Wasn't that enough reason in this place?

Juarez.

People lost their lives here every night over smaller slights than that.

The shards of the mirror were at his feet, revealing his reflection in rogue flashes.

Piranha was the closest thing he had to a friend left, if Piranha could be saved. Even Juan was pissed off at him more times than not, and he swore he was going to fix that, too—starting today. He had to help Piranha get straight, keep his mom and Elvie out of danger, and Pilar, her baby, too. He had to break ties with Luis. He wasn't sure if Luis trusted him, and there was no way he trusted Luis, and if he kept going with that connection, it could only end one way, running, running, running, running, until it ended. This relationship with his brother—the powerful one, was pretty much unsustainable any way he looked at it.

But he did not know how to sustain himself if he ran from this life, or if he could. Maybe he'd be killed, hunted down, and it would all end like that.

Still, he wanted to, wanted to run.

He would not flee as an animal flees in fear, not as an object of prey; he was not that creature, but he would go elsewhere to hunt, to find a new place and establish all he was there. He could be something else. He craved it, and it ate at him now.

Berto reached for the pistol in the end table drawer again, and found it this time, with his good arm. Manny kicked it and it flew in Piranha's direction. Piranha reached down, picked it up. He could smell the gangrene as Piranha stood near him. Manny gagged, covered his mouth. There were scars down Piranha's skin like leather, rippling in scaly folds of pink and white flesh, eaten away where he'd injected the desomorphine, the krokodil. This animal, krokodil, had consumed Piranha's skin in paled rings that looked like oversized cigarette burns on the meaty areas, and it had stripped away tissue, exposing muscle and bone in others.

29

Berto 's hand waffled the pistol imprecise, jerky, as though he was inebriated, or high. He smirked, and he spat on Manny's *charro* boot. The crocodiles on Berto's skin smiled their shit grins. "They come to me when they can't afford anything else."

Piranha did not protest, said, "Manny, I couldn't. I couldn't afford anything. Not even to eat. I bought from him. I'm sorry, man."

Manny spit on Berto, kicked the gun from his hand and twisted the heel of his boot into Berto's shoulder, said, "These boots were my girlfriend's favorite … *pendejo*."

He grabbed the gasoline can on the coffee table and he spilled it about the room. Then he stuck a match and he tossed the match where Berto lay on the floor. He grabbed Piranha around the chest, raced into the next room. A rush of air and an ignition of flames, immediate and hot and bright, covered the rug surrounding Berto.

"You make a mess out of people's lives. Find your way out of this one," he said.

"You and me, we're the same beast," Berto called, batting out the fire where it ignited his sleeve, where the arm had been shot, where it looked numb, hanging, where he clutched it at his side. Berto scrambled to his feet and stumbled on and up toward the front door.

Manny looked back, staring at the blaze, for a moment enjoying in nihilist rapture the image he'd created; yet he was ambivalent, already knowing his revenge would be short-lived. His gaze broke quickly, and he ran out the back, through the kitchen, expecting the place to explode.

And it did.

He threw himself on the ground, holding his head, and his ears, and he dove into a weedy bed of dusty mustard weeds and dead scrub bush, just beside a saguaro cactus, which he missed as he skidded to the ground.

Then the boom came from the kitchen.

30

Piranha was on the ground beside him, covering his ears, his head, too.

He got to his feet and he tossed Piranha the keys to the Maserati, and Piranha followed The Apple out of the valley and onto the highway, all the way to Juarez, fast. The horizon ahead zigzagged purple with heat lightning but there was no rain around, no water to wash The Apple. It was filthy. The lightning stuck close by and several times, he jumped nervously in his seat. He'd been trying to rescue something within him and to find a cure for Juarez by assimilating into himself these ways that disregarded the value of his soul, acknowledging only the tribal and innate and lawless passions that ran machinations, cursed and fallen; but these were contradictory ends that could not both be satisfied.

If he would survive this place, it could be only at the expense of all the once-enjoyed things that had been stolen by it—love, for one, and not only romantic love. There were things that had once made him happy like the smell of cinnamon on bananas, the new smell in The Apple, and every friend he'd ever known. Even if he remained here, still living to hear the rush of the brook at the *estancia*, feeling its coolness over the river stones weathered round by the gentle water, he could only love the effect of nostalgia torturing him, reminding him that there were once things of beauty and pleasure innocent and untested that now were not.

He learned the following Monday, when the moon was full, and he was sitting beside the fountain in the *zocalo,* that Berto had escaped the blaze. The faint scent of something like Alena's gardenia perfume reached him in the air once but he could not find it twice. He worried that Luis would be furious with him for allowing Berto to escape after discovering that Berto was selling cheap heroin on this side of the border to men who couldn't afford any better, because now there was no doubt that Berto was also selling the good stuff, through Luis' *plaza*, on the other side of it.

Luis said nothing to him about it, and he asked nothing of him, but later that week, Berto's body turned up in the *zocalo,* charred, in a steel barrel, and Luis congratulated Manny on discovering Berto's freelance operation. Luis toasted to Berto with a smooth reposado tequila over a dinner of grilled shrimp and skirt steak, though Manny did not tell him then or ever that he had pursued Berto in a fit of rage that had nothing to do with Berto's dealing.

Later that month, on the first day of Holy Week, Manny was minding the store front. He had not gone to mass, but he enjoyed watching the Nazarenes who passed down the *Avenue,* carrying crosses with heads crowned in marigolds, and the women carrying braided palms, enacting the passion play of *Iztapalapa* like the one his father had taken him to see in Mexico City when he was a boy. His eyes glazed over, wet, and he wiped them, and he turned, and he walked to the back and he pulled the curtain to see what was happening in the back room.

Juan was at the wooden table, examining the books. It was Juan's favorite place to sit. He always said that he felt the most in control of his world there, where the gouges on the table told the stories of knives where the table had been scratched. Juan had carved crosses and a rendering of his boat and the sacred heart of Jesus on that table in angst, and he'd filleted fish upon it, and there was still blood on the table from when Gusto had cut off a man's hand for stealing, selling, and not paying his share of the *piso* to Luis. Juan had been unable to wash the blood and the smell of the fish from the table completely, but it did not bother Manny any longer. A lot of things did not bother him as they once did.

Luis was sitting at the table, speaking in a tone indomitable, righteous. His voice intensified, arguing, going back and forth with Juan about not giving him enough of a cut on the totoabas. Manny swallowed, entered the back room; he had to. Usually, matters with Luis were settled quickly unless they were not settled. Luis and Juan had been back there for some time.

Luis offered Juan the chance to step up to the plate more, to help the family, and Juan now refused.

Luis seemed to want Juan's acceptance, his loyalty—but the more he demanded it, the more Juan rejected any sanguine link between them.

Gusto's voice took the shape of a blade now as he said, "A few weeks ago, I happen to be by your mother's place, and I happen to see you digging, so I looked into things while you were gone."

"You were on my property?" Juan placed both palms on the table, rose from it.

"Do you know what I found?" Gusto was rolling a cigar between his fingers. The shiny scar on the finger he'd lost glistened, the amputated digit moving as an awkward stub.

"I found a brass trunk full of money." Gusto held a peso in his thumb and his index finger. He held it up before Juan.

"Stay off my property."

Gusto lit a cigar.

Juan said, "There's no smoking in here."

The tension between Juan and Gusto gripped the two of them; it gripped Manny, too, like the two of them had a vice grip between his legs, punching his groin, knotting his crotch. The look on Gusto's face resembled pleasure and the look on Juan's could not be mistaken for anything but disdain.

"My apologies, *mi hermano*," said Gusto, stubbing out the cigar.

"Anything on my property belongs to me."

"That's not untrue, provided you're paying my boss what you owe him. Isn't that right, Manny?"

"Juan's not keeping anything from you." He surprised himself at how quick he was to defend Juan, and he began to feel the avatar of some sinuous beast rising around them, or a destructive machine that rattled premonitory among the four of them, igniting its terrible engine, ready to grind to pulp everything before it. He picked up the glass on the table and he spat tobacco into it; he'd only picked up the habit of chewing it last week.

"Business has been slow. People are afraid to come out to the market. The violence drives them to their homes, like the people of rocks and caves. Look outside. The streets are empty, except for the eyes and ears and the machinery of the cartels. Even Luis' restaurant is empty."

"I'll speak for my restaurant, Emmanuel," said Luis, picking at his teeth with the edge of a switchblade. The handle had the same skin as his Colt, a black and white skeleton shining with a chrome outlay. Luis put his feet on the table.

"Sorry," he said. "But—"

"*De nada*." Luis drank from his glass, licked his teeth. "Juan, my books suggest that we're short the same amount that we found in your yard, by the river."

"You're full of shit," said Juan, although as he said it, a thick lump in his throat rose quickly and fell slowly.

"Easy," said Luis.

Gusto drank now, too. "There's still the matter of payment, Juan. Each of your special catches commands a filthy sum, an amount shamefully tainted with the guilt of the beautiful, endangered creatures whose lives you risk when you throw out your nets. How many baby porpoises have you ensnared pulling in your totoabas for those small-pricked Brazilian Chinks?"

"I pay you your share. What's mine is mine."

"It would be a shame if the *Federales* discovered your aquatic cocaine operation."

"You can't run your restaurant without my fish market."

Luis laughed, said, "The restaurant."

Gusto said, "The penalty for such an illegal fishing operation must be very stiff."

"What would you know about stiff, you limp-dicked *pendejo*?"

"I said easy."

Juan rose now and grabbed the coin from Gusto's deformed digits. He held the bronze peso before Luis' eyes, asked, "Whose face is on this coin?"

"*Xiuhtecuhtli.*" Luis spit on the floor.

"Octavio Paz." Juan flipped the coin at Luis.

"Pay to Luis, what is due to Luis, *mi hermano*." Luis caught the coin, with basilisk eyes unmoving, that emerged icy, through a smug grin.

"You are not the God you pretend to be," Juan said, "*mi hermano*."

Luis pressed his Colt to Juan's forehead.

31

Luis slammed Juan against the steel refrigerator in the core of the market where Juan kept his unsold catches, the best filets of salmon and tuna and swordfish, and Luis pushed Juan inside, past the strips of clear plastic hanging frosted and stiff, and told him he would let him rot with the fish until he realized where his loyalty was. Then he left him there with the door shut until Manny spoke, calling the bluff.

"You miserable step child." He drew his own Colt and he pointed it at Luis. His hands trembled with a brand of fear he'd never known before this moment. At once, he regretted his words, but he said, quietly, "Let him out."

Luis froze.

"Emmanuel," said Luis. "That hurts."

It was the first time Luis had called him by name. He'd been certain he didn't know it anymore.

Luis opened the door.

Manny knew that Luis was losing money, but it didn't mean that he was increasing his payouts, as he should've been, to save his *plaza*. The cartel could not continue to exist without the layers of corruption the *capo* had built it on, the illusion of law. Instead, Luis had gotten tighter, which was his first mistake.

Luis told Manny that he felt the whole cartel was going to collapse, and now Luis seemed to be holding onto his immeasurable fortune with the fear of a miser. Luis' second mistake was not delegating more responsibility to the other *sicarios*, because he'd grown paranoid.

Gusto was the only one Luis still trusted—and Manny, who shared his blood, which made Manny's decision so much more difficult.

When Manny got home, he started digging.

He dug at every spot he remembered marking on the map, every spot that he'd charted. He'd hidden the map in his mother's hollow bench in the courtyard of the *estancia*—but the map was missing, and the bench was left wide open. The trunks of bills were gone, too. It was obvious from the Mexican cigar stubs, Gusto's shameless calling cards, that Gusto and God-knows-who else, had been there, digging. Manny searched everywhere—there had to be some money left. Between the payments from the totoabas and the jobs for Luis, he and Juan had buried close to a million.

Who knows how long Gusto had been following him, following Juan. Maybe he even had their calls bugged.

He searched another patch of burned-out grass, across the river, a spot where Elvie rode the Appaloosa now through the stream and across from a point that only he knew because it often dried to a trickle right there. And he searched the spot one hundred feet from the almond trees, where his mother liked to nap in the hammock when she drank too much of the *Casa Medero* cabernet wine that against his better judgement, she had him buying by the case. It smelled permanently of bitter chocolate and vanilla and woodsy almonds there where she often spilled the wine, and it often smelled faintly of money and turned earth, but today it did not; it smelled palpably of fear.

Gusto had cleaned out the yard. He swore now and he threw the shovel and he kicked the dirt. He swallowed, and he thought hard, knowing, that Gusto knew that his loyalty was feigned. Those eyes of Gusto's that clouded with cataract in shrewd, blue-grey curtains, saw beyond what Gusto's sight did not. He swore again, and he kicked the dust until his boots were covered red with it, and it made him cough. He punched the oak by the river where it had dried, but the tree did not move.

He squatted, held his head.

Pilar came out into the yard now. She was round and large. Her face was swollen and covered with melasma, like his mother's. Her eyes narrowed, and she offered him a glass of cactus juice and she said that he had looked, from the window, as though he was coming down with tertian fever or had been bitten by a scorpion.

"I'm fine," he said.

"No, let me see," she insisted. "Let me see your hands."

"I'm fine," he shouted. He threw her hand from his forearm, where the skin was exposed and where his sleeves were rolled up past his elbows. He held his hand a moment and then he washed it in the stream, and he sank to the rocks, put his head back in his hands.

He saw her wipe her eye as she turned, and he stood again, said, "I'm sorry. Listen. We're going to have to leave, soon, now. I want you to tell my mother to pack everything she needs in two bags she can carry, and to get Elvie ready, too, be ready when I give the word."

"But the baby, the nursery. Where will I go? I like it here. I like you, Enriqua, I love Elvie. This life is not like in the mountains. I can work here. I cannot return to the mountains."

"Once your baby comes, you'll forget about us."

"That's not true. Don't say these things. You've been good to me."

"You can't stay here forever. You won't want to."

"You don't want me to."

"I have no kind of life to offer you or a child. I never was one myself."

She began to cry.

"Don't do that. I like you, Pilar. You have to trust me, you have to do what I tell you. I'm not going to let anything happen to you. And this is important…you must tell my mother, convince her to do what I'm telling you. Because if I tell her, she's going to beat me like a rattle snake in her vegetable garden and she's not going to listen to a thing I say. She's gonna yell like there really was a scorpion and that scorpion crawled up her ass. And Pilar, I don't know who's listening. I don't. Somebody might hear what we say on the phone, or even in the house. They might know we're going to leave. We can't have any yelling. We can't even have any talking about this, not inside, not on the phone. Do you understand?"

She nodded, gripping her belly.

"Okay, then. When I give the word."

Piranha had been staying at his place since the incident with Berto, but he hadn't left the couch except to piss and to fix himself a drink. He lay there shaking, scratching at bugs that weren't there, and picking at his sores, breathing heavy and moist and hot. The worst of it was when his forehead beaded in sweat and he fell off the couch in unconscious convulsions, violently bucking as the mares did in heat. Manny had taken the keys to the Maserati and hidden the car down the hill. He refused to take him to buy drugs.

"I need a favor." Manny was on the phone with Dr. Manuel Kelley. House calls weren't Kelley's specialty unless they ended with a sewn and tortured corpse. "I got a friend here, and he's in trouble."

"A friend."

"Yeah."

Kelley treated Piranha with an intravenous drip of antibiotics, seemed to find great enjoyment when he incised and drained with scalpels the abscesses in both of Piranha's armpits and on his forearms. Then Kelley smeared the wounds with petroleum and dressed them. He did not offer Piranha pain medication nor anesthesia nor any other drug during the procedure, but he watched Piranha writhe serpentine and convoluted, howling, on the floor, until Enriqua pounded on the door, screaming, demanding to know what was going on, shouting that if there was sodomy taking place, she would burn the house to the ground.

"Relax, Ma," Manny screamed from inside his room. There was an American football on his bed and the smell of sour milk, ripe on his nose, and there were clothes all over the floor. He tried to sop up the mess before Enriqua could get the door unlocked with a hairpin.

32

On Piranha's back were the old scars, pink and white and faded in various stages of healing, the glistening tracks of needles running up his arms where his veins had scarred his skin immobile and leathered. Manny looked then, at Piranha, and he looked at Kelley, and he screamed through the door to his mother to get them some lunch, so that she would leave the door. He saw the true enemy in that room, and he saw everything it had stolen from his friend, and it was not the Sinaloa and it was not Luis nor the Zetas or the Barrios Aztecas.

It was narcotics.

"Once they start krokodil, the life expectancy is under a year." Kelley packed up his medical bag. "Your friend is fucked."

Kelley gave him enough methadone tablets to get Piranha over the worst of the withdrawal symptoms. He said that it would not provide the same high as heroin or krokodil or morphine, but that it would satisfy his body's urge for narcotic.

Manny thanked him, walked him past his mother standing with eyes slit narrow, suspicious, to the door.

Later, long after Kelley had left, he told Piranha that he had fucked up his life and that whether he wanted him to or not, he was going to make sure he didn't kill himself—even if it meant he had to babysit him for the next twenty years. Then Manny hooked up the PlayStation and he went out in The Apple and he brought Piranha back a dinner from the restaurant.

Piranha was sitting up on the couch, but he did not look as though he had the motivation to play video games or even open the Styrofoam container with the grilled swordfish and vegetables and mashed potatoes inside. Piranha only looked at him, weakly, said, "*Gracias, Manny.*"

Manny went to Luis's home later that night. Luis was sitting on the lounge chair and there were two women in the pool swimming naked and Luis told them to get out and to sit beside his brother. One of the women began to kiss Manny's neck and he brushed her away and Luis laughed, asked him if he did not like women.

He said that he did, but there was no smile on his face. He did not laugh at the joke, could not. Luis had stolen his sense of humor from him, too, during that time.

He could not say that he had not enjoyed the company of women since Alena died, but he had not cared for any of them and it was nothing like love. He pitied Pilar, but it was not the same.

Sylvia came out onto the patio with a plate of goat cheese and figs and grilled strips of steak. She was pregnant, though not as large as Pilar, and her face was bruised over the right cheek. There was Bossa nova music playing loud by the outdoor kitchen and a noisy chachalaca calling from the trees beside the pool that could be heard over the speakers. Sylvia looked down and said nothing to Luis, smiled weakly at Manny, turned away.

Manny chewed the steak and he sipped a *cerveza* and he stared off the escarpment at the mountains of Juarez, where they met the sky like an artist had painted them in a chiaroscuro treatment of darkness and light. After a while, he said to Luis, "The job you told me about. I want to take it."

"You want to kill the Sinaloan *capo*. Dolly, are you sure you're up to it?"

"I am."

"Do you know what it means if you do the job?"

"*Si.*"

"It means that every hour of every day, you will be a marked man. And it means that you won't be able to come and go in the little fish market so easily. You won't even be able to show up at the restaurant and dance with the hostesses or have a few drinks at the bar if you like the music that night. And if you think, 'Tonight's a good night to sit out on the patio and watch the *patos* in the *zocalo*,' you cannot always do this. Every time you are seen in public will have to be carefully executed, carefully planned. My security team will have to be there. They'll have to be your security team. You'll no longer be able to drive out to the desert and shoot jack rabbits alone, whenever you please, or drive out to the Valley to play video games with your druggie friend from high school. What's his name?"

"How do you know about Piranha?"

"Dolly," Luis said, chewing. "Come on."

"You've been following me."

"Of course. What do you think, Dolly? I would just allow anyone to access my life, my world, without knowing he was loyal to me?" Luis put down his glass of tequila, dismissed the women, and he hugged Manny and he slapped his back. "Don't worry, Dolly. I trust you. This is a big job, though. Do you understand how big this work is?"

Manny told him he would accept the job, but that he wanted one million in cash and one million dollars transferred to a bank account in his name in George Town.

Luis laughed, tasted his cigar. "Sure, Dolly. I can do that. My money is your money. Our relationship is starting to feel more like family, and that makes me very happy. Does it make you happy, too?"

He swallowed, and nodded, said, "*Si.*"

"Friends like yours come and go," Luis said. "Family cannot be removed. We're tied by blood. You understand now. There's no walking away from family. Not now."

"*Gracias, mi hermano.*" He raised his beer to toast. The glasses clinked, high-pitched, cold, and they sweat beads that dripped as his forehead did now. He perspired thick drops down the valley of his back where it had muscled tense and solid since he'd come to know Luis in this way.

"You'll have the money this afternoon."

"*Gracias.*"

"You going somewhere?" Luis' eyes narrowed.

"No."

"Of course not. My apologies. You've made me so happy, Dolly. Maybe you and I should sail. And Juan, too. It would be good for all of us. Juan, he resists me, but I love you both. We're brothers. You and I, we understand the importance of family. I want to get through to Juan, too. I want to show him my loyalty, if he'll do the same, show me the same respect. We can go to the Caymans and we can go to that little island you like to stop at in the Bahamas."

He did not know how Luis knew about the private island, where the customs guards who worked for the Bahamian government were bought easily, but now he began to sweat more heavily at the collar of his shirt.

"We'll take a trip together soon. We'll sail together. Juan knows the ocean well."

Right then he made his decision.

Luis' promise could have been a moment between brothers that he'd been craving, and it could have been an unconditional love like his fathers' love, and Luis' promise could have led to a beautiful destruction that brought them closer to some ineradicable bond, but it was none of these things on that day or any day; it never had been.

33

That night, he dreamed about doing what he'd promised Luis, and he dreamed about doing a second job, getting the Juarez *capo* out of prison. The dream Alena had had about him in the church seemed far removed from his time, a distant memory, but it was the place he was in now, and he considered how he could ever survive this place.

He could not.

Earlier that night, Elvie had rode her pony around the corral until the sun set. She fed it some apples and carrots and a rutabaga, and she brushed its hair for a long time, and she cleaned its hooves. It was the only time that evening that made him wonder if he could remain here, wonder what sun his life would spin around if he stayed and maintained some allegiance to Luis, if he did not take the money and run.

In the dreams, he was much younger, maybe fourteen again, the age when he had first come to know about Luis' business. In his sleeping mind, he ran as fast as he could, down a narrow alley of Puerto Vallarta, his ankles twisting awry. Uneven cobblestones faulted sideways like tectonic plates that moved mountains from the sea. Beneath his dusty khakis, his black boots were worn, the waxy laces untied. He ran against the wind blowing in off the Bahia de Banderas, panting like a long-coat Chihuahua in heat, darting past a shopfront now in flames, where piñatas blew pendulous in the wind and the mangoes and avocadoes were stacked neatly pyramidal. He could still feel the heat from the blaze, smell the burning gasoline where the garbage in a steel drum had been set ablaze.

The *Federales* followed him on foot.

A left, another left. He looked back. He'd lost them.

He was swift enough on foot to slow down and catch his breath.

It was rainy season on the west coast of Mexico then. Humidity was near one hundred percent in the Jalisco state. Across town, three other set-ups distracted from the more pressing issue.

The *capo's* escape.

Luis had told them to turn their heads, look busy. Be busy with something else, anything else. They'd been told to cover their asses. The guards wouldn't see a thing, his brothers, Juan and Luis, had promised him. He wanted to know how much they were paid.

It was Machiavellian and irrelevant. They'd told him not to worry about such things and that his significance in the plan was more than he could grasp right then, but it would be clear to him as he aged—if he didn't get into trouble and get himself killed first.

A few times, he'd come close.

He'd watched the lieutenants negotiate in the tent, watched the thumping in the men's chests accelerate as Eduardo and Luis spoke. The *capo* was a man with pockmarked skin and his hair was always cut short. He had peppered sideburns, and he spoke in a deep voice and smiled very little. He smoked one cigarette after another and sometimes he alternated them with a cigar.

And in the dream, Luis had explained that the *Federales* would be busy with another matter when the *capo* walked out of prison and that all of the *Federales* downtown would be busy, too, He'd arranged this with the young guard, who would be on duty on the date and shift when the *capo* would walk out of the prison.

In the dream, he'd been there when Luis had had the conversation with the young guard, had given him a clear choice to cooperate or not to cooperate.

Luis had said to the young guard that he could choose not to cooperate, but if he did not, then his men would meet him at his home on the very same evening and tie his entire family to the wooden chairs around the dinner table. First, Luis' men would sit down and enjoy a meal. Then Luis had said, because he was merciful, they would gut his eyes from his skull with a dirty fishing knife because he knew that the man wouldn't want to see what else they might do to his wife and daughters. And Luis said that after it had been done, and he had finished listening to their screams, he would feed his wife the alabaster globes from the tip of the blade and then douse them all in gasoline and light the entire house on fire and watch it burn, said he would feel nice and warm under the stars, watching it burn.

Manny had stood against the prison door and watched silently. They'd agreed to cooperate with the plan. They'd all agreed. *Si. Si.* They'd nodded, their faces only partly feigning humility, pretending to hide the change overtaking them from within, but he'd seen it, the internal contest between good and evil. It was a brief passage of conscience, almost instantaneous, or maybe there was no contest at all except as a matter of pride. They left clutching their automatics a little tighter, their sweaty-palmed left hands over their pounding hearts. Right hands poised near their belts.

He raced across town now. The *Federales* wouldn't be available for backup at the prison. They'd be busy with robberies at grocery stores, a car theft, a stolen purse. Gusto and his brother, Ernesto, were creating similar situations about a block away. A car with its hood in flames and a roadblock, where the *capo* could pass in the town car, safely, until he could get into the Unimog that would climb the ruts and muddy roads coursing into the jungle, to the safe house, hidden even from satellite view, high in the mountains of palms and almond trees and jungle vines. Gusto had orders: shoot down anyone who stands in the way, including the *Policia Federal de Caminos*.

In the dream, Gusto was machine-like, his Spanish militant, and he fired rounds from an HK G36 German assault rifle when he was held up.

Manny had watched Gusto many times at crossing points, out in the middle of nowhere, not too far from Ciudad Juarez and El Paso where Gusto had taught him to shoot a rifle. He never missed a shot—he would lie on the dirt, motionless, for hours, just poised there in the arroyos, sweating in the sun, waiting for his game to come to him. The tortoises would turn their heads from time to time and Manny would smoke weed, waiting there beside Gusto, silent. There were plenty of animals out in the desert Gusto could've shot, bunchy jackals and armadillo and mangy coyotes. Even wild horses.

Gusto was a sick fuck who would practice his fire on real targets, migrants and Sinaloan dope runners, as they came over the hills from hundreds of yards away. If he had the Ruger, he would place the bolt in the gun and the first shell would fall out and he'd pull back the bolt and push it in and aim and shoot the next target while the first one was still wondering what had happened.

Gusto's brother, Ernesto was older than him, forty-five, maybe, with scars from stab wounds, a C-shaped scar on his cheek. When Ernesto took his shirt off, he'd seen his big linear scar down the middle of his abdomen, made by a surgeon who'd removed a bullet from his intestines, saving his life. He wanted to ask where Ernesto had gotten the disfiguring mark on his face. It made him very ugly, he thought. One day, when he was staring at Ernesto, Radolfo, another one of the Juarez lieutenants, had noticed that he was staring. Radolfo told him to cut it out. Radolfo told him that Ernesto had been maimed by his own parrot, and Radolfo said that the animal was reaching for a handful of macadamias and Ernesto had grabbed its beak and twisted it and told him, *Stop,* just as he always did—but that time, it did not stop—it retaliated and tore a flap from his cheek that bled for hours and should have been sutured but was not. And Radolfo said that Ernesto at once took the animal, which he had held in high regard as his companion and friend for more than ten years, and clamped its beak shut and ripped out handfuls of red and yellow and blue plumage, listening to its squawking, looking like he was quite enjoying it, before he twisted its neck in a full circle until he heard the avian bones crack.

Manny glanced at his own reflection in the dirty store front window he passed now.

He swallowed.

He turned down the alley and he pushed a *nino* off his bike. The bike was blue with chrome handlebars and the back tire was almost flat. The kid was about fourteen, not much younger than himself, with skin just as smooth, hair as slick as oil. The boy's mother was selling fruit in the street. She screamed, clutched her cheeks.

"Shhh," he said. "*Vamanos.*"

The woman grabbed the boy and pulled him back and she screamed, and she tore at his shirt, but he flung her off him. He kicked the boy, who was almost as tall as the woman, and the boy fell to the ground and he got back up.

Manny started the scooter and sped off down the narrow street. He circled back around the back of the Oxxo mart, where he'd smashed the glass with his 9mm and set fire to the pumps just after he'd bought a carton of chocolate milk. The owner was cursing. Police barricaded the storefront. The hitmen from the *plaza* fired a hail of bullets that hit two officers. One sank to the pavement. He sped away from the breezy *Bahia de Banderas* and down the *Avenue Mexico* and he made several quick turns in succession and he rode for a while and he got onto Highway 200 south to Manzanillo.

34

Friday found his duffels loaded heavy with bills and his heart suffused with angst, though he did not reveal this to his mother or Pilar. Elvie knew, though. She knew.

She made a sour face when she placed her arms around his neck. "You're all wet, sweaty, like a hog," Elvie said.

His mother was at once guarded. It had taken a great deal of convincing to get her to leave the *estancia*.

"We should go back." Enriqua crossed herself and she looked to a sky pink and smeared wispy with cirrus.

They were almost at the crossing point at the Zaragoza Bridge. Soon, the customs inspector would ask for their identification and he would accept or deny them entry to the United States. He had a duffel of bills for the inspector, too. Everything depended on finding the right inspector. If they changed booths, randomly, or changed shifts, or something fell out of place in this plan at the last minute, it might get them all pulled into custody, cost him his life, his family.

There were hundreds of ways he could have left. It could have been a mile to a safe house in a barrio or it could've been halfway to Columbia. He could've written his story any way and still left behind the same thing, but there was no way to remove the uncertainty, the hesitation falling in the pit of his stomach that his way of life could never be put back just the same. He would pick fruit in California if it meant he could get away from there safely, away from this war, the irreverence for life, the indignation.

He could not be sure they would be safe in Mexico, nor in the United States, nor anywhere. Luis' ties ran deep.

Still, he moved forward. On the bridge, The Apple was stuck behind ten or fifteen other cars, but it inched forward, too.

Juan told him then what Papa had always said—that there is the family you are born with in blood and the family you make, and Papa had said that only if you are very lucky might these be the same people.

He looked around now at the motley band of misfits they were. Elvie giggling, missing the Mary Jane slipper on her left foot. Juan, with his arms crossed. Pilar nearing the end of her confinement, swollen *campesina,* unable to read or write. Piranha, with his skin torn up and purulent like he'd walked over smoking coals in hell, through brimstone, emerging vagabond and derelict with one leg in the next world and one here with loose footing only.

The Apple rattled, its engine jerking forward, sputtering at the ground beneath them in chugging jolts. He had not changed the brake pads on it and it squealed as it slowed, and they approached the border crossing. Enriqua looked uncomfortable with her wide hips and shoulders settled next to Pilar and her patchwork memory bag of photos and Elvie all spread over her lap. In her bag were her letters from Papa, and her *Tia* Maria's rosaries, her own slippers, snacks for Elvie.

About halfway over the bridge The Apple began to smell of burning rubber. The needle on the temperature gauge leaned right.

"Not now," he said.

"What's wrong?" his mother asked. "Go back, Emmanuel."

"It's too late, Ma. It's fine."

"Emmanuel, go back."

"It's fine, Ma."

But the engine was getting hot.

Elvie was waving her unicorn so that its pink tail whipped Enriqua's cheek every so often. She was taller now and her hair had curled throughout. Her shoulders were brown and there were freckles dusted across her nose and she had a very warm laugh that made him smile even now. The air was thick, stagnant on that day, and the horns on the bridge were layered on top of one another, drowning his speech.

"Are we really going to the U.S.A.?" asked Pilar. "It looks beautiful."

"It looks the same," said Elvie. "I'm hungry. Ma, I'm hungry. I want frijoles and beans and juice. I want some juice."

"Okay, shhhh, Elvie. Shhhhhh," he said, putting the car in park. It was smoking from beneath the hood.

"Just a little further," Juan said. "Not now, anytime but now."

Traffic was crawling, came to a stop then. He turned off the engine. They were stuck behind a freight truck and the customs agents were searching the manifold and under the seats. They had the dogs out, sniffing.

Ten minutes passed, fifteen.

The truck moved forward. It was being pulled off to the side.

He restarted the engine, approached the customs booth, the agent.

"It looks so beautiful," said Pilar.

"It does," he said. "It looks great."

"So beautiful."

It was not a novel observation, he understood, though novel to him, and to each one who had passed before him.

With these travelers he carried with him, away from the war behind him, moving forward uncertainly, with the family he owned and the one he'd made, he crossed then.

Enriqua was staring back over the bridge, down at the water, and every so often she would swat back at the unicorn, brush it out of her field of sight, out of her face. In the rearview mirror, a solemn look fell over his mother's face and he could tell that she was collecting every memory and thought, acrimonious or joyful or ambivalent, of guilt and loss, of regret, and in her suffering, he saw an uncertain, ephemeral glimpse of satisfaction. In that mirror was everything he could not leave.

"Listen to your brother," his mother whispered.

The memory of his last moments at the *estancia* punctuated his thoughts, made hopeful the road before him, the image of their home as it was, before he'd lit it up in flames, right before they'd left under a noon sun. The *estancia* had burned, raising in great plumes pointed in tongues of fire, licking the sky, with smoke white and streaming in cottony billows and rivulets of carbon twisting aloft, and some voice in him he could not understand had told him then that this was what he must do, leave this war. He'd watched the fire for some time before they piled in The Apple. And some great fire kindled in him, too.

www.ingramcontent.com/pod-product-compliance
Lightning Source LLC
Chambersburg PA
CBHW071723190726
48292CB00003B/592